EASY Tiger

by USA TODAY bestselling author
GINGER SCOTT

EASY TIGER

BOOK 1

THE BOYS OF SWEETWATER SPRINGS

GINGER SCOTT

For Carol.
<3

ONE
HUNTER REDDICK

I'm fucking good.

No. I'm the fucking best.

Yeah. That's the mantra. I'm the best they've ever had pass through this place. After today, the press is going to buzz about how short my stint here will be. Texas will call me up after the first month. They won't be able to deny how much they need me. I was the number one pick on purpose—with purpose. I came to dominate, and that's exactly what I'm going to do.

Starting . . . right . . . now!

I open my eyes and focus on the stocky three-hole hitter named Todd something or other. I tuned out the announcer when I marched around the mound after striking out the last batter, and I wasn't focused so much on this kid's name during my prep as I was his batting habits. He likes fastballs. *Loves* them, in fact. So he won't see a hint of speed from me. He's getting the junk.

I nod to Roddy, my catcher, and feel the threads on the ball inside my glove as I prepare to throw the best slider of my life. I give a quick sideways glance to the dugout to take stock of how many eyes are on me, and when I note the important ones, I step into my windup and set my attention on the invisible path I've mentally planned for the ball. The batter flings his bat at my slider, both late and nowhere close to putting wood on the ball. His chuckle is the best compliment, so I smirk when our eyes meet.

"That's nasty, Reddick!" He knows my name. Everyone does. I'm *that* guy. *The* guy.

"Saved it just for you," I bark. "Todd," I mutter when my back is turned, in case I've got that wrong.

The ump lifts his chin when I step back up on the mound. It's a subtle check on me to keep the banter friendly. It's early yet, the regular minor season for the Mavericks still two weeks out. Extended spring games are a bit looser, but I'm smart enough to know not to push the envelope, even when the league is giving us wiggle room to act like fools. Those eyes watching me from the dugout aren't simply clocking my speed, they're looking for reasons to hold me back. It costs the team less if I stick around Sweetwater Springs for a while. It also gives them an extra year on my contract before I get to ask for what I'm worth. I've seen attitude problems take down a lot of guys who can throw hard. They're either in bullpens now or working in sales and living off their former-pro image.

I make sure to flash Todd my best smile, keeping it friendly as I listen in for the next call on the PitchCom.

"High fastball," the robotic voice announces.

I shake my head at Roddy, and he repeats the same call in my ear. I pull my hat off and shake my head at him, calling him out to the mound as I fake a problem with the device. I'll only have a second or two to get my point across before the ump trails behind him, so I'm ready with my words.

"It's working fine. Quit calling for fastballs. Not for him." My eyes meet Roddy's, and I'm hit with the fatherly glare he's known for. Roddy's been catching for nearly two decades. He's here to finish out his career. Maybe he feels as though he has something special to pass along to the youngins. Who knows? Like hell am I going to stand by and let him tank me, though.

"Everything all right here?" The ump eyes me, then turns his attention to Roddy.

"Yeah, it's working fine. Little shit just wants to tell me he knows better than me. Let's go." Roddy leans to the side and spits in the grass before dropping his facemask back over his eyes and marching back to the plate with the ump.

Fuck.

I'm sure they're still ripping on me. I can see the slight quiver in the ump's shoulders. He's amused. Two old dudes loving putting the young kid back in his place.

I take a deep breath and glance to the dugout again. Coach Shuster doesn't seem to care about my rigged timeout. He's still leaning on the railing alongside the pitching coach, Abe Burdick, and spitting empty seed shells onto the ground. I turn my attention back in Roddy's direction, and the radar gun raises behind the backstop about a half second before I get the call through the PitchCom.

"High fastball."

Goddammit.

I can literally hear the ump's chuckles from ninety feet away. I'm sure Roddy said something. Rather than shaking off the pitch again and throwing a diva fit, I take my licks and will my arm to throw the hardest fastball of my life.

"One-oh-three!" the assistant with the gun shouts when the ball snaps into Roddy's glove. It didn't earn me a swing and a miss. It's a ball. A fast, loud, pointless ball. But fine. I threw it. I got the lesson. My job is to listen to my catcher.

I settle back into my stance, foot dug into the divot I've formed at the front of the rubber and look to Roddy.

"High fastball."

My eyes flutter shut. The lesson isn't over yet. And more people are laughing this time. It seems coaches Shuster and Burdick are more aware of what's going on than I thought.

"Brace yourself, kid. He's throwing the high heat again," Burdick shouts.

I roll my neck to brush off the frustration before readying myself for the windup. If I just clip the top of the zone, I can turn this around. I feel the ball, situating my hands for a solid two-seam toss, then unleash everything I've got toward Roddy's glove. I manage to get the top of the zone; unfortunately, that seems to be Todd whatever's sweet spot, and he sends the ball four hundred feet, over my head and into the grass area where local college kids sit on blankets.

"Shit!" I hiss through gritted teeth, punching the pocket of my glove.

"Hey, it's all right, Hunter. We all miss our spots sometimes," Todd mocks as he makes the slow turn toward third base.

"Ha ha," I unload, my tone clearly full of irritation.

I walk around the mound and meet Roddy at the front, where he slaps a new ball into my glove but quickly grabs my wrist below the leather.

"I'm not out here to pull pranks and haze the new kid. That shit right there is on you. I told you to hit a spot. You missed because you got mad at being told what to do. Learn from that. You throw that pitch higher, you're going to get swings. Especially off fastball addicts like Tyler Padilla."

I am not the most coachable. I know this about myself, which is, I suppose, a good step toward self-improvement. I nod at Roddy and make a mental note to shore things up in front of the coaching staff when we get back in the dugout.

He lets go of my wrist.

"His name's Tyler? I thought it was Todd," I say, halting him before he heads back to the plate. He chuckles and shakes his head.

"Fucking starting pitchers, man. You are all the same." He holds out a fist, and I pound mine on top of his. "His dad won the Silver Slugger the year you were born. Do your homework."

I swallow as Roddy walks away, then shift my focus to Tyler's back as he celebrates outside the dugout. Number twenty-three, Padilla, high fast balls. I'll never forget.

Three innings of work, four strikeouts and one run. Not bad for my first outing in Sweetwater. I'd rather not have the dinger on my record, but I seem to have made headway with Roddy. At least, enough for him to buy me a beer at Earl's Big Easy, the local pub that's perfectly situated between the state university's campus and Sweetwater's minor league stadium. I didn't want to start in Triple-A ball, but everyone starts somewhere. And Sweetwater is full of beautiful women, thanks to a thriving college scene and one of the country's best nursing programs. My time here promises never to leave me lonely.

Speaking of . . .

"What's her story?" I nudge Roddy with my elbow. The cutest damn blonde swivels through the crowded bar while balancing a tray of pitchers and mugs over her head.

"That's Renleigh. She's not for you." He coughs out a laugh and turns back to his conversation with the other guys.

"What makes her not for me?" I interrupt Roddy as he's talking, and he snaps his mouth shut and blinks his way to meeting my gaze.

"You're a cocky little shit, aren't you?" He takes a long sip from his beer, foam coating his upper lip.

I waggle my head and put my beer down, dropping my hands in my pockets as I take a step back.

"You say cocky, but nah. I'm just confident. I've found that women are attracted to a guy who believes in himself, and gentlemen, I might be *exactly* the kind of guy this . . . Renleigh?"

Roddy nods and grunts out, "Uh huh."

"The kind of guy Renleigh needs," I finish.

Roddy's lip ticks up, and I anticipate his dare before he has a chance to fish the twenty bucks out of his wallet. He slaps it on the table a second later and glances to the other catcher and the two pitchers hanging out at our table. They follow suit, all three of them laughing as they slam down twenties to match Roddy's. He scoops them into a small, neat stack and swivels his head to meet my eyes.

"Eighty bucks. It's all yours if you can get that girl right there to go home with you." Roddy picks up his beer and takes a drink as he studies me. His sureness is a tad unnerving, but also, I meant what I said about having confidence when it comes to women. I *know* it's an attractive quality. Shit, it's been getting me laid well above my level for four years. I'm not like the other guys who pop in and out of Earl's. I just need to get this Renleigh girl to notice.

I slide my wallet from my back pocket and pull out the hundred-dollar bill I've been saving for emergencies. This seems like a good use.

"Deal," I say, dropping it on top of the pile of cash. "I'd say keep the change, but I'll be back for that stack in a few minutes."

I chug what's left of my beer and slam the mug down, wiping my mouth along the sleeve of my Maverick's long-sleeved training shirt. I'd prefer to be dressed nicer, rather than like I just got off the field, but at least I can pull off the compression-pants-under-shorts look.

There's a decent crowd for a late afternoon, so I slip into an open space at the end of the bar and wait patiently as Renleigh returns with a tray filled with empty steins and pitchers. She discards the dirty dishes into a bin, then nods to an older man wearing a Harley-Davidson bandana on his head. He says something that makes her laugh enough that she leans forward and slaps her palms on her thighs before snagging a clean glass from a rack and filling it with Kentucky bourbon. He gives her a nod and a wink, then slides a twenty across the bar. She's still chuckling softly as she heads my direction.

"Is it always this busy in here?" I ask as she punches a few keys on the register and changes out the twenty, pocketing the change in the apron around her waist.

"Sure is," she says in a snappy tone. She doesn't even glance up at me. "What can I get ya?"

She grabs a wet cloth from behind the bar to clean the bar top around me, and I smirk at how hard she's working to not make eye contact. I see why Roddy thought this would be a sure bet. I'm guessing Renleigh gets hit on a lot. Why wouldn't she? The woman is gorgeous, hair pulled up into a tight pony-tail that whips against her bare shoulders when she turns. The black Earl's tank top clings to her body, showing off the toned muscles of her arms, and her dark blue jeans hug her ass. I made note of those the first time I spotted her. So yeah, I'm certain Renleigh's been told she's hot, pretty, gorgeous, smokin', fine, and every other term assholes shout as they ogle her while she's on the job. It's a good thing I shoot my shots differently.

"What's good here?" I squint my eyes as I lean into the bar and pretend to read the list of specialty brews scribbled next to the TVs mounted behind the bar.

"Uh, let's see . . . we got an early case of the summer brew from Oklahoma City. It's an IPA with a hint of citrus." She stows the washcloth beneath the bar, then spreads her palms out along the bar top and tilts her head, finally looking me in the eyes.

A faint smile pulls on my lips.

"I'll try that, then. If you recommend it." I maintain eye contact, and our gaze lasts that little extra second that usually tells me everything I need to know. She's intrigued by me, I'm sure of it. She didn't look away first. I did.

"I don't drink, so I can't recommend anything. But the guys seem to like it, so . . . comin' right up." She pats a hand on the bar top and steps back a few steps, keeping her eyes on me before glancing over my shoulder, then turning around.

I twist my neck to see what caught her attention and find Roddy and the guys all staring our way. I grimace and shake my head. Fuckers are going to make this hard. They all lift their beers, and Roddy gives me a thumbs up. I don't have to see or hear it to know they burst into laughter the second I turn around.

"So, how much?" Renleigh slides my beer toward me, then rests her elbows on the bar top as she nods over my shoulder.

"Huh?" My pulse kicks into a higher gear as I try to play dumb. Thankfully, her gaze is fixed on the guys behind me rather than my throat, because I just swallowed an invisible rock.

"They bet you to come talk to me, yeah? Or . . . is this one to take me home?" Her eyes flit to mine, and I freeze, instantly trapped.

"Oh, uh . . ." I puzzle my face, pulling my brow in as I glance down at the beer, rotating the glass with my fingertips. "That's not why I came over here, but they did . . . uh . . ." I grab the back of my neck as nervous laughter slips from my mouth.

A mischievous grin snakes into her cheeks.

"I'm caught, aren't I?" I give in, dropping my chin into my neck as I squeeze my eyes shut.

"'Fraid so, rookie," she says, patting the space next to my IPA. "Good news, though. This one's on the house."

I chuckle softly and utter, "Thanks."

I linger, not ready to abandon my quest, while Renleigh takes care of a few customers on the other end of the bar. I take a few sips from my beer and hold up a finger to my teammates, buying myself time. I can salvage this. A guilty smile has always worked for me.

"So, what do you think?" Renleigh nods at the beer as I pull it down from my lips.

"*Mmm*, it's good. I taste the citrus." I don't taste shit, but I need this banter to continue.

"Good to know. I'll keep pitching it that way," she says, her gaze flitting to me in fits while she busies herself making a rum and Coke.

"Speaking of pitching," I segue, squinting my eyes at the cheesiness of my line. I went for the cheese on purpose. It's better to look like a hapless fool than an asshole.

"Oh, wow. So, you're a pitcher, then, huh? I wouldn't have guessed."

I roll my shoulders back and cradle the half-empty beer mug in front of me.

"You were right about the rookie thing, but I don't plan on being here long. I was the number one draft pick," I say, whispering that last part, though loudly enough that the guy sitting next to me turns to give me a once-over.

"Well, shit. You are Hunter Reddick. You really throw a hundred pitches during that college playoff game?" the guy says.

I smirk boastfully on the side closest to him but keep my eyes on Renleigh.

"One-hundred-fifteen, actually. Could have gone a dozen more, too, but ya know . . . coach didn't want to stress the arm."

More like I was starting to get a little wild, but nobody needs those details. Coach pulled me in the ninth before I gave up the winning run. Saved that for our bullpen.

"Ha, well. You better worry about stressing the arm in Texas when you get there. They can't hit worth shit, so it's all on you, buddy. Good to meet ya, though." The guy pats my shoulder with a heavy hand as he heaves himself from his stool and carries his drink to the pool tables in the back of the bar.

"Number one draft pick, huh?" Renleigh's tongue is pushed in her cheek, and even though she's teasing me with her words, I sense she's also a touch impressed.

"Yep. Seeing my mom cry happy tears was probably the coolest part about it all, to be honest."

I'm not making that part up. My mom put in a lot of hours driving me from camp to camp, practice to practice, game to game. My dad's job requires a lot of travelling for sales, but he showed up for the big things. He was there for draft day, too. No tears from his eyes, though. Just lots of bragging, which also felt pretty nice.

"All right, rookie. How much is on the table for this little wager?" She pushes a few buttons on the register again, this time counting out bills in the drawer before zipping them into a deposit bag.

"I put up a hundred, and they put up eighty," I say, smirking through another drink from my beer.

"Wow, you paid the vig, huh? That confident?"

I tilt my head to the right and pull my lips in as I shrug.

"More like going all in when I want something. Money is money. But making quality conversation with the coolest girl in Sweetwater? No price tag for that."

I step back, abandoning the rest of my beer and feeling rather pleased with my final shot. I think I may have tilted this entire thing in my favor.

"Tell ya what? Wait for me to lock up this deposit, then I'm off for the night."

"Yeah?" I raise my eyebrows.

"Yeah," she says through adorable laughter.

My grin stretches as I nod.

She holds up a finger, then skips into the back room. I turn around and shove my hands in my pockets as I make wide eyes at my doubters. Roddy's brow lowers with what looks like skepticism, but the other guys punch each other's shoulders and cover their mouths.

"Let's go, rookie," Renleigh says, popping up next to me with her hair down and apron long gone. The black work boots she's wearing add to her tough girl persona, which I'm beginning to think is rooted in fact.

"You lead the way," I say, trailing behind her as we head for the table where my teammates are suddenly straightening postures and putting drinks down to appear less like an unruly crew and more like gentlemen.

"That his, Roddy?" Renleigh's eyes glance toward the pile of cash at the center of the table.

"Yep," Roddy grunts, his cocky smirk long gone.

"Well, then," she says, sweeping the cash into one palm as she takes my hand in the other. "You ready to get out of here?"

Her heated stare hits me from over the smooth curve of her shoulder, and I'm not sure which has me more mesmerized—her words or the look in her eyes. Maybe it's the slight upturn of her top lip. Or the fresh touch of pink she's put on her cheeks. Or maybe the raspy tone of her voice.

It's all of it. It's the whole fucking package.

"Yes, ma'am," I say, snagging the keys and phone I left on the table just before she rushes me to the exit.

Her hand drops mine the second the door slams shut behind us, and the harsh glow of the afternoon sun warms my face. I stuff my keys and phone into my pocket and hurry to keep up as her feet crunch across the gravel parking lot.

"You live far from here?" I ask, squinting into the sun. The way it lights up the curled tips of her hair as she flings it over one shoulder is almost angelic.

"I don't. But you're not coming with me." She spins and walks backward, looking me in the eyes as my steps slow and eventually stop. "It was nice to meet you, though . . . Hunter Redding."

"Reddick," I say, somehow picking that out as the thing to respond to. "It's Hunter Reddick."

"Right," she says, pulling a key fob from her pocket and beeping a nearby ragtop Jeep. "Hunter Reddick, the number one draft pick. Enjoy your short stay in Sweetwater."

She winks before hoisting herself into the driver's side of the Jeep, and I stare at her taillights like a damn fool way longer than I should.

TWO
RENLEIGH BLACKWOOD

A symphony of garlic and peppers assaults my nose the moment I crack open the front door. I love it when my sister, Lindsey, stops in for dinner. She doesn't only visit me and Dad on these occasions; she cooks. That Dad and I have mastered two-and-a-half recipes between us has made for a fairly repetitive menu over the last year.

"Please say that's stuffed bell peppers!" I shout my wish from the foyer just before my sister's twin boys wrap themselves around my legs.

"Mine!"

"No, she's mine!"

I drop my keys and phone on the nearby entry table before bending down and scooping up my three-year-old nephews. Riggs and Deacon are a handful, but they're a lot of fun in doses. Being the cool aunt is a gig I relish.

"I found the meatballs. Is the pot ready?" I sway my hips, a toddler balanced on each, as I make my way into the kitchen.

"I think those two are over-seasoned. They might need a bath before we eat them," Lindsey says over her shoulder.

"You can't eat us!" Deacon giggles against my right hip.

"I can't, can I? I don't know about that. Maybe we should ask Pap."

I lean to the side, putting Deacon's head within reach of my father as he sits in his wheelchair by the dining counter, a knife in one hand and a fork in the other like a wild zombie ready to feast. It's nice that despite his stroke and subsequent uphill battle with rehab, my father has maintained one hell of a sense of humor.

He growls at the boys playfully, licking his lips as if he's about to take a bite, and their legs kick wildly against my thighs until I let them go. They scurry down the hallway and up the stairs to my washroom. I cup my mouth as I prepare to shout.

"You best not be using my expensive soap!" I wink at my sister as the boys giggle from the bathroom upstairs. I don't have expensive anything, but we've discovered when I refer to the soft hand soap as expensive or fancy, the toddlers are more apt to wash their hands for real.

"How long do you think we can run with that trick?" my sister asks.

"Bah, still works on . . . you . . . . two." My father's words come out between breaths. He's come a long way with his speech therapy, but every sentence is still a challenge to get out of his mouth.

"I wash my hands just fine, thank you very much." I bend down and kiss my dad's cheek before adding a *humph*.

"Sure, but if something is . . . expensive, you two . . . sure need to have it!" He coughs out his laugh as my sister purses her lips in response.

"Not gonna lie. You're right, Dad," I admit. My father lets out a quiet but satisfied grunt.

I pull the wad of cash from my day out of my pocket and flatten the bills on the counter. Lindsey spots the crisp hundred the moment she turns around.

"Damn, who gave you that tip?" She swipes it and holds it

up to the light. I think she's inspecting if it's real. I sure as shit hope it is.

"I won a bet. Well, more like I got a commission for *helping* someone win a bet." I shrug as I slide onto the stool next to my father.

"Okay, how does that work? Are you a bookie now?" My sister slaps the hundred-dollar bill back down in front of me and arches a brow before turning her attention back to the stove pot. I can see the cheese-encrusted edges of the peppers in the oven, and my stomach growls.

"No, Lindsey, I'm not a bookie. Just the usual antics from the latest crop of ballplayers at Earl's. You know how they like to haze the rookies. I felt bad for this one, I guess."

I can sense my sister itching for more details. She puts out a vibe, like shockwaves, when she's about to get nosy. Thankfully, she pulls the peppers filled with meat sauce from the oven before grilling me with more questions. My rambunctious nephews buy me more time, fighting over who gets to sit next to me until I solve everything by giving up my seat and standing between them as Lindsey dishes out our portions. My knife is halfway through its first cut into the stuffed pepper when the interrogation resumes.

"Felt bad for him, huh? What was this bet? Did they make him embarrass himself in front of you? Was there a strip tease involved?" She smirks after chewing through her words, and I'd kind of like to flick her stuffed cheek with my finger.

"No, they didn't make him strip for me." I flit my gaze to either side to remind her that her impressionable toddlers are right here.

"I'll strip tease for you!" Deacon announces. I glare at my sister, expecting her to drop her face in her palm in shame, but she continues staring at me with her smug grin, unfazed.

"He doesn't even know what that means. It's fine. So, spill it. What made this one different?" She takes another massive bite of her dinner, something I have yet to do.

"I don't know. He was sweet, I guess. I mean, cocky like the rest of the players, but he was also nervous. The guys prodded him to try to take me home, and I wanted him to save face, so I walked out with him and let them think whatever they want. I kept the money, though."

I shove a massive bite into my mouth before another question comes, and the euphoria from eating cancels out the stress of enduring my sister's enquiry.

Lindsey quakes with a silent laugh, then glances at my dad.

"Don't look at . . . me. She's your . . . sister."

My sister rolls her eyes at our dad but quickly turns her attention back to me.

"That's a lot of money he let you walk away with. Those boys don't make a lot playing for the Mavericks, so you must have made an impression on him."

There is so much insinuation to her tone, I don't have to look at her expression to know it's tongue-in-cheek.

"Or . . . he's already loaded from a signing bonus, so a couple hundred bucks walking away isn't something he'll miss." I shrug and quickly dive back into my meal. I make it through two bites this time before Lindsey hits me with a follow-up.

"What *kind* of signing bonus?"

I bother to look her in the eyes this time, and the arched brow I expected to see greets me.

"I don't know, a big one?" I mumble, no longer caring that I'm talking with food in my mouth. Lindsey's lucky this pepper is the best thing I've ever eaten because I'm willing to overlook her meddling just to get to eat it.

"Did you hear that, Daddy? A *big* one. So, this guy—he must be a pitcher!" My sister's guess isn't as impressive as she makes it sound. Nearly half the players in Sweetwater right now are pitchers. Every season starts this way, and having grown up here, she and I both know the ebb and flow of rosters. Several of the rookies will get sent to other affiliates in the next few weeks, as the coaching staff evaluates them.

"And she said he's loaded from a signing bonus, so that leaves us with . . ."

Shit. I sometimes forget how well-studied my sister is in baseball.

"Brooks Callahan isn't a pitcher, and Proctor McQuistion was a rookie last year, plus he's still rehabbing from surgery. That leaves . . ."

Fucking hell.

I lift my gaze, mouth full and stomach heavy, and my sister slaps her hand over her mouth as soon as our eyes meet.

"Hunter Reddick tried to sleep with you!"

When my sister's kids are called into the principal's office in a few years, I'm going to be sure I bring up this moment.

"It was a bet. It wasn't like he *actually* wanted to . . . ya know." I waggle my head, feeling the heat of being between my nephews and in the same room with our dad.

"Oh, Renleigh. Don't play dumb with me. Of *course* that man wanted to—"

"Could I get some water?" my dad pipes in, saving both of us from hearing my sister get explicit about my potential sex life.

"You sure can, Dad." I jet up from my seat and head into the kitchen to fill a glass for my father.

I pinch my sister's earlobe as I pass her on my way back to my seat, and she swats at my hand. My father takes the heavy glass in both hands, still needing assistance from his left hand to steady anything he grasps with his right.

"This discussion is to be continued," Lindsey says, dotting each word in the air with her index finger.

"We'll see," I mutter, devouring the rest of my stuffed pepper, then promptly copping myself seconds.

Lindsey manages to hold off her pressure campaign long enough for her kids to fall asleep on the couch and our father to become engrossed in his nightly routine of watching SportsCenter.

Of course my sister and dad would know who Hunter Reddick is. Our dad spent thirty years coaching baseball at Sweetwater High. You don't grow up in our house and not follow baseball news, at least the major headlines. And Hunter? He's a pretty damn big headline. I played aloof with him, but I recognized his tall frame and blue eyes the moment he slid up to the bar.

And yeah, I'm sure if I let things play out the way Hunter planned, we would have been in his apartment within minutes, and I would have been hemming and hawing my way through stripping my clothes off or marching out the door in protest. But I know better than to get mixed up with the summer boys. And Hunter Reddick is going to be out of Sweetwater and on to the next mound in weeks, months at the most.

I pop the final dish into the washer and nudge the door shut with my hip before pressing the start button. My sister hands me a glass of wine, and I follow her to the front porch where the two of us fold up our legs as we sit in the pair of rickety lawn chairs parked on the wood planks. This place needs some love. My dad talked about painting the exterior of the house two summers ago. That was before his second stroke wiped out the use of most of his right side. He's getting stronger, but I'm not sure he'll ever have full function in the way things like hammers and nails require.

"He should sell this place," I sigh out, patting the chair cushion by my hip so it emanates a poof of dust.

"He'll never sell it. Besides, what will you and I fight over when he's gone?" She winks at me and I chuckle before sipping some wine.

One of our dad's go-to jokes is talking about the fortune he'll leave me and my sister. The man has existed on a teacher's salary his entire life, and the district pension barely covers his bills. Honestly, if it weren't for his disability assistance, I'm not sure where my father would be able to live. Certainly not his house. Paid off or not, the taxes for this place are too much for his dismal savings alone to cover.

"Brandon coming to pick up you and the boys?" I nod to my sister's full glass of wine.

"Yeah," she sighs before taking a long sip.

It's her second glass, and she's a lightweight. My sister and her husband live about twenty-five miles away, closer to the city. Brandon works at the university's downtown campus, but occasionally, he has workshops or lectures at the main campus here in Sweetwater. My sister always tags along so she can visit Dad and me.

"He's cute, you know," Lindsey says.

"Who?"

I know who.

"I'm just saying, if I were twenty-four and single, I'd let myself enjoy a little fling from time to time with a nice set of abs and some gray sweatpants magic."

"Lindsey!" I tease, stretching my leg toward her chair and poking her knee with the toe of my sneaker.

"What? Girl, I'm turning thirty, and my boobs were milk trucks for piranhas for two whole years. I'm simply saying you're young and hot, and he's young and hot, so why not be young and . . . *hot* . . . together?"

My sister's brow waggles as she says, "hot." I snort out a laugh.

"I don't know, Linds. You know how those guys are."

Unserious. Uncommitted. Selfish.

A lot like our mom.

"I'm not saying you have to marry him, for Pete's sake. I'm just asking you to be open-minded about seeing him naked. And then telling me all the details." A devilish smirk pulls up both sides of her mouth, and I shake my head at her. The wine is hitting her hard, and I have no doubt she'll be projecting these thoughts onto Brandon when they get home. He's getting lucky for sure.

"He is fine," I finally relent.

My sister sits up tall and leans toward me, slapping the tips of her fingers against my knee. "That's what I'm talking about!"

We both laugh and act like giddy schoolgirls for the next thirty minutes, gossiping about cute boys we went to school with and espousing the perks of baseball pants. But after my sister's husband shows up to sweep my sibling and their kids off to her fairytale life, the reality of mine sets in.

I clean up the clutter of toys left in Riggs's and Deacon's wake, then help my dad maneuver his wheelchair so it lines up with the adjustable hospital bed we set up in the space that was once his home office and our mother's library. Mom's books are long gone—one of the few things she took with her when she packed up and moved to Houston. My dad's coaching books and trophies remain clustered on the few shelves she set aside for him. Everything else in here is medical.

"Ready?" I hunch down so my dad can swing his right arm around my shoulders and use me for leverage.

"One, two, *three!*" We grunt the final number as my dad uses every muscle he's retrained, and I lock my legs and core in place until he's able to transfer himself to his bed. The nurse comes in the morning to help with his bath, and then we're back at it with his physical therapist. He's so close to walking without having two people at his sides to brace him. His doctor thinks he could very well regain full walking ability within the year—two and a half years after he lost the ability to do everything.

Two years after I left college—a semester away from

finishing my degree—and moved back home to help him after my mother decided that while she loved the man, she didn't love him quite *that* much. So, while my sister means well, the state of Hunter Reddick's abs will remain a mystery to both of us. I barely have time to sleep, let alone hook up with this season's hottest prospect.

[illegible]
[illegible]
[illegible]

THREE
HUNTER

Oklahoma and California are very different. I didn't think I'd miss the ocean air as much as I do, and it's humid as fuck here—every damn day.

I run my forearm across my forehead, then push my hat back down, pulling the brim lower to block the sun. Rosin and sweat do mix, for a nasty curveball at least. I should be able to throw some crazy pitches while I'm out here, though I'm not used to a hard limit on how much I can throw. I get twenty in today's session, all breaking balls. I suppose when people pay more than a million dollars for an arm, they want to do all they can to protect it. I'm not so sure coddling it is the way to go, however. Nolan Ryan threw his ass off back in the day, and he was the best there was well into his forties.

I wind up and release my last pitch for the day, and it snaps in Roddy's mitt. He holds it in place for an extra beat, letting Coach get a good handle on my spot.

"Good work, Reddick. Your curve looks solid today. Hit the trainer and take the arm care seriously."

Coach Burdick slaps my back with his massive palm, then heads toward Roddy to chat. The two glance my way while I'm packing up.

I sling my bag over my shoulder and meander toward them. "Did I miss my spot or something?"

Roddy shifts his glove from over his mouth, revealing the hard line of his mouth.

"You did fine today, Hunter. Go take care of your arm," Coach repeats.

I nod and their eyes linger on me for a beat before Roddy's glove comes back up to cover his mouth. He's clearly talking about me. I thought the little bet incident was our icebreaker. I don't know what the fuck I did to make this guy hate me so much, but I can't have him fucking up my path to the show.

I spin around again and their gazes zip to me.

"You know, if I need to work on something, I can take it. You can tell me."

I shrug, because I've grown up with coaches barking mean shit at me. A lot of dudes *say* they can handle criticism, but I really mean it. I didn't get to be this good because my coaches were nice to me. They pushed my ass, every day. Hell, *I* pushed myself twice as hard as they did.

"You know what you need to work on, Hunter? Your arm care." Coach's expression matches Roddy's now. I'm fucking this up.

"Yeah, okay. I got it," I mumble. I head out of the bullpen and up toward the clubhouse without looking back again.

The trainer is finishing up my massage when Roddy makes his way into the room. I lift my chin when our eyes meet, and he rolls his eyes before heading to the other side of the room where one of the young catchers is working on hip mobility.

"*Pfft*, whatever. Maybe spend more time with the catchers and leave me alone," I mutter.

Mike, our trainer, stops his compressions and follows my gaze to where Roddy and the young catcher seem to be getting into it.

"Roddy's old school, ya know," Mike says.

"Oh yeah, believe me . . . *I know*."

Mike chuckles and heads toward the ice machine to fill the bag for my wrap.

"He's the best, though. And people he's caught for? They win Cy Young awards." Mike drops the Ziplock of ice on the table next to me, then tugs my sleeve down before holding the ice in place against my bicep tendon. I wince from the instant chill.

"Yeah, I know his story. And he's good. I'll give you that. He's just so . . . prickish. I mean, why does he have to fuck with that kid's head too? Look at that. Kid's marching out all angry. I bet he's going to have a shit practice thanks to Roddy's words of advice."

"I'd be careful here," Mike warns.

I glance at him but before he can explain things further, Roddy is at my side with his mask tucked under his arm.

"You should know you threw some great stuff today. That conversation I was having with Coach? It wasn't about you." He holds my stare for a few painfully long seconds, and dammit if I don't swallow under his scrutiny.

"Thanks," I eek out.

"Also," he begins.

My head falls back and my eyes flutter shut as I exhale. Here comes the lesson. It's bad enough I'm trapped here to take it, thanks to Mike wrapping ice against my arm.

"Not everything is about you. When you were at San Diego State, it probably felt like it. Hell, I'll give you that— you put that team on your shoulders. But out here, you're one of many. And I do mean *many*. So, do your job, work hard, and when you finally get called up, remember to listen to your fucking catcher."

I drop my chin back to my shoulder and meet his hard stare.

"That what you tell the kid?" I shift my eyes toward the exit, where the rookie marched out a few minutes prior.

Roddy chuckles, and I can't be certain, but I think Mike just tsked under his breath.

"You're good to go. See you in two days," Mike says, slapping the end of the wrap along my shoulder before making eyes at Roddy.

"Take it easy on him, boss," Mike says to Roddy before packing up his tools and moving to the next massage table to work on one of our infielder's hips.

I swing my legs around and move to slide from the table, but Roddy cages me in before I can, leaning over me with his hands on either side of my body, forcing me to lean back so far I fear I might flip backward and tumble to the floor.

"Shit!"

"Yeah, shit is right. Now, listen to me when I tell you this one . . . last . . . time."

I'm done playing tough. Roddy's shorter than me, but he's twice as thick. And being this close gives me a clear view of what looks to be a well-earned scar that cuts from under his right eye toward his jaw. I'm sure it was baseball related, but I also wouldn't be shocked to learn that he got it when some mugger slashed his face with a knife. Just like I wouldn't be shocked to find out he then made said mugger swallow the knife whole.

"Not everything is about you. Tell me you hear me."

I nod, but that doesn't seem to be good enough. He slaps the bench on either side and lunges a few extra inches closer to me.

"Say the words," he commands.

"Not everything is about you," I say, repeating verbatim. Fuck if I can't help but be a smartass. If I get my teeth knocked out right now, I deserve it. But I'm not going to let this guy think I'm a total pushover. There's a line, and while I see he's to be respected, he himself has a few things to learn.

His pupils dart from left to right as he focuses on each of my eyes for milliseconds at a time, and I swallow down the dry razors taking over my esophagus just as he steps back with a hard laugh.

"Well, fuck if you aren't one tough rockhead," he says, holding out his hand. I blink at it for a moment, then grip his palm for a shake as he helps me to my feet.

"I've been called worse," I say, adjusting the fit of my wrap around my arm.

"I'm sure you have," Roddy says through a chuckle. "You bust your dad's balls like that? Or is that something you save for grizzled old athletes like me?"

Roddy moves toward the locker room, so I follow.

"I have two sisters, and if you think I'm bad, you should meet them."

It's true, too. Bethany and Isabelle are two and four years older than me, respectively, and the amount of shit I took from them growing up should have put me in the manure business.

"Two sisters, huh? I know a thing or two about that. Try four!" Roddy flings open his locker and tucks his mask in the cubby at the top before unsnapping his chest protector.

"I wouldn't have survived four," I laugh out.

Are we . . . bonding? Finally!

"I barely survived, and I'm twice as tough as your ass," he says.

I laugh at the joke at my expense, but Roddy doesn't, so I quiet down quickly. After a few awkward seconds, though, he cackles and snaps his clean shirt at me.

"Just giving you shit."

"Ha, yeah. I get that. Now." I exhale and take a seat in front of my open locker before pulling my turf shoes off.

We change out in semi-comfortable silence for the next few minutes, and Roddy finishes first.

"Tell me one thing, rookie. Did you really spend the night with Renleigh when you left the bar a couple nights ago?"

My lip twitches and eventually gives in to a lopsided smirk, and for a moment, I consider lying to him. With my luck, though, this is another one of his tests, and he'll catch me in it and hang it over my head for the next week. I meet his gaze.

"I spent about three minutes with her that night, all the way to the parking lot, where she pocketed the cash and told me to have a great season." I shrug and he chuckles, leaning forward and patting my shoulder in what very much feels like an act of solidarity and consolation.

"You're not the first, young man. And you will likely not be the last with that one. That girl doesn't date. And she doesn't trust. And maybe around here that's a good thing, ya know?" He glances around the empty locker room, and I get his point—there's a lot of single, and not-*actually*-single assholes coming in and out of this place.

Except, I don't really think I'm an asshole. Confident to a fault? Sure. Maybe even cocky. But when it comes to women, I've always been a gentleman. I've even had relationships that lasted more than a season, which I bet a lot of the dudes on this team can't say. My college freshman girlfriend and I are still friends on social media. Hell, she even invited me to her engagement party set for November.

"What if I'd still like to give it a try?"

Roddy spins around and walks a few steps back toward me.

"Try and sleep with her? I mean, she'll probably throw a drink in your face the next time you hit on her, but—"

"No, no. I mean, like, take her out and shit. You know? Take her to dinner, maybe a show. Whatever people do around here." I wave my hand around the room, acknowledging the limited entertainment in Sweetwater. It's a cute place, but it's harsh on the fringes. And other than the college town part and the rivers and ranches, there aren't a lot of places to take a girl you're trying to impress.

"You mean you want to date her?" His brow arches.

I lift my shoulders.

"Yeah. And if it leads to her place some time, well, okay. I mean, I'm not blind. But, I don't know, there's something there. Maybe it's the challenge. She reminds me of my sisters, giving me shit right back. I'm into that, I guess."

Roddy chews at the inside of his cheek and lets out a breathy laugh.

"Well, goddamn. I don't know what to tell you, rookie. Like I said, that girl has a fortress up. But it doesn't hurt to try, I guess. Just don't think I'll be buying you a beer to nurse your wounds in every time she shoots you down. I'll cover the first one, but that's it."

I chuckle as I stand, then grab my phone and keys from my locker to shove into my pockets.

"I'm persistent. It's only one of my charming qualities," I say with a grin.

Roddy, however, grimaces.

"I'm not so sure I'd call it that. Annoying? Yes, but it falls short of charm."

We walk out together, reaching his lifted pickup truck that looks like it's seen more seasons than he has.

"Maybe you can teach me how to be charming, old man," I say, only half teasing. I don't really need nice guy lessons from Roddy, but I would like the two of us to get along.

"Ha, I'm not the one to go to for lady advice. Trust me. But I'll get that beer ready. And piece of advice?" He stops with one foot in the truck, leaning into the open door.

"What's that?"

"Not everything is about you. Same advice goes for shooting your shot with Renleigh. Remember that."

I nod, though I'm not entirely sure what he means. Besides, I've got a feeling about her. Maybe I can help her shake up those walls for a bit and let herself have a good time.

FOUR
RENLEIGH

This is what my life boils down to. Mango smoothies.

It's truly the one thing that brings me joy, and I look forward to this damn cup of pureed fruit every Monday, Wednesday, and Friday while I wait for Dad to finish with his physical therapist. I join his therapist, Heather, for the first half most mornings, which ends up being a bit of a workout for me, so I feel like the sugar reward is warranted. Plus, I like this lime green chair with the bright yellow pillow shaped like a giant Tootsie Roll. And I *love* the romance book swap in the corner.

I'm tucking my latest read back on the shelf and pulling out *Wild Kiss* by Kacey Shea when a shadow casts over my lap, blocking the light from the nearby window.

"That looks like a good one."

I don't know how I recognize Hunter Reddick's voice, given I've spoken to him for no more than a total of ten minutes, ever. But there he is, confirming my hunch when I glance up at him.

I nod toward the counter.

"You going to order something?"

"I'll get to it," he says, perusing the selection of books.

"You read romance?" I arch a brow, expecting him to make some crack about my choice in literature. That's what most people who don't really read the genre do because they're missing out, but instead he leans in and pulls out the Amalie Howard historical I just put back, and thumbs through the pages before meeting my gaze.

"This one was good, but have you read her romantasy?"

My mouth falls open, because *how the hell does he know that word?*

"Uh, yeah. I have." I'm blinking more than normal. I feel it. It's because I feel like I'm being pranked.

"I got it for my mom for her birthday, and she sent it to me when she was finished. Which reminds me, I should probably give it back. Mom's funny about keeping her paperbacks on her shelf. She probably still has the placeholder there." He chuckles and slides the book back in place while I continue to stare at him.

"What?" He moves toward the smoothie counter and pulls a menu from the plastic stand. "Is it so shocking that I read?"

I huff out a single laugh.

"No, but yeah. Maybe. A little. You read romance? And you know the word *romantasy?*" I realize this is the pot calling the kettle and all that by judging him, but also, he does not fit the romance reader profile. Like . . . at all. And maybe I'm a bit protective of it.

"I read everything. Sometimes I need a happily-ever-after to follow a good thriller, ya know? Not every book ends happily. And some shit gets dark."

He slumps into the chair opposite me as I shake my head and blink a few more times before deciding to just let him have this one. Hot, romance-reading pitcher. So, he gets one green flag. It's still in a sea of red ones.

"Shouldn't you be at practice or something?" I flip my phone over on my thigh, checking the time. My dad should be done soon.

"Off day for me. I threw a bullpen this morning. I don't throw again for two days. You should come. We play Tulsa." He shifts in his seat and pulls his phone from his pocket.

"Thanks, but I've seen my fill of Mavericks games. I grew up here." I wrinkle my lips and shrug.

"I get that, but . . . you've never seen *me* pitch." He's persistent, and I almost reply that I *have* seen him pitch—on TV. But I don't want to give him that satisfaction.

"Tempting, but I work nights," I say instead.

"Well, good news—it's a day game. Here, give me your phone." He sits up tall and holds out an open palm, which I stare at skeptically.

"I'm not going to hack it. I just want to transfer the tickets to you."

My brow puckers.

"You already got tickets?" I have yet to accept this invitation. Is that what he was doing on his phone?

"Yeah, Jackie sent them over when I texted her just now. You know Jackie, right? She's in PR or something—"

I raise a hand, but keep my phone where it rests, on my leg.

"I know Jackie. We went to high school together. And you're awfully presumptuous, aren't you? I haven't said yes yet."

"Exactly. *Yet.*" His lips twist up on the ends into this fucking charming smirk that pulls a light laugh from me. Damn him.

"Fine, I'll *think* about it."

I hold my phone out but keep a good grip on it. No way am I giving him full control. He scoffs but lets me have my way, cupping the back of my hand in his palm as he taps his phone against mine. His fingertips brush against my knuckles when he's done, and the tickle nearly makes me drop my phone. I clutch it fast, then pull it into my lap and bury it beneath my hands.

"Are you going to order something? Or are you just here to harass me?" My hands are still buzzing, which I don't like at all. I need to regain my cool.

Hunter tilts his head, his eyes crinkling a little on the edges with his soft grin as he rests his elbows on his knees and clasps his phone between his hands.

"I did come in here for a smoothie. You're right. You're also very distracting." He waggles a finger at me as he stands and makes his way to the counter.

"I'll have what she's having," he says to the college girl working the counter. He leans against the counter as he taps his phone to the payment device, and it's obvious he's waiting for the sweet blonde with her hair pulled into a net to swoon over him. She doesn't as much as remove one of her AirPods, however, which gives me smug satisfaction.

"They get ballplayers in here a lot. Just so you know. I'm sure you're used to the smoothie girls fawning over you back home at—" I stop myself from dropping the name of his college, Pacific Coastal University. "Wherever you went to school."

"You got me," he says with a wink. "Some guys are players, but me . . . I only love and leave the smoothie employees. If a woman can't blend ice and banana, I'm not interested."

I purse my lips, staving off the itch to laugh at his joke.

"You know, it's possible you're all wrong about me," he says.

My head falls to one side as I study him for a beat.

"*Hmm*, is that so?" He has a point. He did surprise me with the romance books.

"Absolutely. For starters, I happen to believe in exclusivity when it comes to dating," he says, taking his smoothie from the employee and pulling the wrapper from the straw.

"Okay, that's fair. But . . . how often do you start and stop these exclusive arrangements?" My gut says he's working with a loophole in this argument.

"Well, I've had four girlfriends. The shortest relationship lasted six weeks—*she was a football fan,*" he whispers as he sits across from me. He wraps his lips around his straw, puckering as he glances up and squints at the ceiling tiles. "I guess maybe four or five short dating attempts, too, after the draft."

"Dating." I call out that word as I narrow my gaze on him. He means sleeping around. He can play gentleman all he wants, but no pitcher with his body and buzz is a saint.

"I mean, yeah, there was always a dinner involved. But I'm an adult. The women are adults. We're adults. Like you and I . . . *we're* adults." He waggles a finger between us, as if we're a thing.

I shudder with a silent laugh.

"Yeah, we're adults. And that's where that connection stops. I can buy my own dinner, thank you very much." I palm my phone and wake the screen to distract myself with the news or some doomscrolling.

"I'm fine skipping the dinner part, too. I mean, I prefer a little romance. You know, some good foreplay. But if you're not into that type of thing . . ."

I glance up through my lashes, a little shocked at his brazen proposition.

"Are you serious right now?" My brow draws in tighter.

Hunter pulls the straw from his lips to stir it in his cup. He sucks in his bottom lip, and I brace myself for his next line. He blows out hard, though, practically raspberrying his lips.

"What flavor is this?" He pulls the lid off his cup and sniffs inside.

"Mango," I respond.

He nods slowly, getting up from his seat and heading toward the trash can. He tosses his nearly full cup away, then waves a hand to get the attention from the worker, who is deep into her phone and AirPods.

"Huh?" She pops her head up.

"I'm having an allergic reaction. Can I get a big cup of

water?" His words are starting to slur, and the plumpness of his bottom lip is becoming noticeable. Holy shit, I may have inadvertently just killed Hunter Reddick.

The worker fills a large cup with water from the rinse sink, but she's moving pretty slowly, so I get to my feet and step up beside Hunter to keep an eye on him. His cheeks are puffing out now, like a chipmunk storing nuts. It's terribly unattractive, but of everything he's tried so far today, there's something about this that gets to me. He's on the verge of anaphylactic shock, and here I am about to give him his shot.

"I'll come to the game," I say, moving a palm to his face. I press my thumb into the swollen cheek as he lets out what I *think* is a laugh.

"I'm not faking this just for sympathy. I'm incredibly allergic to mango." He takes the cup from the worker and gulps down water while pulling at the collar of his T-shirt.

"Do you need an EPIPen? Or do you have pills or something?" Shit, I'm panicking now.

He shakes his head and continues to stare at me over the rim of the cup as he gulps down water.

"I think I'm okay. I didn't drink much. Can I get more of this?" He shakes the cup toward the worker, and she rolls her eyes, annoyed.

"Uh, maybe hustle," I snap at her. That earns me a glare. *Wow.*

I turn my attention back to Hunter to find him chuckling. He's still puffy, but the expansion seems to have paused. Now, we just need it to reverse.

"If I knew all I had to do was flirt with death to get you to go out with me, I would have led with a pack of peanut M&Ms and a melon spread." He takes the refilled cup and drinks immediately, but the smile remains in his eyes as he stares at me over the cup.

"Don't get ahead of yourself, Tiger. I said I'd come to your game. I didn't say anything about a date." I'm entertaining the idea, though. I'll keep that part to myself.

"Ah, okay. Well, I better kill it on the mound. Maybe then . . ."

His eyes soften on my face, and the damn tingles that struck the back of my hands when he touched me rush down my arms this time. Thankfully, my phone buzzing against the chair I left it in gives me an excuse to gain a little space.

I answer when I see my father's name.

"Hey. You all done?" I stuff my keys and wallet into the pocket of my hoodie and hold up a finger to Hunter. My dad usually waits for me in the physical therapy facility lobby so I can help maneuver his chair through the doors and down the curb.

"I am. Look out the window."

I pop my head up at his clue, and when I spot him standing, albeit with a walker wedged into his gut, my knees buckle a tad.

"Holy shit, Dad!" I end our call and leave Hunter alone to deal with his allergy as I push through the smoothie shop door to greet my dad.

"Did you know this was coming today?" I circle him, checking out the various tools on the walker, like the variable brakes that will keep my dad from accidentally falling into a downhill sprint.

"Not at all. Heather surprised me . . . with it. She said . . . I can still use the chair . . . you know. Fatigue."

I nod through my grin. I know my dad, and now that he's made it to this step, I'll be hard pressed to get him to take it easy in that chair. There's no such thing as too much practice in his mind. Coach mentality, I suppose.

"I survived. Thought you'd want to know." Hunter's voice breaks into my celebration bubble, and my pulse ratchets up. My dad recognizes him immediately, and despite the way his stroke sometimes distorts his mouth, it seems to have left his smirk unscathed. My dad's eyes shift to me and I immediately look away. It feels as though I've been caught. Doing what? I have no idea. But definitely not something I want to be caught doing.

"Sorry I abandoned you in there. Glad the water worked. You should probably be more careful with your allergies." I clear my throat, doing my best to sound platonic, almost clinical.

"That's quite . . . a fastball you've got."

I squeeze my eyes shut, knowing my father's fan fest has now begun, and Hunter's ego is about to shine.

"Thank you. See? I was trying to tell Renleigh here that I'm pretty good at this baseball thing. It took me an hour to talk her into coming to one of my games. And they're great seats!" Hunter steps toward my dad, reaching his hand out to shake. My father adjusts his grip on his new walker and takes his hand awkwardly. Still, though, I notice the slight flex in my father's forearm. He put as much squeeze into that as he could to make his point—he's still *Dad*.

"If she won't . . . go, I will." My dad coughs out a laugh as Hunter's gaze shifts to me.

"Why don't you join her?" he suggests.

Son-of-a-bitch!

"Love to!" My dad's enthusiasm leaves me zero excuses. Looks like I'm locked into watching Hunter's game. An afternoon at the ballpark with my dad isn't the worst way to pass the time. In fact, most of my favorite memories involve this very thing.

"Sounds like I'll see you two on Thursday, then." Hunter turns his body toward mine, mouth curved up on one side. "It's a date."

"It's not a date," I respond under my breath, thankful that my father is busy working to turn his walker in the right direction.

Hunter's head tilts when our eyes meet.

"*Hmm*, it's kind of a date."

"Yeah? That's how your dates roll, Mr. Number One Draft Pick? You take fathers along to chaperone?" I roll my eyes as I laugh, and turn to follow my dad along the sidewalk, ready to support him as he takes slow steps toward our car.

"If that's what it takes for a date with you, Renleigh Blackwood, then yes. I welcome Mr. Blackwood's company," Hunter hollers.

"You can call me Coach . . . Blackwood." My dad's been paying more attention than I thought.

"Yes, sir. Coach it is," Hunter says, and I don't bother to fill him in on my father's history with the game. I don't need them bonding any more than they have already. I'm doomed enough as it is.

FIVE

HUNTER

Tulsa is an offensive beast. Of all the games to invite Renleigh to, I go and pick the one where I'm going to have to work my ass off.

On the iPad screen, I run my finger along the player and review the compilation videos of Tulsa's heart of their lineup. Again. It doesn't help that two of these guys are on rehab assignments from the Pirates. Even with oblique strains, they'll be tough outs to get.

"You getting nervous, rookie?" Roddy passes behind me as I pause the video on Tulsa's clean-up hitter.

"Nah, I don't get nervous. Just doing my homework." I slide the iPad on the top shelf of my locker and swing a leg over the bench while Roddy shoves his helmet into his locker and runs a towel over his sweat-drenched face.

"Good. If you listen to me, you'll be just fine."

He chuckles, but I know he's not kidding. Just like I know if I blow off his pitch-calling against Tulsa, he'll tell the four-hole hitter exactly what's coming just to teach me a lesson.

"Right, hit my spots, throw what you tell me to." I salute him, then lean back on my palms, propping one leg up along the bench while I weigh whether to get Roddy's advice on another matter.

"So, Renleigh . . ."

He's laughing under his breath before I say another word, shaking his head as his eyes shut.

"You knew I wouldn't be able to leave it at one and done, Roddy. I'm a glutton. Hard-headed. I need a woman to shoot me down at least six times before I even think about giving up."

It's never taken six times. It's never taken more than once, to be honest.

"Some might call that stalking, you know." He puffs out a short laugh, then slings a towel over one shoulder before pushing his locker door shut.

"Persistence. Stalking. Same thing. Anyhow . . ." I push my tongue into my cheek and let my focus get fuzzy as I stare off to the side for a moment. I fix my gaze back on him with a shrug.

"She's coming to the game. *My* game."

"You mean *our* game." He's quick to correct me, and I roll my eyes as I drop my leg back to the floor.

"Yeah, fine. Whatever. *Our game.* Now, are you going to help me out or not?"

His head falls back with a bark of laughter.

"Oh, hell no. I'm not getting involved in this. I mean, it's bad enough I've gotta catch for your ass. No way am I feeding Dale Blackwood's daughter to some rookie on an ego trip."

"Come on, man," I groan, sitting up straighter. "I promise I'm not a dick. And I'm not just trying to score points or one-up the other guys. There's something about her. I don't know what it is, but I feel like I've got to put in the work and see this one out, ya know?"

He stares at me, almost like I left him speechless. He's not saying anything, so I suppose I did. Finally, he exhales and meanders toward me, straddling the opposite end of the bench.

"Okay, so give me the lay of the land. What's your progress?" He drops his chin a touch as he glares at me.

"I talked her into taking my family seats for Thursday's game. She's bringing her dad. He seems to like me more than she does."

Roddy laughs out hard.

"I bet he does. Dale's a retired high school baseball coach. Won a few state titles here in Sweetwater. His uncle used to work for the Mavericks as a hitting coach. The Blackwoods are a bit of a baseball family. They've also got deep roots in Sweetwater. And Dale Blackwood is beloved by this town."

I nod, taking it all in.

"What's his deal? I mean, what happened to him? He had a walker, and he seemed to struggle when he spoke." I don't want to make assumptions.

Roddy nods slowly.

"Yeah, he's had a couple of strokes. The last one was two years ago, and that's when Renleigh came back home to help him out. He's come a long way, though."

"I see," I say, sucking in my bottom lip as I let Roddy's words sit with the picture I'm beginning to paint of Renleigh's situation. I'm about to ask Roddy for tips to ensure Dale is in my corner when his gaze shifts over my shoulder. I follow the path of his stare and notice the young catcher he was arguing with the other day has walked in.

"You're late," Roddy says, and there's something in his tone that makes me think I should busy myself and give the two of them space.

"I was with the trainer. Coach knows." The young catcher doesn't look Roddy in the eyes. He doesn't even bother to glance over his shoulder, in fact. He simply grabs his gear from his locker and snaps the door shut before walking back out without another word.

"Wow, and you thought I had an attitude," I mutter.

"Yeah, well . . . he's got a better reason than you do," Roddy says, getting up from the bench and heading toward the showers, pausing just long enough to say over his shoulder, "He's my son."

My attention zings to the exit where the young catcher is long gone. Despite that, I try to reconstruct his build, the color of his hair, his eyes, the sound of his voice—all of it. It's fucking uncanny how alike the two of them are. I feel stupid for not putting it together earlier. Hell, I'm probably the last to know, which I guess goes along with Roddy's assumption that I'm some self-absorbed egomaniac. I guess, in a lot of ways I am. It comes with the pitching gig. It's hard to be so responsible for a win or a loss and not shoulder some of the God complex along with the burden. But if Dale Blackwood is as passionate about baseball as Roddy says he is, I think he'll be the first one to defend me.

I'm definitely going to need him on my side.

Looks like it's time to pay the old guy a visit.

There are a few perks to living in a small town, at least as far as I'm concerned. I like my congested cities and various strip malls, crowded rooftop restaurants, live music venues, stadiums . . . *plural.* But I can't deny there is a charming quaintness to places like Sweetwater. The fact the addition of the second stoplight, something that occurred about a week before I got here, was a media frenzy for this town is amusing. And the way everyone looks familiar, even after only being here for two weeks, does lend to the sense of home. But perhaps the best advantage I've come across so far is how easy it is to find literally anyone who lives here in under an hour.

One visit to the main market was all it took for me to

figure out where the Blackwoods live. I did have to hear the produce man's favorite story about playing ball with Dale Blackwood back in their day. It was a good tale, even if I'm not quite sold on his recollection that Dale hit a ball so hard the cover came off during their state title game thirty years ago.

With a six-pack of Sam Adam's tucked in my arm, I take a deep breath and march onto the porch of the white and gray Craftsman home on the corner of Fifth Street and Gully Ranch Road. I glance to my right and note the long ramp that appears to have been built more recently, probably after one of Dale's strokes. I rap my knuckles on the screen door, then take a big step back to make some space. I can hear the hum of a television behind the door. It sounds like one of the afternoon news programs, or maybe commentary from a daytime game.

"I'm coming!" I recognize Dale's voice from the day before, so I pull the screen door open in anticipation.

A chain sliding from a lock precedes the wood door's opening, and when Dale spots me waiting on the other side, he laughs so hard it turns into a coughing fit.

"I'm not sure why my visit is so funny, but can I get you some water, Coach?" I'm proud of myself for remembering his title request.

He coughs a few more times into his fist, then scoots back from the doorway, pulling his walker with him.

"I had a feeling . . . you'd be by . . . is all. And screw the water. Hand over one of those beers." He nods toward my hospitality gift.

I promptly hold it up and step inside.

"Coming right up, Coach." I scan the wide-open living space, and smirk when I see the Yankees game on the television in the other room.

"Put the rest in the fridge, after you take one for yourself, of course," he says. I guide myself into the kitchen, pulling a single beer out for him and tucking the remaining ones next to a gallon of orange juice and a wrapped head of lettuce.

"Wish I could, but I'm throwing tomorrow. I like to detox the day before." I unscrew the cap and toss it in the trash before handing the cold one to Renleigh's dad.

"You pitchers are . . . a weird bunch. If you think . . . drinking a single beer . . . is going to screw up your rhythm, you've got bigger problems." He brings the bottle to his lips and tilts his head back, taking a big drink before releasing an, "Ahh."

"You're probably right," I relent, sliding onto one of the nearby stools.

Dale rests his elbows on the high-top portion of the counter and cradles his beer, his walker tucked into his belly. He's thin, but there's muscle to his arms and chest, probably from the rehab work he's been doing.

"So, I've been schooled on all things Coach Blackwood," I confess. *All things* might be a bit overboard, but enough.

"Is that . . . so." He smirks at me over the lip of his beer before holding it to his mouth and tipping it back.

"Yeah, Roddy McKinney is a big fan of yours."

Dale chuckles.

"He is now. He sure . . . wasn't a fan of mine . . . when he played for me."

I narrow my eyes as I mentally piece it together. Makes sense that Roddy would have grown up here. And that he knows the Blackwoods better than most because of it.

"Don't suppose you have tips for how to handle him?" I quirk a brow, and Dale sucks in the right side of his top lip. I don't think he has full control over it.

"Just listen to what he says." He sets his beer down and fixes his hands on his walker.

"Yeah, I'm learning it's better to have him on my side."

Dale maneuvers his walker toward one of the leather chairs in the main room. He awkwardly glances over his shoulder toward his beer, and I gather he means for me to bring it with me, so I do.

I set it on a wooden Maverick's coaster on the nearby end table, then sit on the sofa across from Dale.

"How long have you been working with the walker?" I glance at the fancy contraption he's parked next to him.

"About thirty-six . . . hours." He chuckles, a bit out of breath.

I nod.

"I thought about going into physical therapy my freshman year of college, but then I topped a hundred miles per hour with my fastball. Talk of anything other than going pro seemed silly. Besides, it turns out I don't like blood."

Dale's expression morphs into an almost suspicious smile. He probably thinks I'm feeding him bullshit so I can get the secret code to crack his daughter's armor. I really did set out to be a physical therapist at first. Mostly because being an MLB pitcher seemed like a pipe dream. I grew two more inches when I turned nineteen, though, and something just clicked.

"The girl likes . . . her steak medium rare." He folds his hands over his belly and tilts his head as he continues to smirk at me.

"Renleigh?" I mean, duh. Of course, Renleigh.

He nods.

"I think I've got to get her to dinner first. I'm not sure I've earned my way past the smoothie shop yet."

"You got her . . . to go to a game." He takes a deep breath, then continues. "That's more than most. Just . . . don't fuck it up."

My swift laugh surprises me. His candor is refreshing, if not harsh.

"I'll try not to. Mind telling me how?" I squint one eye.

He picks up his beer, tipping it toward me.

"Don't let Tulsa . . . jack a bunch of homers." His silent

snicker tells me all I need to know about his and Roddy's relationship. I see why Roddy is protective of this man. And vice versa.

"Got it." I get to my feet and step around the table, holding a hand out to shake his again. His grip is surprisingly firm this time. "So, basically, don't look like—"

"An overrated jackass," he finishes for me.

He winks, and I somehow feel less sure of myself than I did before I came over here. But I've accomplished one thing. Dale Blackwood might just be in my corner. And if it doesn't piss his daughter off too much, she might just let me buy her a damn steak.

SIX
RENLEIGH

It's been a while since I sat in these seats. My sister and I used to come to the Mavericks games with my dad when we were kids to catch any of his old players taking a crack at the big leagues. Roddy McKinney's the only one who ever hit it truly big, but a lot of my father's former athletes got their shot on the field.

"Are you sure . . . you don't want one of those? It's a . . . classic." My dad gestures toward the wilted poppyseed bun hugging a blistered hotdog clutched in the palms of the man two rows in front of us, and I scoff and shake my head.

"Now that I know what those things are made of, I just can't," I laugh out. "And no, you can't either. Those things probably got you into this mess."

I prop my feet up on the seat in front of me and dig into my popcorn instead, leaving my dad with his celery and low sodium dip.

"You think that butter . . . flavor is any better than a hotdog?" He chuckles his way into a cough, and I shrug.

"Probably not." I lean to my right, pressing my shoulder against his.

Spending an afternoon out at the ballfield with my father isn't the worst way to give in to Hunter's advances. I'm still not sold on my sister's position on the whole thing, though. Flings aren't exactly my thing. Though, now that I'm watching the six-foot-plus man saunter onto the grass in tight baseball pants and a compression shirt that does literally everything for his physique, I'm more open to the idea.

"I told him . . . to listen to Roddy," my dad says, nudging my arm with his and jostling me out of my temporary drool fest. I guess I have been in a bit of a dry spell since I left the university. I haven't exactly had time to date.

"That's good," I say, not fully unpacking my father's tidbit until I'm well into chewing another handful of popcorn.

"Wait," I cough out, dropping my feet to the ground and twisting in my seat to face my dad. "You told Hunter to listen to Roddy?"

My eyes narrow, and my father practically smirks his way into a massive bite of a celery stick.

"Oh no, you don't. You don't get to fill your mouth with food I know you don't really want just to get out of this. When did you tell him to listen to Roddy? Because I was there when you met, and I don't remember any such conversation."

My father's smirk is itching to turn into laughter. He's loving this. My dad has never been the kind to ward off pursuers. I'm probably the only daddy's girl whose father actively tries to marry her off to ballplayers on the regular. I'm shocked he hasn't tried to broker a deal with Roddy to have me marry his son, Jake. My gut says that's because Roddy and Jake have their own messy relationship to sort out first.

"He stopped by . . . the house. Real gentleman." My father snaps off another bite of his stalk and turns his attention to the field, where Hunter is now warming up with some long toss.

"Real gentleman, huh?" I sink back in my seat and pop

another handful of popcorn in my mouth while I study Hunter with a bit more scrutiny.

How the hell did he find out where I live? And shit! He knows where I live!

I mesh my father's commentary with my experience so far, and I can't deny the fact that cocky or not, Hunter Reddick doesn't seem to be an asshole. Perhaps I'm being a bit unfair to him. I mean, he does have nice arms. And legs. And his thighs . . . I do like his thighs.

"You gonna pick . . . your chin up?"

I turn to my right and glare at my father.

"My chin is just fine," I protest. I may have been gawking a bit. Fine. A lot.

I've always liked watching long toss. When I was a kid, I would bet my sister on how far one of the players could throw. I always believed they could throw farther than she did, and I won those bets half the time. Hunter, however, moves farther than my longest expectations. By the time I shift my gaze back to the field, he's moved to the opposite foul pole and is easily zinging the ball across the outfield to Roddy without a single hop. When he starts to jog back toward us, Roddy holds up his glove and props his mask on top of his head as he saunters toward my father.

"I thought I saw a familiar face over here," he says, tucking his glove under his arm before stepping over the base-line wall to visit my father.

A hulk of a man, Roddy bends in half and hugs my father to his side before reaching his hand across my father's body to shake mine. I give his palm a squeeze and smile, a little embarrassed to be here. Of all the Mavericks players, Roddy is the one to know my hardline stance on dating these guys— *any* guys. He doesn't seem to be judging me with his gaze, though, and that's probably because he's happy to see my dad.

"How are you feeling, Coach?" Roddy kneels to make it

easier to look my dad in the eyes and hear his start-and-stop speech, and I let the two of them catch up while I focus on the leg stretches Hunter is completing mid-field.

He squats, facing me, and pushes the brim of his hat up just a touch as the sun catches his blue eyes. He's a hundred feet away, and I can't be certain, but I think he's staring at me. He pushes one knee toward the grass, stretching his quad. His chest puffs up with a deep breath, his shoulders somehow widening their span before he switches legs and repeats it all again.

"He's the real deal, you know?"

"Huh?" I snap out of my stupid, embarrassing trance again to meet Roddy's eyes.

He nods toward Hunter.

"The kid's the real deal on the mound. He's got the stuff to go far. But don't you dare breathe a lick of that to him, you hear?" Roddy stands but keeps his chin low and his eyes on mine.

"I wouldn't dare. Hell, I might not even talk to him after this game." That's a lie, and we both know it.

Roddy chuckles.

"Sure, you won't," he says, pulling his mask down and turning his attention to my dad. "Enjoy the game, Coach."

I stew with my thoughts, mentally protesting what I know is true—I'm a little into Hunter Reddick. He's fucking hot. And I'm so very single. And yeah, maybe it would be nice to feel a man again. For a little while. What's the harm?

"He's got you figured . . . out," my dad teases.

"Who does?" I pull my water bottle from the cupholder in front of me and unscrew the cap.

"They both do," my dad huffs out with a laugh.

"*Hmm.*" I hum because I'd like to think I'm more complicated than the cliché girl who crushes on the hot, young pitcher.

Hunter finishes his stretches, picks up his glove, and makes his way toward us. I force myself to look away. I busy myself with my phone at first, then lean forward and look down my aisle to count the bodies in the seats, squinting to pretend I'm looking for someone. When enough time passes that I feel good about the coast being clear, I turn my attention back to the field, and Hunter is long gone. My stomach tightens, and the squeeze grows stronger the longer I scan the dugout and then the bullpen in search of him.

I'm such a hypocrite.

"Ladies and gentlemen. Welcome to Sun Oil Stadium, home of *your* Sweetwater Mavericks."

I stand and hold out my hand to help my father steady himself on his feet. We brought the chair today because I wasn't sure how easy it would be for him to navigate his walker through this old stadium. There are a lot of quirks to the layout, including random chunks of concrete where walls once stood. We parked the chair at the back of the section near one of the seat attendants, and despite the awkward length of the stadium steps, he managed to tackle them on the way to our seats with my help. I'm proud of him.

The announcer goes through the usual drill, mentioning all the quirky mom and pop businesses in Sweetwater that sponsor the summer season every year, and I whistle when there's a shoutout to Earl's Big Easy. I think half the team does the same. In a college town where most of the bars are wannabe clubs with loud dance tunes blasting until midnight, Earl's remains tried and true to its roots. It's a pub in every sense, with giant TVs sketchily hung on walls and Mavericks gear as well as some from the college slapped on the walls. The pool tables are well-worn, but the Saturday night bets still get placed between old timers. Every new class of Mavericks players gets schooled in darts and served some of the best microbrews in Oklahoma until the weather turns cold and they all head off to warmer places for the off-season. Earl's daughter, Daisy, was nice enough to give me a job when I came back home, despite my lack of bartending experience. I'm a quick study. It's why I did so well in school until I had to drop out.

My palms sweat as the players' names are announced one at a time and they line up for the national anthem. It's a decent crowd for a Thursday game, and I'm beginning to realize people came out here today for one reason—*him.*

"Your starting pitcher, the number one draft pick by the Texas Rangers out of Pacific Coastal University, Hunter Reddick!"

There's an audible roar from the few thousand gathered for today's game, and my father's voice is in the mix. He cups his mouth and does his best to holler as he jabs me with his elbow, urging me to join in. I roll my neck reluctantly and push two fingers into my mouth so I can whistle. I normally use this skill to break up fights, but I guess I can use it in support of Hunter today.

We quiet down for the anthem, and I keep my gaze fixed on Hunter's back the whole time—number thirty-four pops from the crisp white in blue lettering. How fitting that he's wearing such a storied number, Nolan Ryan's. I wonder if he really is as good as Roddy says.

My dad and I settle into our seats, and Hunter takes the mound. He's methodical through his warmups, snapping the ball into Roddy's mitt and walking in a slow half circle around the mound after each pitch. His jaw works, and I hold my breath waiting for him to spit to the side. Of course he never does though, instead blowing a massive pink bubble before snapping his gaze to me and fucking grinning. Dammit—not only am I caught, but I also can't ding him for chewing tobacco. He just keeps notching out green flags.

He makes quick work of the first three batters, getting a fly out to right field from the first hitter, and striking out two and three with a total of ten pitches for the inning. He pulls his hat from his head and runs his hand through his wavy brown hair as he nears the dugout, and his cheek dimples with the smile he sends my way.

I hold up my hand and wiggle my open palm side to side, as if I'm scoring him a fifty percent for what was clearly an A-plus outing. Hunter grips his chest and mouths, "Ouch." And then he dips into the dugout and out of sight.

"Yep," my dad utters.

"Shut up," I snap back.

His stubborn, smug laugh is the last word.

Hunter makes it through five innings, and other than an iffy call that earns him a walk, he finishes with four strikeouts and one earned run. Just over sixty pitches, too, which I know from being schooled by my father, is pretty fucking efficient on the mound.

"Looks like Roddy . . . was right," my dad says. I've been waiting for him to pipe up.

"Yeah, I know," I sigh. I'm playing up my disappointment for show, and I think my father can tell. There were a few times I was audibly impressed, breaking out the finger whistle more than once when he strutted off the field after closing out an inning.

He is the real deal. And I don't have to know a lot about baseball to see it. It's in his presence. It shows in the hard line of his jaw that flexes when he digs in to throw with a little extra *oomph*. It's obvious by the way he sits away from the rest of the team until he's done pitching, locked in, and studying whoever is coming up to face him next. And it's in the way he takes it all in and never makes the same mistake twice.

Hunter might not realize it, but Roddy's tough love is also genuine love. He likes him. He meant it when he said he saw the talent shining in his heart. It also might be why he made that bet with him the other night and urged him to talk to me. Perhaps there's a part of Roddy that thinks Hunter Reddick might be good for me, too.

"Hey!" A short whistle chirps from the dugout.

I lean forward and find Hunter's blue eyes peering at me from beneath his Maverick's hat. I can't quite see his entire face, but his brow rises, lifting the brim of his cap with it, and he holds up a ball. He flicks it forward and back with his wrist a few times, and I hold out my hands ready for him to toss it. I'm relieved that I catch it when he finally does, especially given the anxious middle schooler perched on the edge of his seat down our row. That kid has been grabbing foul balls left and right.

"Souvenir, huh?" My dad brushes his hand against mine, and I unfurl my fingers to show off the ball. Only then do I see the note scribbled in blue ink between the seams.

Did I earn dinner?

My lip pulls up on one side automatically, and my cheeks warm as I glance back to the dugout to find those same blue eyes peeking back at me and awaiting my answer.

Hunter's brow lifts again, and it tickles me the way his hat raises every time.

"I don't know," I ruminate, knowing full well I've crossed that mental barrier when it comes to him. I'm going to say yes.

Lucky for Hunter, he doesn't have to wait through me toying with him.

"You can pick her up . . . at seven," my dad says, somehow finding enough breath to really shout his words to Hunter—as well as the dozen or so fans seated immediately around us.

A few people giggle, and a pair of college girls sneer at me. They have not been shy about ogling the taut fabric hugging Hunter's thighs and ass every time he walks back to the mound. To be fair, I've ogled too. I'm just a lot more subtle about it.

"Fine," I finally say.

Hunter jumps up from whatever step he's perched on, and for a fraction of a second, I get a glimpse of his entire face, boastful smile and all, before he drops back below the dugout roof for the rest of the game.

SEVEN
HUNTER

This truck is literally the only nice thing I've bought with my money. You can't head to Oklahoma and Texas in your mom's old sedan and get taken seriously. These parts call for a truck. At least, that's the excuse I made to justify blowing through seventy grand on something that started depreciating the moment I drove it off the lot.

Dad was on board, which helped ease the guilt.

Mom was not, which ramped the guilt right back up.

That's how it goes when you're the son of an accountant and a salesman, I suppose. Two schools of thought when it comes to money, though even my dad has to admit my mom is right about all things financial more often than he is.

Still, the lift kit and running boards are pretty tight, and the roll bar I absolutely do not need but had to have adds a certain legitimacy to the entire vehicle. The splurge felt warranted. I worked my ass off for that signing bonus. And the sponsorship deal I inked with Big Man Protein Drinks has already more than replaced the funds.

But now that I'm parked in front of the Blackwood home, checking my breath for the tenth time, I worry that this truck gives off the wrong impression—at least for this audience of one.

It's a bit flashy—the dash has more touchscreens and tech than steering wheel and odometer. And these new jeans I'm wearing, fuck if they aren't tight. I adjust myself and bend my knees to work out a little more space, but to no avail. There's zero chance I'm not going to sport obvious wood in these things. Only way to avoid it is if I strap my cock to my thigh with duct tape.

The sky is a dusty blue, striped with faint purple clouds that are quickly disappearing as dusk turns to night. The air is sweet from the flowering milkweeds and holds crispness as if the temperature is deciding whether or not it wants to be chilly. This place is a long way from home and full of possibilities. I breathe it in and take my first step toward the front porch, and the door swings open before I can knock.

"Took you long enough," Renleigh huffs, popping the screen door open and nodding over her shoulder to urge me inside.

The television is on in the background, and it sounds like one of those reality shows where contestants have to nearly die or eat dirt to win a hundred bucks.

"You were waiting for me to pull up?"

I shut the door behind me as she moves into the sitting room toward her dad, a sweatshirt slung over her arm, along with a green fanny pack-looking thing.

"I'm starving, so yeah . . . I was waiting for you to pull up. And then you were standing out there for what felt like forever. I was ten seconds away from heating up a frozen dinner and calling it a night." There's a twinkle in her eye, along with a slight lift on one side of her mouth, as she glances at me with what I'm going to classify as a smirk.

"You're giving me shit," I say.

"I'm giving you shit." She bends down and kisses her dad on the cheek, and he offers me a thumbs up when her back is turned. I cross my fingers, then do the sign of the cross for good measure, which makes him chuckle.

"All right, I'm separating you two," Renleigh says as she faces me.

She's putting up a tough front, but a few signs point in my favor. For one, her hair is down. I've only seen her a handful of times, but it's always pulled into a ponytail or bun when she's in work mode. It was up for my game today, too, which is probably normal for a game. But wavy blonde hair that she's clearly styled, probably with one of those styling tools, is definitely date hair.

Second, she's wearing heeled boots, black ones, up to her knees. Sure, they're over tight jeans, but also . . . those are *tight* jeans. And the black shirt she's wearing is fairly see-through, enough that I can see the details of the black lace bra underneath.

She's going to be pissed when she finds out we aren't going out for steak.

"Don't wait up," I say over my shoulder as I trail behind Renleigh to the door.

"I'll be home early," she adds, hitting me with a swift glare and pouty lips.

"We'll see," I hum.

The nerves I felt before have been replaced with a familiar rush. There's something about being around Renleigh that makes me feel as though I'm stepping on the mound, about to face off with some fierce competition. While some guys might find it intimidating, my reaction is far different—I'm intrigued. No, more than that. I'm driven by it, and if I can somehow convince her to let me kiss her, just once, it might just shock my heart out of rhythm.

I hold the truck door open for her, and she actually takes my hand when I offer it to help her climb inside. Her skin is cool to the touch, and her nails glimmer with a shimmering white polish that reminds me of snow. They're cut short, probably because it's impossible to sling beers with talons on your hands, but they're long enough to dig into skin if the mood is right.

And that thought right there tests my hard-on theory.

I shut Raleigh's door and take a slow walk around the back of the truck to give me time to adjust myself. Fucking tight-ass jeans are doing the job.

"This is nice," she says as I slide behind the wheel. She runs her fingertips across the dashboard screen, hovering over the temperature controls and turning her side up a few degrees. I keep the air low because this humidity is the real deal. I wasn't prepared for it.

"Thanks. Not like I made it or anything. I mean, I basically picked it off a lot in Irvine, California, so really . . . zero skills on my part were involved. In fact, maybe I should write the CEO at Ford and pass the thanks on to him, since it's his design and all that." I buckle up and rev the engine before shifting into drive.

"I doubt the CEO had anything to do with it either. You can just hang on to the compliment, and if you ever sit next to some design engineer on a plane one day, pass it on to him."

I chuckle and sort of love that she can bullshit with me.

"Will do," I say with a nod.

I force myself to keep my eyes ahead as I pull down her street, despite the fact she's running her palms and her perfect fingertips along her thighs.

"So, where did you want to go? There's not much in town, but over in Jacksonville, there's a smokehouse that's pretty good, or—"

"I was thinking maybe we could drive into the city. It's a little over an hour, but there's somewhere I need to go, and I could really use your advice." I glance at her to gauge her reaction, and am met with bunched lips and a wrinkled brow. "I take it you weren't kidding about that being hungry bit you said earlier."

She shakes with a single, silent laugh, then folds her arms

over her chest as she sets her attention back to the roadway ahead.

"It's after seven, and I've only had a bucket of popcorn. I wasn't kidding about being hungry." Her tone is legitimately grumpy, and I'm tempted to abandon my grand plan altogether and ask for her directions to the smoke house. But then, she gives me an inch.

"What do you need help with?"

I smirk. I don't have a sister nearby to run this stuff by. They live in California. So, I'm going on instincts with this one. Taking a big swing, so to speak.

"You know IKEA?" I quirk a brow, and Renleigh stares at me in dead silence.

My pulse speeds up a tick, and for a beat, I worry I played this wrong. Women love IKEA. I read it on some influencer's post a few months ago and tucked the idea away for the perfect moment. I was really sure this was it. But maybe—

"Are you kidding me?"

Her statement is devoid of emotion, so I'm still not sure.

I shake my head and utter, "Uh uh." She might smack me and jump out of the truck. Damn it all if I played this wrong.

"What are we buying?" Her eyes light up a hint, I swear.

"I need everything. Basically." It's not a lie because my rental is bone bare. I have a mattress on the floor and a folding table, and a sofa that came with the place that I refuse to lay on because there have been a lot of renters before me.

"Everything. So like, bookshelves, dresser, table . . ."

"I mean, I probably don't *need* bookshelves."

She waves me off.

"If we're going to IKEA, you're getting bookshelves. Unless you were lying about being a big reader." She stares at me with the intensity of a detective trying to work me for a confession.

"I wasn't lying. I read, yeah. I mean, I didn't exactly haul my books down here with me for Triple A ball, but—"

"Right, right. Because you're just passing through. You'll be called up soon. Short stay in Sweetwater and all that." She throws my words back at me swiftly, and I can't help but wonder if my short tenure in this town is part of her hesitation to give me a shot.

"I didn't really want to haul books from place to place. Eventually, I'd like to have a home somewhere. And I don't know if that's Sweetwater or Dallas or . . ."

She's turned her attention back to the roadway, and her arms are once again folded over her chest.

"It's not Sweetwater. This isn't the kind of place people choose to make home."

There's a slight bite to her tone, so I let her words simmer in the air for a few solid minutes as I pull onto the highway and head toward Oklahoma City. I wait until her arms untangle and she appears to relax a touch before I broach the subject of her dad.

"Your dad coached in Sweetwater for a long time, huh?"

She shifts in her seat, her blue eyes flitting to me briefly. A few strands of hair have blown across her face, so I reach over and tuck them behind her ear. She stiffens at my gesture, but her gaze follows the movement of my hand, and her lips form a faint smile.

"Thanks," she says, her voice softer than before. "And yeah, my dad was born in Sweetwater. He went to Florida State for college, though. He played there, met my mom, and they moved back to Sweetwater when the coaching job opened up. So, thirty years or so? He'd still be out there if he could handle the stress of it all. It's not so much the standing, but not being able to kick dirt on the umpire that really holds him back."

She breathes out a soft laugh that I mimic. I can see the coach's fire in her dad based on the few interactions we've had. He reminds me a lot of the ones I've played for.

"Did you ever think about leaving Sweetwater?" I chew on the inside of my mouth when she sighs.

"I did leave, for three and a half years. I went to Tennessee to study psychology. I'd like to work in family therapy. Of course, I need a license to do that, and since I'm twelve credit hours shy of my degree, it looks like I'm more likely to renew my liquor serving license before I ever get an opportunity to help people navigate complex relationships."

I give her a half-hearted smile.

"I mean, isn't that sort of what bartending is?" I shrug, and she laughs.

"Yeah, I guess. I don't know that anyone in Sweetwater listens to the shit I say, though."

It's quiet for a few long seconds before I respond.

"I listen to you. For example, I now know I should ask what's in a smoothie before I drink it."

"You probably didn't need me to tell you that," she says with a short laugh.

"I *shouldn't* have, but clearly, I did." I rub my palm along my neck, the visceral memory of the itching and swelling still very front-of-mind.

"Okay, well, one person listens, then. Of course, you aren't from Sweetwater, so do you really count?" She scrutinizes me with one eye squinting, and I slap my palm to my chest.

"Ouch! I'd like to think I count. Man, you are harsh!"

"I warned you I was hungry."

I nod, checking my mirrors as I switch lanes to the left so I can lay on the gas and get us to the city a few minutes faster.

"You did. And I listened. One order of IKEA meatballs coming right up."

I manage to get to the IKEA parking lot in under an hour, and as promised, I have a dish of hot Swedish meatballs in Renleigh's palms, and we're on our way up an escalator with enormous blue shopping bags looped over our forearms.

"Are you sure you don't want one?" Renleigh holds a single meatball out on a fork, but I shake my head. I got a glimpse of this girl in hangry mode. I'm not denying her a single calorie.

"I'll wait and grab something on the way out, maybe a smoothie," I tease.

She smirks, then pops the morsel into her mouth and chews.

"Let's do this," I announce as we set off into the maze of strangely spelled closet organizers and end tables.

Renleigh takes a seat at one of the kitchen counters while I peruse the first mock apartment. She swivels in the bright orange circle poised atop a chrome pole, and I flop back on the oversized canvas sofa.

"This feels like me," I say, glancing around what is definitely a masculine, college-aimed space.

Renleigh wrinkles her nose as she gets up and tosses her empty carton in a nearby trash.

"It looks too messy. You need something that looks like you cleaned it even though you didn't. Let's keep going." She holds out a hand and helps me to my feet, and our fingertips tangle for an extra second that feels both awesome and awkward.

"Messy, got it. What exactly makes a living room messy?" I back up into the next design, running my hand along the wooden back of a chair. There's a black leather sofa in this space, and the walls are covered in dark wood paneling. I don't know that I want to rework my rental condo so much that I have to completely dismantle the walls when I leave, but I do like the rich wood look.

"This is neater, but still not quite right. You want the upholstery to be low-maintenance, and black is good, or brown. But this feels too cold. We need something that also says . . . *take a nap here.*"

"Nap. Yeah, I like naps."

I follow Renleigh through a few more spaces, and when we come to a soft leather sofa, we both pause with our hands cupping our chins.

"What do you think?" I quirk a brow and she meets my gaze.

"We should test it," she says, rushing around the gold and white coffee table to slouch on one end of the sofa while I do the same at the other. We prop our feet up on the coffee table, and stare ahead at the cardboard television propped on a matching entertainment center across from us.

"Yeah," I say.

"See? Home. You can practically envision your Sunday night here, winding down with a good bowl of cereal, the remote stuffed somewhere between these cushions," she says, her hand diving into the space about a half second before mine.

"Oh, sorry," I say, my palm pressed against the back of her hand in the crease. I don't pull away because her eyes flashed to mine, and time has stopped.

"It's okay," she says, dragging her hand away slowly. The feel of it grazing along mine produces a pleasant tickle. My fingers curl in response as I pull my hand into my own lap.

"It's a good nap couch, don't you think?" I twist so my back is against the armrest, and I pull one leg up so I'm facing her with my body open and ready for her to crawl into the space I made.

She shakes her head with a sharp laugh, and gets up from the sofa.

"Nice try, Hunter."

I exhale and lick my wounds, but I'm quick to rebound from rejection. I have to be. I play a sport where failure is built into the stats. Achieving thirty percent at anything in this game is to be highly successful. I didn't expect to bat a thousand with Renleigh tonight.

I pull the card for the sofa, along with the matching living room pieces, then follow Renleigh into the next department where she helps pick out a dining table, dishes and silverware, and some linens. By the time we make it to the register, I've rung up about ten grand in Ikea furnishings and décor, most of which will be delivered. I do, however, get to take home one very important item—the bookcase.

Renleigh waits near the exit with the long box on a rolling cart, and I back my truck to the loading area. It's starting to sprinkle, so one of the employees rips off a large sheet of plastic to use as a tarp, and Renleigh helps me wrap the box as I slide it into the truck bed.

Our ride home is a lot lighter, and I'm careful not to drill too deeply with questions about her dad and her coming home to care for him. I gleaned enough details for now on the trip out, and I get the sense she isn't keen on sharing personal information with people she doesn't know well. So, that's my next step—getting to know her well. And to do that, I think the two of us should spend a lot more time together.

Maybe, say, a sleepover.

"You know, I could really use a hand putting the SNUFLEUPERGIS together." I make up the name of the shelf because there's no way I am ever going to remember what it's really called. My attempt makes Renleigh laugh.

"You should call Roddy. I bet he's got a free evening." She smiles at me with tight lips, and I groan teasingly.

"Are you really relegating me to spending my night with Roddy? I'm trying to be smooth here." I pull off the highway and turn down the long rural road that leads toward Sweetwater's town center.

"*Mmm*, you are smooth, Hunter Reddick. And I bet those lines get the job done with most girls." She flashes me a smug grin, and I hate that she thinks I'm a player.

"I can't say I've thrown out that line before."

"Oh, am I your first IKEA date?" Her expression reads that she's sure she's not.

"Uh, yeah. I'm not buying out the IKEA catalogue every weekend to impress the ladies. I honestly thought we'd have some fun. And didn't we? Have fun?"

She blinks a few times when I glance at her, and her lips part but remain silent. I sigh through my nose as I look back to the roadway.

I turn into her historic neighborhood and wind my way toward the Blackwood home. As I pull to a stop, Renleigh unbuckles her seat belt and lunges across the center console, pressing her lips to my cheek. I freeze at her touch, then slowly swivel my head as her fingertips graze against my jawline and I turn to face her.

"I did have fun. A lot of it, actually." She sucks in her bottom lip, and her eyes flit to my mouth.

Fuck it.

I wrap my hand around her wrist, holding her hand against my face while my other hand moves to nudge the bottom of her chin, coaxing her mouth up just enough that I can press a soft kiss to her lips. I restrain myself, limiting our kiss to a chaste, dusting of skin on skin, though it takes every ounce of will power in my body to stop myself from nipping at her plump bottom lip and dragging her body into my lap.

"You sure you don't want to come back to my place and help me build the . . ." I look up through my lashes, and she chuckles.

"The SNUFLEUPERGIS?"

I drop my gaze back to hers, and my mouth curves into a faint grin.

"Yes, the SNUFLEUPERGIS. What do you say?"

My knuckle tickles her jawline, and her gaze narrows and grows more certain.

"They give you one of those Allen wrenches for that. I

think you'll be just fine." She slides back into her seat and pushes open her door, letting herself out before I have a chance to run over there and do it for her.

"I had a nice time, Hunter Reddick, number one draft pick."

And for the second time in less than a week, she leaves me with those words and a cock so hard I could use it to pinch hit in tomorrow's game.

EIGHT
RENLEIGH

I don't sleep well. If I can make it through the night without waking up a dozen times with a racing mind, I call that a win. So the fact I'm blinking my eyes open and it's bright in my room has me scratching my head a bit.

I didn't drink last night. And while I don't know Hunter well, I don't get the sense he's the type of guy to roofie a woman with laced Swedish meatballs. I sit up and stretch my arms over my head, expecting to feel achy or sore perhaps, but no. I feel . . . great.

Taking advantage of this rare gift, I slip out of bed and pad down the hallway to the bathroom with my Earl's T-shirt and clean jeans tucked under my arm. When I push the handle, however, it doesn't budge.

"What the . . ."

I press my ear to the door and clearly hear water running. The television is murmuring from downstairs, and I can't fathom my dad making miraculous overnight strides to the point he's climbing stairs to use this shower rather than the one on the main floor.

"Hey, Dad?" I holler down the stairwell.

He coughs but doesn't answer, so I step to the edge of the

steps and lean around the corner to peer into the living room. My sister is sitting on the sofa, and my dad is in his recliner with a plate of what looks like egg whites propped on his chest.

"Hey, Linds?"

I get my sister's attention, and she flips around to flash me a toothy grin that reads more like a warning. I'm doing my best to work through the clues when the nightmare she was trying to warn me about exits the bathroom door behind me.

"Looks like someone slept in today."

My mother's voice sends shivers down my spine, and I visibly shudder as I turn to face her. She purses her lips while leaning her head to one side and scrunching her wet hair with *my* towel.

"Really, Renleigh? You're not a teenager anymore. I figured you'd outgrown the whole *my mom is the bad guy* phase." She's wearing one of her matching workout sets, lavender yoga pants with a white stripe on either leg with a matching sports bra-type top. My mom is in incredible shape. She still runs several miles a day. She gets up at four to get the miles in so she can spend the rest of her day ruling the business world on her computer or in boardrooms.

She's a shark. Literally, that's what the people who hire her call her. She's both a legal expert and a master of crisis communications. And she's obsessed with her work. So much so that the thought of slowing down and staying in Sweetwater when my father needed her was basically, well, unthinkable. The lure of a big oil company job was simply too strong.

"Nope. Still smack in the middle of that phase, it seems. Can I have my towel back so I can run it through the dryer before I shower?" I hold my hand out, and she dumps the damp cloth in my palm.

"I didn't want to disturb your dad's space, and it is still my house, you know." She nails me with her signature superior glare before heading down the stairs to join my sister and father.

My eyes widen with fury, but I bite my tongue instead of uttering, "Half of it." I toss my wet towel in my hamper and pull a clean one from the folded laundry on my dresser. I lock the bathroom door behind me and pound out a message to my sister before starting the shower again. Who knows how much hot water my mom saved for me.

> ME: When did she show up? Is she here for long? WTF!

I pace in the tight space while my sister types her response.

> LINDSEY: She's in town on business. I didn't know. I'm sure Dad did, but you know how he is.

I stare at my sister's words and sigh before texting back.

> ME: Yeah. He's a sucker.

I reflect on those last few words before hitting send, then delete them and send a simpler *yeah*.

My parents are divorced, but the hostility that usually resides between spouses is instead between my mother and me. Even Lindsey seems more willing to go with this strange arrangement my parents chose. Probably because she doesn't like to look at things critically the way I do. I look at my parents' situation and see a man so in love with a woman that he's willing to accept whatever relationship he can have with her just so he has a piece of her in his life.

Lindsey once called it romantic, but I think it's selfish. My mom is exploiting my dad's soft heart so she can keep her toe in this life whenever she wants to pop in for a visit. She says she loves him, but I think if you love someone, you make sacrifices. Of course, I have yet to come across another person who is willing to pick someone else over themselves, so I'm pretty sure love is a farce.

I can't pretend I'm here to be noble. I'm here because of duty. And guilt. And because hiring a full-time caretaker in my place would require my dad to sell this house or accept financial help from my mom, which, *I'm* not willing to let pass. She doesn't get to ease her guilt by buying her way out of this situation. She should be here. And yeah, I'm petty enough to play martyr since she's not. And I know deep down, that really eats at her.

The hot water runs out on my shower before I'm done having practice arguments with my mom in my head, and the unexpected start to my day leaves me feeling unsettled while I finish drying my hair and getting ready for my shift at Earl's. By the time I get downstairs, there's a plate of toast and cold egg whites waiting for me, and my sister is hovering around the kitchen, probably positioning herself to step between my mom and me if I decide to escalate things. Lindsey has never been a fan of conflict. Apparently, I am.

"Hey, Dad. I'm getting off at four today, so I can pick you up from physical therapy." I make eyes at my sister as I slide the cold eggs into the trash and wrap the toast in a napkin to take with me.

"I'll take him today. I'd like to see this progress he's been bragging about," my mom says.

I purse my lips and hold my sister's gaze. She drove over today to take my dad to his appointment so I could get to work on time. I'm sure she rearranged her schedule to do so, planning care for the twins while she's gone. This is what happens when my mom shows up on a whim. Plans go out the window.

"Right. Well, enjoy the show," I huff, shaking my head as I snag my jacket and head out the door. My chest burns with a hint of guilt, but only because I don't like being a brat with my father. My sister can handle me. I'm frustrated by the whole arrangement, and if I stick around, I'm going to level my mom with a lot of cruel stuff my father doesn't deserve to hear.

My phone buzzes in my lap once I get in the Jeep. It's a text from my sister. I sigh but read it, knowing she's going to call me out for my behavior.

LINDSEY: You really need to get laid.

A short laugh shakes my chest. At least she let me have it with humor. Although she's probably not wrong.

ME: I'll keep that in mind. Sorry for being a bitch.

LINDSEY: Good. And don't be. If you weren't one, how would I look so good?

I laugh louder this time, then toss my phone in the passenger seat and head to work.

The main bar is packed as I tie my apron around my waist. Today's another home game, and it's Friday, so anyone within an hour's drive snuck away early and is crowding us here. Draft beer at Earl's is about half the price of what it is at the ballpark, so people came here to pre-game before walking to the stadium for an afternoon game. It's good for tips, but it's hard to handle a rowdy bunch with less staff. Thank God Daisy shows up for early games. All the muscle in the world at the doors is still half the deterrent of the fiery brunette who runs this place.

"I've got this handled. Why don't you take care of the crew in the back." She nods to the tables, where a dozen or so Mavericks players are clustered. Empty pizza pans are stacked atop metal stands, and there's a lone piece left on the one closest to Hunter.

"Shouldn't y'all be warming up or something?" I nod in

the direction of the stadium as I gather the empty pans, minus the one with a single slice left. There are a few soda pitchers on the table, and half of the guys are rubbing their eyes with the butts of their palms, likely nursing decent hangovers.

"None of us are starting today. We've got an hour before we have to report," one of them explains.

"Ah," I say with a nod, my gaze sliding over to Hunter. He's sitting back in his chair, his arms crossed over his chest and a smirk on his face. My body rushes with sudden heat from his attention, and my cheeks burn as I wonder if anyone else at the table notices my physical reaction. This isn't like me. Maybe my sister is right.

"I tried, but they won't let me start every game," Hunter jokes.

I give him a soft laugh. His cockiness is a little cute.

"Yeah, well, if you want to be able to shift a car from park to drive when you're thirty, you probably should take your off days seriously. Arm care and all that." I squint one eye, and he shakes with a silent laugh.

"I take care of my arm, Renleigh. Believe me, I take care of my entire body when it needs it." His brow quirks, and the damn heat wave strikes my core again.

"Well, good thing it's an off day for you. You can take care of yourself all damn day." My lips buzz with nervous energy, but I manage to form a smirk anyway.

"Ohhhh, that's rough, man!" One of Hunter's teammates nudges him in the bicep with a balled fist, but Hunter's gaze remains fixed on me, his sure smile still locked in place.

He licks his lips as he sits forward, resting his elbows on the table.

"I was up all night putting together my . . ." He sucks in his lips as his brow furrows, I think trying to remember either the real or fake name of the bookcase he purchased.

"SNUFLEUPERGIS?" I help him out.

"Isn't that from *Sesame Street?*" one of the other players pipes in.

I chuckle because it's close to the name of one of the show's characters.

"I finished at two a.m. If only I had an extra set of hands to help." His gaze follows me as I round the table, picking up empty glasses.

"You had an Allen wrench. That's better than hands."

"Ha!" He busts out a laugh at my terse response, and as I pass behind him, he twists in his seat and catches my wrist with his hand.

"Hands are always better than some tool," he says in a low voice. His eyes glimmer with what I'm pretty sure is innuendo, and my stomach tightens in a way it hasn't in years. I lean forward and put my mouth near his ear.

"Depends on the tool," I say, pulling back and giving him a wink.

His mouth forms an O that he hides with his palm before his teammates catch it.

"Tell our boy to get off his ass and come camping with us Sunday, Renleigh," says Jasper, a regular here given this is his fifth year playing for the Triple-A team. I have to hand it to him—he's not giving up. He must be twenty-seven or so by now, and in rookie ballplayer years, that's nearing retirement.

I shrug and glance at Hunter, whose gaze is waiting for me.

"You should go. Camping by the stream is a thing around here. Maybe one of the guys can teach you how to fly fish."

"*Pfft*, doubt that," Jasper laughs out. "We can teach him how to drink, though."

I roll my eyes.

"Well then, maybe you've got the right idea. That's not camping," I say, scolding the crew along with him. I recognize Jake, Roddy's son, at the end of the table, and I give him a nod. "Of everyone here, you should know how to camp by the springs."

He lifts what looks like a beer, something he should not be drinking before a game, even if he's not playing.

"You say that like I had a dad around to show me how," he says, and a collective wince hits all our faces.

I think *I* have family problems. Jake's literally on the field with his.

"Wish I could help," I say with a shrug. I head to the back to dump the dirty dishes before my red cheeks burn off my face.

"You all right, hon?" Daisy says as she nestles in next to me at the wash station. We're down a dishwasher until early afternoon so maybe I should offer to hide back here until the guys leave.

"I'm fine. Just the usual sexual harassment from entitled ballplayers," I say with a laugh.

She grimaces and glances through the open window to the back area.

"You want me to deal with them?"

"I have it handled. Thanks, though," I say, stopping her from going full bouncer on the country's top pitching prospect. Besides, this might be the first time I've wanted attention from a guy in this joint. In fact . . .

"I'm going to go close them out," I say, drying my hands and leaving the rest of my glasses with Daisy.

"Give 'em hell, girl," she laughs out.

I'm sure she thinks I'm looking to spar with the guys. It would be typical of me. But there's something about this day that has me looking at things through a new lens. Maybe it's the good night's rest. Or that my mom is here. Or, like my sister said, I really need to get laid.

Whatever it is, I'm about to do something reckless for once. And I refuse to feel bad about it.

I step to the head of the table while the guys are pooling

cash to pay their tab and, hopefully, tip me well. I cross my arms over my chest and wait for Hunter to glance up and see me waiting.

"I'll go."

His brow lowers, and his eyes haze.

"Camping. I'll go with you guys. I haven't been in years, and frankly, I need to get out of my house. So, I'll go. And I'll show you what Sweetwater camping is all about."

Hunter blinks a few times and glances to his right, meeting Jasper's stunned expression. I don't hang with these guys. Not ever. Even Jake, who I technically grew up with, isn't someone I spend free time with unless it's running into one another at the market.

"Do you need me to get my gear out of storage, or—"

"I . . . I have gear," Hunter stammers out. His surprised reaction is sweet.

"Okay, I like a thick sleeping bag, so if you don't have that, I'll get mine. Head up there at ten, get there for lunchtime?" I scan the table, and the dumbfounded group of guys look at each other and nod. I have a feeling packing in beer was the only plan they truly thought out for the getaway.

"I'll pick you up at your place," Hunter says, and I bite the inside of my cheek, because I was planning on driving myself. There's freedom in a getaway car. But I don't want to give myself an out. I want to do something wild for once, even if it's just spending a night under the stars with a bunch of dudes.

"Okay," I relent.

And then I push things into new territory.

"It's a date."

[illegible]
[illegible]
[illegible]
[illegible]
[illegible]
[illegible]
[illegible]
[illegible]
[illegible]
[illegible]
[illegible]

NINE
HUNTER

I didn't tell Roddy about Renleigh joining me on this trip when I borrowed his camping gear. He's made his opinion about her and me quite clear, so I'm pretty sure he'd have words about me showing up with a tent and sleeping bag meant for one with the hopes that two of us fit inside. We won't fit comfortably, but that's kind of the point.

We pull up to the campsite after a few of the guys have already arrived. Jasper has his fishing gear ready, and two of our teammates seem content to kick their feet up on a log while lounging in two old-ass lawn chairs with a cooler of beer between them.

"Thank God for girlfriends," Renleigh says as she steps around to the front of my truck and ogles the two shirtless dudes now sunning with their cold beers clutched at their bellies. "Aren't you guys supposed to be in tip-top shape?"

She gives me side-eyes, and I scoff before lifting my shirt and slapping my tight abs.

"Don't look at me. It took a lot of sit-ups to get here. Brady's a bullpen catcher, though. And Adler isn't really motivated to get called back up. He's trying to get traded," I whisper.

"Not sure how many teams are in the market for beer-chugging slowpokes." Renleigh makes her way to the back of the truck, so I follow behind.

"He's not as slow as he looks. Besides, he's a first baseman. He just has to hit bombs."

I flip the tailgate down and snag Roddy's tent and sleeping bag, which are tightly bound together in a hiking pack. Renleigh pulls out two fishing rods, along with a gear box. I don't know how any of that stuff works, but she was excited about showing me, so I'm willing to wade in the cold stream for a few hours if it means we might have to sit close after to warm up.

"He ever hit a bomb off you?" She glances at the now snoring Adler, and I laugh and shake my head.

"Nobody on our squad hits home runs off me," I scoff.

Renleigh's eyes narrow, and I mentally replay my tone. This must be what Roddy means when he rips on my ego. Yeah, I hear it now.

"Not that he *couldn't*. We haven't done that many live at bats," I explain, image clean-up in full effect.

"*Ooooh*, was that you being humble?" Renleigh teases.

I drop the tent pack on the far corner of the campsite, far away from the lawn-chair boys. "I am humble; what do you mean?" I give her a crooked smile, and she laughs.

"Yeah, Mr. Modest. That's you."

Shit. Roddy is on to something.

I shrug nonetheless, and take one of the poles from her before following her lead toward the stream. We tread along a small trail cut through the rustling trees, and I give in to my most basic urges and study the smooth curves of her shoulders and her long, tempting neck. She's wearing a tank top under denim overalls that she's rolled up to her knees, and her shoes are a slightly beat-up pair of blue sneakers. Her dirty blonde hair is poked through the back of a white ballcap with a maroon S on the front. My guess is it's from the high school and her dad's team. She seems so comfortable in her own skin, and she's right at home out here in nature's playground. She's completely unbothered when one of the legs of her overalls unravels enough to touch the water's edge as she steps into the stream. She simply giggles and rolls it back up.

"It's not that cold if you want to take your shoes off. I brought spares," she explains.

I'm wearing slip-on sneakers and socks, and I wasn't as thoughtful with my packing. I was too damn focused on getting a tent and a warm sleeping bag.

"Okay," I say with a shrug before slipping my shoes off and tucking my socks inside. I tread into the water carefully, my toes flexing against the smooth, moss-covered stones. If I slip, I'm going to break my ass and get soaked head to toe. Rather than pushing my luck, I halt when I reach a wide flat rock, then look on while Renleigh ties a tiny fly to the end of my line. She hands it to me then steps back, as if she's expecting me to . . . *oh.*

"I've never fished with a hook. Not sure why you think I know what to do here." May as well build on this new humble, modest guy persona.

Renleigh chuckles, then maneuvers herself behind me, balancing her rod on an outcropping of rocks while sliding her palms along my biceps, then forearms. Her fingers wrap around my arms as she nestles in close.

"You want to make sure you have good balance, so unlock your knees." She nudges her knee between mine. I feel a bit dominated, but I'm surprisingly okay with it. I do what she says, relaxing my legs. "Good," she says, her breath tickling the skin of my bare bicep and making goose bumps rise.

I glance to my left and find her close, her gaze flitting up to meet mine, her blue eyes mesmerizing me through the hood of her golden lashes. She's a fucking angel.

"I respond well to praise." My devilish smirk earns me another knock on my legs, this one less gentle. "*Oww!*" I play along, and she shakes her head at me. Her smile gives her away, though. We're flirting. She can call this fishing all she wants. "Okay, okay. I'm listening." I breathe in deep, then let out a heavy exhale, relaxing my arms under her touch.

"Have you ever skipped stones on water? You do have water in California, don't you?"

Even her sarcasm is cute.

"Uh, does the Pacific count?"

"Right, that little body of water. Well, there aren't waves here. The ripples are more subtle. But there's a rhythm to them. You want to use that. Feel it when you cast your line."

She glides her hand over my left one, unraveling a few feet of line with me, then adjusting my grip on the rod before guiding my right arm up and back.

"When I count to three, we're going to flick the line forward a few times. You ready?" She's basically driving my entire upper body, and still, I'm perfectly fine with that.

"Let her rip," I say.

"One . . . two . . . *three!*" she whisper-shouts, urging my arm forward and back as the line stretches out across the water. The tiny fly splatters across the surface, then quickly sinks under the current.

"Is that what you mean? About the ripples and that rhythm stuff?" I squint one eye as I glance at her. She's tucked close to my arm, and it's tempting to throw the rod into the water and swoop my arm around her, but there's this proud glimmer in her eyes as she smiles up at me that makes me want to keep the lesson going a little while longer.

"That's *exactly* what I mean." Her gaze settles on mine for a quiet moment, and it's strange, but I feel oddly proud of myself. I also feel like maybe, just maybe, I understand Renleigh Blackwood a little more than I did before we stepped into this freezing cold water.

"Let's go again," she prompts.

I chuckle through my shivers and nod.

"Okay."

We repeat the steps, and while her touch isn't as firm, it's still there. In fact, the graze of her fingertips along my forearms as I whip the rod through the air is somehow better. It's doing things to my chest, to my heart. Fuck me, I'm full of nerves.

"You know that move is usually the other way around, rookie," Jasper says, breaking our quiet little solace with his wisecrack.

"Ha ha," I say over my shoulder. Renleigh takes a step back and her hands fall away, and I consider slapping Jasper in the neck with my rod for being such a cock blocker.

"This your first time?" he asks.

I nod, still a little pissed that he didn't read the room before wading in near us.

"Don't be mad if you don't catch shit. It takes a while."

No sooner did the words leave his mouth than there was a slight tug in my line.

"Holy shit!" I pull the rod toward my body on instinct, but my gaze zips to Renleigh for help. Her eyes widen, and she steps to my side, grabbing the rod with me and pulling up the line in fast swoops.

"What is it?" I don't even know what types of fish are in these waters, but something is floundering near the surface as Renleigh and I tug at the line.

"Trout," she says, a grin plastered on her cheeks so wide her dimples have quotation marks around them.

"Is that good?"

I'm clueless, which amuses Jasper, who laughs and says, "It's amazing you caught anything your first time. You're one lucky fucker, Hunter!"

With a final jerk on the line, a tiny fish pops out of the water, swirling through the air as it struggles to break free. Renleigh grabs hold of it within half a second, and without pause, she pulls it free and releases it back into the water.

"Wait! We're not eating that?"

I'm kind of bummed I didn't get a photo with it, at least.

Renleigh's palm flattens on my back, drawing my attention back to her pink lips and blue eyes.

"That was the size of a pet, Hunter. I don't even know if there would be food left after we skinned it and put it on the fire. But . . . nice work. You can officially say you've caught a fish."

I stand taller and grin like a stupid fool, but damn it . . . I am proud. And I'm going to tell every person I know that I caught a fish, and it was massive.

We spent a solid three-and-a-half hours flinging line over the water and came back to camp with nothing to show for it. Renleigh did catch another trout, and hers was bigger than mine, but we decided it wasn't worth the effort to cook a single fish. Especially when Jasper told us Adler brought up a kettle of his famous chili.

Dinner is nearly ready, in fact, when we get back to camp. And everyone's finally arrived. I don't know many of the guys well, but I recognize everyone. We buzz through introductions around the campfire, and Renleigh is surprisingly at ease— even more so than the two girlfriends who are clinging to the guys who brought them.

Once dinner is dished out, everyone starts sharing war stories from their time in the minors. Jake and I are the only true rookies, so the only stories I have to share are from my days at Pacific Coastal. I have the benefit of having played on national TV a few months ago, and the guys are interested in my tales from our play-off run. Though even those don't quite measure up to their stories of late-night travel bus drives through Missouri or Kansas.

"Dude, hope you know we don't get first class from Sweet-water," Jasper jokes.

"*You* fools don't. They're picking me up in one of those ride-share jets," I joke. Jake pulls one of his shoes off and tosses it at me before jokingly calling me an asshole. I promptly toss it into the woods, which earns me a less gentle *fucking prick*. It does make everyone else laugh their asses off, though, so worth it.

"Dude, you'd better get your tent set up. We're all done, and it's hard to hammer shit into the ground when the sun fully sets," Jasper says, and then offers me a hand up from the boulder I've been using for a seat.

"Yeah, probably . . . I'll just . . ." I turn to face the spot where I left the gear. Jake has made his way back with his shoe and is standing right over it.

"You're sleeping in that piece of shit?" He points at the bound tent, and chortles.

"Tent's a tent, right?" *Fuck if I know, but I sure hope it is.*

Jake snickers and utters, "Good luck with that."

"Come on. I'll help," Renleigh offers.

I unfurl the slick fabric wrapped around a set of folded poles, and a few metal stakes clank together as they fall to the ground.

Fucking Roddy. Man has major league money, and this is the piece of shit tent he sends me out into the woods with.

Renleigh studies the various pieces before us, her hands tucked into the back pocket of her overalls. "Well, let's get started."

Her shoes are drying by the fire, and I'd give anything to have a pair of those fuzzy boots she's wearing right now. My feet have yet to recover from the cold water, and the hems of my jeans are never going to dry.

Renleigh picks up one corner of the tent, so I take the opposite side, and between the two of us, we manage to poke poles into the right seams and produce a semi-stable structure. A triangle tent. Perfect for one.

"Please say you have two of these." She blows up at the flyaway hairs that have slipped from under the brim of her hat.

"I don't even have this one. It's Roddy's," I confess.

Her gaze sticks to mine for a few long, quiet seconds. Everyone else has drifted off into their own thing, the couples in their comfortable, double-wide tents, the single guys either crashing out under the stars or chugging more beers with Adler near the log. And then there's me and Renleigh, and a situation that seemed way sexier in my head but is starting to look more like I'll be sleeping in my truck.

"Yeah, so I'll just . . ."

I thumb over my shoulder, toward my pickup, and Renleigh laughs out, "Yeah, you will."

She unfurls the sleeping bag next, holding it up to her body and glaring at me as if to say, *Duh, you idiot. It's meant for one.*

"Like I said, I'll just . . ." I tilt my head toward the truck this time.

Renleigh nods.

"Uh, yeah," she breathes out. She scoots me in that direction with a hand in the air, and I follow orders, opening the king cab door and investigating the back seat for comfort. At least I'll be warm . . . *ish.*

Renleigh has already slid the sleeping bag into the tent. The backpack she brought is in the passenger seat, so I snag it and carry it to her as she's fastening the closure on the tent.

"You probably want this stuff," I say, holding her bag out and making my best sad puppy face.

"Thanks. I brought sweats for the night. I don't suppose you did?" She lifts a brow and chuckles. "You really are bad at this."

I wince and hold my palms out, holding out hope for a last-second invitation to join her inside.

"Well, good night, then. Your truck should be warm enough. And at least you won't have to worry about the bears." She starts to snap the opening shut again, but I hook a finger in and catch her gaze.

"You're joking about bears, right?"

She maintains her serious expression for several long seconds, but her lips finally pucker into a tight smirk.

"Yes, Hunter. I'm kidding about the bears. Not that I would count on you to know what to do with them." Her eyes roll back as she presses the final snap in place and shuts me out of the tiny tent for one for good.

[illegible] [illegible] [illegible] [illegible]

[illegible] [illegible] a [illegible] [illegible] [illegible] [illegible] a turn
[illegible] [illegible] [illegible] [illegible] [illegible] to [illegible] about the
[illegible] [illegible] [illegible] [illegible] but there.

[illegible] [illegible] [illegible] [illegible]
[illegible] [illegible] [illegible]
[illegible] [illegible] [illegible] [illegible] [illegible]
[illegible] that [illegible] [illegible] to [illegible] finding [illegible] [illegible] [illegible]
the Figure [illegible]. [illegible] above the [illegible] are [illegible] that I
[illegible] [illegible] [illegible] [illegible] follow [illegible] to [illegible] with them. The
[illegible] [illegible] the [illegible]. [illegible] [illegible] opportunity [illegible] [illegible] [illegible]
[illegible] [illegible] [illegible] [illegible] [illegible] be [illegible]

TEN
RENLEIGH

It's been years since I did this—slept on the hard ground. I have so many fond memories of camping trips with my sister and dad, but this . . . *this* is miserable.

I've tossed and turned for two hours. The giggles from the tents across the clearing have stopped. The two couples have either fallen asleep, or they're . . . *busy*. The hum from Adler's speaker is still low, but I haven't heard his voice singing along for at least an hour. I'm likely the only one awake. And I swear it's because of this poor excuse for a sleeping bag. I may as well have layered a few paper towels on the ground to sleep on.

It couldn't possibly be the guilt.

No. Not guilt. Nah. Nope.

I'm sure Hunter is comfortable in the truck. He's inside. On a leather bench seat. He may as well be on some fancy couch in an apartment. Yeah. I'm sure he's sleeping just fine. *Way* better than I am. He's probably actually sleeping. I guess that's good since he'll need to drive in the morning. *How close is morning?*

I pull my phone from my backpack pocket where it's plugged in to my charger. It's just after midnight, so I can't really say it's morning. But it's the next day. I made it over the hump into tomorrow.

Go me!

I still feel guilty, though.

Shit.

It's the thoughts I'm having.

Not the ones about forcing myself to sleep. Those are just excuses I'm telling myself.

No. I feel guilty because of the mental torture I'm trying to bury and rewrite. I want to do something bad. Not *bad* bad. Just *bad idea* kind of bad. And I'll regret the decision by morning, I know I will. Hell, I might regret it minutes after orgasm.

But I do want it.

I want him.

In this fucking tent.

Fucking me.

I bury my face in my hands and laugh silently at what I've become.

Get it together, Renleigh. You're a twenty-four-year-old sexual being. You're single. You're in a tent out in the wilderness, albeit not totally alone, but for all intents and purposes . . . you're alone. With a hot professional athlete.

Who clearly wants to fuck you.

Just let him, for Pete's sake!

I kick off the top flap of the thermal-lined sleeping bag and get to my feet. Shaking out my hands and feet, I let the cool air spike my courage. I run my fingers through my hair, combing the wavy ends and resting them over my shoulders. I'm wearing a double XL pale pink sweatshirt and equally baggy gray sweatpants. It's my go-to pajama choice, and it seemed practical when I shoved it in my backpack fifteen hours ago. Now, though? I feel pretty fucking frumpy.

I stare down at my legs, then bend to pull the elastic up my calf on one leg before rolling the waist band so it sits below my belly button. I feel like I'm wearing a fleece innertube.

Gah!

I pull my pants down and dance my way out of them, kicking my feet free so I'm now wearing nothing but the calf-high tube socks with pink stripes across the top to match my favorite sweatshirt.

Okay. This might be sexy.

I pop my hip out and turn my knee in, practicing what I'd like to think is a rather coy pose. Demure, as that influencer says. I run my fingers through my hair one more time, scratching at my scalp to give my locks a bit of body, then shove my feet into my warm boots. One more deep breath and exhale, and I unbutton the tent closure and step out into the starry night.

"Jesus," I whisper, hugging my body as the breeze cuts right to my bare legs. Goose bumps rise on my skin.

"Can't sleep?"

I jump at Hunter's voice, and it takes my eyes a few minutes to adjust to the landscape and moonlight. He's sitting on his tailgate, leaning back on his palms while his legs dangle. He isn't asleep. And he isn't inside the warm cab.

"Why are you out here?" My inner thoughts pour out before I think to answer his question. "And yeah. Can't sleep."

He raises a hand.

"Guilty. Turns out, I'm really bad at camping."

I laugh quietly and step toward him. My arms are still wrapped around my midriff, and I'm so cold and nervous that I've nearly forgotten about not wearing pants. Hunter quickly reminds me.

"Well, fuck me." He plasters his palm over his mouth and jaw while his gaze fixes on my bare legs.

"I got hot. I'm not now, though. Clearly," I say through a shiver.

"Yeah, I can see that. Also, you're still hot. Just . . . different hot." He laughs quietly at his own joke as his gaze lifts to mine.

I stop a few feet out of his reach, my chest tightening with fear of rejection—and a bigger fear of acceptance, which leads to a whole new rabbit hole of emotions. But it also leads to feeling something . . . *anything.* For just me. Satisfaction and appreciation.

Pleasure.

Hunter sits up tall and crooks his finger, motioning me to him.

"Come here."

I bite my bottom lip. Cliché, but what the fuck. I'm going with it.

"Hi," I utter, my voice soft, my hands cold.

I unfurl my grip on my sweatshirt and reach forward to take his waiting hands. He holds them out as his gaze scans down my body.

"You took your pants off because you were cold, huh?" His eyes flit up to mine as he bites his bottom lip, his fucking adorable smirk pushing a dimple into his cheek.

I shake my head.

"No."

His lip comes loose as his grin widens.

"Why did you take your pants off, then?"

I step between his legs and guide his hands around my body, urging them lower until his palms cup my ass.

"Oh," he groans.

"Yeah," I breathe out, lifting myself on my toes. He drops his chin and tilts his head just enough that our mouths line up perfectly.

He nips at my top lip, and I nearly jump to catch his. He toys with me, though, lifting his head and smirking at me with playful hunger in his eyes.

"Confession?" His eyes narrow on mine, the curve of his mouth remaining unchanged. There's a mischievous side to his expression. And it's sexy as fuck.

"*Hmm?*" I lift my chin again, wanting to feel all of his

mouth on mine. The warmth. What I predict will be strong lips. His tongue.

"I borrowed that tent from Roddy, knowing full well it was meant for one. And I kind of hoped . . ."

He bites the tip of his tongue and smiles, a downright bashful look in his eyes.

"What did you hope for, Hunter Reddick, number one draft pick?"

He nips at my upper lip again, and his hands slide up my back, under my sweatshirt, lifting the fabric up my spine and exposing my nearly bare ass and midriff to the night air. Rather than kissing me hard like I want, though, he holds me in this infinite purgatory of almosts.

It's intoxicating, and the longer I stare into the deep blue of his eyes, the more I want to stay here on the verge of feeling something. Because the edge is powerful. It's enticing. It's like getting away with making bad choices without fully accepting consequences.

"I hoped," he begins, his bottom lip full and open with his intensifying breath as his gaze drops to my chin and then my chest.

"Yes?" I whimper.

His fingertips scrape around my rib cage, his knuckles brushing against the sides of my breasts, then roaming to the hard peaks of my nipples. I arch toward him, gasping. If Adler isn't really asleep, he's getting a full show right now. At the very least, an audio porn. But fucking hell, what is this touch of Hunter's? It's literal temptation.

"That you," Hunter continues, his hands forming around the fullness of my breasts as his mouth inches closer. His tongue swipes at my upper lip, and I shudder as his thumbs rake over my nipples.

"Would let me," he says, his lips brushing against mine with his words as his thumbs and fingers position themselves to pinch my hard buds.

"Fuck you," he finally says, rolling my nipples in his vise grip, pinching them so hard that the ache and pleasure filter to my toes and I pool between my legs.

His mouth covers mine, and I grip the front of his hoodie in my fists, pulling him toward me. His hands move from under my shirt to either side of my jaw, holding my mouth to his as he drops from the tailgate to his feet. He walks me backward while we kiss, and I feel for the edge of the tent when I know we're close.

I peel the flap back and dip inside, breaking our kiss just long enough for Hunter to follow me in and push the opening closed enough for privacy. His hands fly back to my face the moment he turns back to face me, and mine gather the front of his hoodie, along with the T-shirt underneath. I push the material up the center of his chest, and he breaks our kiss long enough to pull his shirts over his head and toss them to the ground.

"You're fucking unreal," I say through a giggle as my hands splay along his hard muscles. His obliques are so tight, and his chest and abs move with his laughter in response. My sister will be so proud of me when I tell her about this.

"I work out a lot," he chuckles, lifting my chin with his index finger and sucking my top lip between both of his.

"Your turn," he says, pulling the hem of my sweatshirt up my body. I step back enough to raise my hands in the air and let him undress me. My tits are basically missiles at this point, swollen and hard, begging to be devoured.

"Goddamn," Hunter breathes out, dropping his mouth to my right breast as his hands swoop to the small of my back, lifting me to him.

My hands fumble with the button on his jeans, but I get it undone and quickly work down his zipper before sinking my hand inside his pants and cupping his hard cock under his boxer briefs.

"Oh, fuck . . . yes. Yeah, just . . . yes." His words are

wrapped in nervous, quiet laughter, which emboldens me as I begin my descent.

Hunter gathers my hair as I press kisses to his chest then stomach, finally situating myself on my knees before pulling his jeans and boxers down to his thighs so his cock springs forward.

"Renleigh, you don't have to—"

I wrap my lips around his crown before he can finish his sentence, and his head falls back as his mouth opens with a low groan. I tease his tip with my tongue, tasting the precum that drips out before wrapping my lips around him fully and taking his cock into the depths of my throat.

"Oh, fuck," he pants, his hand twisting in my hair, his grip tight as he coaxes my head forward and back along his length.

I never considered myself good at this. It's not a thing I practice, and I've only given two other blowjobs in my life, both to boyfriends who, upon reflection, did not deserve them. But there's something about Hunter that makes me want to do dirty things. He's like a hall pass. And I'm going to use every bit of him he's willing to give to me.

I wrap a hand around his cock, sliding my grip along with my mouth as I coat him with my saliva. My gaze flits up through my lashes just as Hunter drops his chin, and our eyes meet. There's a devilish smirk on his lips, and his head tilts like a king pleased with his servant as he guides my mouth down his cock, holding me still when he's deep inside my mouth.

"I'm not coming in your mouth, Renleigh," he whispers.

I moan, a little disappointed but also very excited.

"I'm coming in your sweet cunt, if that's all right with you?" He pulls my hair back, taking my mouth away from his cock. The wet tip paints my lips and chin as I gasp for air and nod.

"Please," I add, moving to my ass, then laying back on the sleeping bag so I can wriggle my panties down my legs.

Hunter licks his lips as he pushes his pants and boxers all

the way down his legs, his heated gaze centered on my swollen pussy. I'm so glad I thought to tidy things up down there yesterday. Nothing special, just a small landing strip that I hope he likes.

He kneels between my feet, then pushes my knees far apart, exposing me to him and leaving me in the most erotic, vulnerable position I've ever experienced. I bring my hands over my head, giving myself to him completely as he sucks on his thumb, then presses it to my swollen clit.

"I knew it," he says, gliding his thumb along my soaking wet skin and teasing me.

"What?" I rasp.

"I knew this would be the prettiest fucking pussy in the world." He smirks at me then, winking as he lowers his entire body until his mouth is sucking my clit. My knees come up on reflex, but Hunter is quick to push them back down, his palm flat on my right inner thigh as his tongue flicks my sensitive skin.

His hand inches toward my center while his tongue continues its assault, and when he finally sinks a finger inside of me, my body writhes with pleasure. It's as if I've had an itch for years that he's finally scratching. Like a salve for a troubled nerve, a treat for a worried soul. Bliss for a broken heart, perhaps. Whatever this is, it's the most sensual journey I've ever taken, and I want nothing more than for it to never . . . ever . . . stop.

"Come for me, Renleigh. Come on my mouth, then you can come on my cock."

His tongue makes slow, languid strokes against my swollen center while he pushes two fingers inside of me, hooking them slightly when pressure begins to build deep in my core.

It turns out that pitchers are indeed quite good with their hands . . . and tongues. And Hunter Reddick has me coming in his mouth in seconds. My hips buck with this need to rub myself against his face, to gain more friction, to feel him deeper.

I exhale as his mouth leaves my soaking pussy open to the cold air, the exposure sudden and painful, yet so, so sweet.

"Ah, I need. I need," I beg.

Hunter feels inside the pocket of his jeans, then pulls out a gold packet. He tears the foil with his teeth, then slides the condom down his length. I arch my back, opening my legs to him wider as he guides himself to my pussy. He coats himself with my arousal, sliding his cock up and down my still-pulsating pussy until finally pausing to sink deep inside.

I gasp as my head falls back, louder than I want to be, but fuck it. I don't care.

"Fuck, you're tight. So fucking wet, too."

He sinks in completely and holds still for a moment, letting my body adjust to his girth. I steady my breath and straighten my spine so I can look him in the eyes. When his gaze is waiting for me, it takes me by surprise. He's smiling faintly, and his eyes wander the expanse of my body in an incredibly adoring way. He studies my face, sliding his cock out slowly as his hand comes up to cradle the side of my face. His weight held up on his left arm, he pushes back in and draws a soft line along my jaw with his right hand.

"Come again, Renleigh. Come *with* me," he says, his thumb grazing my open lips before he pushes it in my mouth. I bite him gently with my teeth, smirking around him before closing my lips and sucking his thumb as he sinks into me again.

"Yes," I mumble, my mouth occupied by his thumb he repeatedly runs along my lip then sinks into my mouth, matching each thrust.

"That's it," he coaxes, dropping his mouth to my ear as his hips continue to thrust.

My tongue swirls around his thumb as his dick pummels me below, every pump hitting me just right, building something that's full of promise, until I feel myself begin to lose control.

"Hunter," I pant, the pad of his thumb pressing on my lower lip.

His rhythm gets faster, and my hands move to his hips, pulling him into me with every drive as I chase my release. The sensation builds to an unthinkable peak that nearly knocks the wind from me until I'm nothing but pulses and waves. My body goes numb as his hips pump into me, his mouth panting heavy breaths at the base of my throat. I take every surge of pleasure, the world suddenly bright and full of color.

"Fuck me, Renleigh. Fuck, fuck, fuck—" Hunter pumps into me a few more times, stilling deep inside of me on the last one, and I make a mental note to have my IUD checked stat. The next time we do this, I want to feel his hot cum inside of me.

The next time.

Yes. I've made a choice. And I'm going to make it again. And probably again. Until it feels like a mistake. But for right now, all it feels is good.

So. Fucking. Good.

ELEVEN
HUNTER

I may suck at camping, but I'm absolutely going again—assuming Renleigh comes along. And maybe we lose the others.

Someone is brewing coffee. I'm not sure how that's achieved on a campsite, but bless whoever figured it out and thought to bring it along.

Renleigh's hair is splayed along my bicep, her cheek pressed against my bare chest. Her lips are barely parted, and tiny breaths slip between them. The guys aren't exactly being quiet outside, so I'm sure she'll wake soon. I just can't seem to rush her, though.

The girl I was with last night was a complete one-eighty from the one who swore off ballplayers and blocked my best flirting attempts at Earl's. This version of Renleigh Blackwood was forward, aggressive, and so fucking sexy. Not that the other version isn't all those things too, it's just that this Renleigh let me put my dick inside her, so at my base self, I'm kinda biased.

I might also be in trouble because last night wasn't just wild, it was the best sex of my life. Which brings me back to the whole camping thing, because if the wilderness had anything to do with it, I'll start working on my troop badge right now. Sign me up. Fuck baseball.

Okay, maybe not *fuck baseball*. But I can make time to get more outdoorsy and shit. With Renleigh.

I'm musing over all things she and I could do together out here, alone, when she stirs against my body and stretches her arms over her head.

"Hey," I breathe out.

She turns into me more, rubbing her face against my skin, her eyes squinting against waking up.

"What time is it?" Her voice is raspy. That's sexy too.

"I think six, maybe? It's not bright out yet, but the sun is coming up. And someone is making coffee."

She cracks one eyelid open, and even in the dim shelter of the tent, the light blue looks like diamonds. The subtle curve to her lips tips toward a bashful smile. She shifts her naked body against mine, careful to keep herself covered with the top layer of the sleeping bag, and when our eyes meet again, she quickly drops her forehead to mine and closes her eyes. She's adorable when she's embarrassed.

"You want coffee?" I sweep the stray hairs from her face and smooth them behind her ear before guiding her head to my lips and pressing a soft kiss to her skin.

"Yeah, that might help," she says in a whisper.

"I'm going to assume you mean help with waking up and not help processing what went down, because I have zero regrets." I'm being honest as I pull the top of the sleeping bag open so I can get to my feet. I reward myself with a solid glance at her naked body, however, and take a mental snapshot of her ample breasts and the thin trail of hair that leads to her fucking goddess of a pussy.

"I'll answer that after the coffee," she says, which feels a bit like a backtrack. I wince as my back is to her while I pull my jeans on and shove my feet into my still-damp shoes.

"If I learned anything on this trip, it's pack backup shoes,"

I grumble, my feet squishing against the sole as I amble my way through the tent opening with my shirt in my hand.

"Well, good morning, stud," Adler teases. He's in charge of the coffee, it seems, which is fitting since he probably knew he'd need to nurse a hangover this morning. He pours a cup from a large silver pot and hands it to Brooks, our rookie shortstop. I played with Brooks in high school, and he went to Iowa for college. He's quiet, though it looks like Adler may have gotten him to open up last night, probably more than he wanted to. Brooks seems to be paying the price this morning, too.

"Hey, can I get a cup?" I ask, snagging a black travel mug from the top of the now-empty cooler and hold out it while Adler pours.

He gives me side eyes, and his smirk seems to be holding something back. I think I know what that is.

"No, this coffee is not for me. Yes, Renleigh is in my tent. And no, I am not going to give you any more details." I take a sip from the full mug and keep my lips closed as I swallow down the hot, strong drink.

"Dude, you may just be a legend. Renleigh Blackwood hates ballplayers," he says through a gurgled cough-laugh.

I gesture the mug toward him and squint one eye.

"Maybe she just hates bad ones," I tease.

"Fuck off. You lucky fuck." He tosses a hand towel at me that hits my back when I turn to walk away.

I leave the two of them with their hangovers and coffee, then dip my head as I slip back inside the tent. Renleigh is fully dressed when I get inside, and I'm not even shy about being disappointed.

"It's not a nude camp, Hunter," she scoffs, teasingly.

"But it could be," I say, quirking a brow.

I kneel next to her as she slips on her boots and offer her the coffee. She clutches it in both hands once her boot is tugged up her calf, humming as she takes a long sip.

"This is so terrible but so very good."

I chuckle.

"Adler made it, and I have a feeling he just boiled coffee grounds into liquid.

She nods, still sipping, and utters over the rim of the mug, "Makes sense."

I lower myself to fully sit on the ground, and I'm about to swing my leg around her so I can hold her against my chest, when she gets to her feet and backs up a few steps.

"So, this is Roddy's stuff, huh?" She gestures to the rumpled sleeping bag that, in the light of day, is clearly too small for a couple. It's barely big enough for a single, and definitely not one my size.

"It is. I borrowed it. I wanted to look like I knew what I was doing . . . with the whole camping thing."

I grab the back of my neck as Renleigh smirks at me. I think I'm blushing because my cheeks feel tight. What the hell?

"You knew what you were doing. I mean, in here. The whole camping thing was a bust. But in here . . . it was good." She's blushing now.

"Good, huh?" I'm fishing for more. I'm fishing for *again*.

She waggles her head side to side as she pulls her phone from the back pocket of her overalls.

"You were all right," she says this time, clearly teasing me. She must be teasing. There's no way last night was just all right. Last night was incredible. The two of us together are incredible. And I *know* I satisfied her. She was quite vocal.

She winks at me as she holds up a finger, and I relax a little. She has me all kinds of unsteady. I'm usually the confident one. I'm also usually the one who's dressed first, who's ready to leave, who's in charge of a second date. Renleigh, however, holds *all* the cards in this scenario. I'm holding an empty box and maybe a Jack of diamonds.

"It's in the cabinet by the glasses. Everything is labeled. He can handle it, Mom. You don't need to—"

She's steps outside while she talks on the phone, her fingers woven into her hair and her palm on her head.

"You need to go?" I whisper.

She glances my way, her brow furrowed, and she holds up a finger again.

"I'll just . . ." I gesture to the tent, and she nods.

I pull the sleeping bag out first, shaking the dirt and leaves from the flannel side before rolling it tight. I think I'll toss that in the wash before I give it back to Roddy. Someone is bound to gossip in the locker room, and when he finds out I was in his sleeping bag with Renleigh, he'll probably knock my teeth out, then burn his sleeping bag on principal. Maybe if I bring it back clean and fresh, I'll get to keep my teeth.

I start taking apart the tent, piling up the poles with the stakes before moving on to the fabric, when Renleigh groans to my right.

"Everything okay?" I fold the tent canvas around the various other pieces and bundle it together with the sleeping bag.

"No," Renleigh says, her answer swift and surprisingly honest.

"Can I help?"

She's already begun marching toward my truck.

"No," she says again.

She flings her backpack onto the back seat, then climbs in the passenger side. I drop the camping gear in the back, then walk over to Adler to let him know we're leaving. He snickers and winks, still impressed with my conquest, I suppose. He really knows how to cheapen it.

I climb in next to Renleigh, and glance toward her lap, where she's texting someone on her phone.

"Is your dad okay?" My stomach tightens as my mind

races with negative thoughts. I hope he didn't have another stroke or fall.

Renleigh doesn't answer immediately, still firing away texts, line after line. I let her work through whatever is happening, biting my tongue—literally—as I drive us along the dirt road back to the highway. She finally drops her phone between her thighs and promptly bites her thumbnail as she stares out the passenger window.

"Are you going to tell me what's going on?" I finally say.

She huffs, rolling her neck before moving her gaze to me. I glance to my right a few times, balancing my sight between her and the roadway.

"My mom is trying to help my dad. She hasn't been here for years, but today, right now, she wants to help with his physical therapy. And she told my sister to go home and enjoy herself, because she 'has it handled.' And you know what my sister did? She went home."

Her words fly out in a single breath, and my muscles tighten on instinct, the tension rolling off her and bleeding into my body.

"That . . . sucks? I'm sorry?" I don't know the full story, but I glean enough from her tone.

"It's . . . fine," she sighs out, dropping her shoulders and turning her gaze back out the window.

"It doesn't sound fine," I continue.

She shakes her head but doesn't respond.

We drive in quiet for the next several minutes, Renleigh continuously checking her phone while I mentally riffle through the right words to say. I come up empty, and she doesn't seem to be hearing from whomever she's trying to get hold of. The air is practically boiling with anxiety. It's palpable, and I'm half-tempted to pull over for a short walk to get my head right.

"This was a stupid idea," Renleigh mutters.

I think she both didn't and *did* want me to hear her.

"I'm sorry?" I squint one eye and tilt my head as I glance at her.

"This. Me coming out here. I shouldn't have come."

My chest tightens. Fuck, she actually regrets this. Me. Last night.

"I'm sorry. I thought we could have a good time. *I* had a good time . . . with you. And not just because——"

"It's just that I don't do this. *This!*" She sweeps her palms out in front of her, like a conductor, and I try to regain my train of thought before she hijacked it.

"I'm sorry. But . . . what do you mean by *this?*"

Her sudden laugh doesn't really make me feel better.

"Exactly. See? This is nothing. Which is why I shouldn't have come." She huffs again, her eyes darting around the cab with her stream of thoughts. She's freaking out. And as bad as it feels to be summed up as "nothing," to some degree, it's my fault she feels like this.

"I didn't mean to pressure you, and I didn't really have expectations or hopes. Well, no, I had hope. Gah!" I pinch the bridge of my nose as I pull up to the stoplight right off the highway.

"You didn't pressure me. I made a mistake. This was a mistake, is all. I'm sorry. It's me, okay?"

I laugh, but then realize she's being serious, and the sound drops from my mouth.

"Oh, wow. You're really giving me the *it's not you, it's me* bit. Wow. Just . . . huh." I stroke the stubble on my chin with my palm, my elbow balanced on the driver's side door.

"Because it's not you. Trust me," she says.

If I had half a clue what the hell was happening, I might be apt to trust her. But this actually might be a genuine case of someone getting cold feet. And all I wanted was a second date.

I pull up to her house, her Jeep parked out front alongside what looks like a pricey Mercedes sedan. The black paint is coated with a thin layer of Oklahoma dust.

I shift into park and reach into the back seat to hand Renleigh her bag. She grasps the top strap, but I hold on to the other side for a beat, coaxing her gaze to me.

"We're heading to Nashville tomorrow. Three days. Maybe when I get back?"

She blinks, her expression devoid of all the passion that colored it pink just hours before.

"Good luck in Nashville. I hope you get the W."

I let go of her bag, and just as fast, she slips from my truck and shuts the door behind her.

How the hell is this my lot in life—always watching Renleigh Blackwood walk away?

TWELVE
RENLEIGH

How did I get here?

I've heard people utter those hypothetical words, and I used to scratch my head and wonder how they could be so obtuse.

I get it now.

I have always been a driven, focused, independent woman. And I can't fathom for the life of me how I landed my ass back in my hometown and put myself into a situationship with, of all the men in the world, a ballplayer. And not just any ballplayer. I went and picked up a number one draft pick. A guy whose face has already been in the media. *A lot.* A guy who is going to be in the media a whole lot more. A guy who, by his own accord, is only passing through.

And fuck if I don't kind of like him.

The good news, at least from this warped perspective, is I don't have time to mentally work through that mess right now. I've just learned that my mother isn't simply visiting. She's staying. As in . . . *moving in.* And yeah, it's her house still and all —half of it—but does she really need to be in her old bedroom? The one I've made myself comfortable in? FOR TWO YEARS!

"Renleigh, this doesn't have to happen today," my mom says, though her actions contradict her words as she hangs a collection of pantsuits on the right side of the closet.

I glare at her as I grab a handful of my clothes—all mismatched sweatshirts and over-sized T-shirts—and carry them to the spare room I once shared with my sister. Now, it's the place where my father's card collection is stored, along with every other abandoned trinket this household has ever seen. The purple floral wallpaper remains; it's yellowed a lot, and the seams are peeling.

"No time like the present," I utter, my tone clearly unamused.

My mom sighs behind me, but I leave her with her self-righteous thoughts and close the door with my foot as I enter my *new* room. A puff of dust kicks off the nearby dresser as I drop my clothes on the sitting chair in the corner. I wave my hand through the air, coughing my way to the window so I can crack it open. This space is the very definition of musty. And I'm sure there are ghosts in here—fragments of every life decision I've ever made.

I didn't want to get into the history of my parents' bizarre arrangement with Hunter during our drive home. It was bad enough that my mom insisted on stepping into the caretaker role without me around. Then she dropped her little bomb about moving in, and my brain simply shut down. I may have channeled that frustration toward Hunter, and I'm only now reflecting on my behavior.

I sit on the edge of the mattress and stare at the specks of dust floating through the beam of sunlight. My phone buzzes at my hip, so I fish it from my side pocket and see my sister's incoming call. I pinch the bridge of my nose and press the phone to my ear.

"I'm surprised I can get cell service in the guest room. It feels kind of like a scene in one of those horror movies where they send the bad children to starve."

My sister snort-laughs at my tasteless joke.

"You're being dramatic," she says.

I pat the folded bedspread, and more dust puffs into the air.

"Am I?"

My sister is quiet for a few seconds, which pretty much answers my question. I know she hates what's happening as much as I do, but the brunt of it is happening more directly to me. Regardless, I am glad I have her to commiserate with. Just like I'm glad she agrees that I shouldn't pack up and head back to school right away. My mom's been impulsive about her relationship with Dad before. This could very well turn into a pit stop . . . *again.*

"I can't believe you're giving her the room without a fight," my sister finally says.

I shake my head and utter, "Yeah," because my move surprises me a bit, too. I'm usually more stubborn than this. But my dad seems so happy to have her here. And he's doing so well. I don't want to be the downer. At least not this time.

Lindsey and I have always been embarrassed by our parents' arrangement. They never told us they got divorced the first time our mom left, when we were eleven and thirteen and Mom went to Boston to work for a congresswoman.

Now that I'm an adult, I think she probably also moved to Boston to be with another man—Collin. They both worked at the same crisis communications firm, and Collin represented this exciting life that was nothing like that of a small-town high school baseball coach's wife. My mom was only in Boston —aka with Collin—for two years. She was back home with us when I started high school.

She left again a few times, usually for work. Six months in Chicago was followed up by a year in Northern California. She was just settling back in Sweetwater again when my dad had his first stroke. She stayed for the first one, which wasn't as severe. Then, conveniently, the Houston opportunity showed up around the time Dad had his second stroke. And she was gone again, leaving him to do the hard stuff alone.

"Do you think Dad's a sucker?" It's a blunt question, and it tastes bad on my tongue, but I have to ask it. And Lindsey's the only one I can say it to.

"Sometimes," she says, her response equally honest.

My sister and I make plans for her to come over for dinner next Monday, along with the boys. That's another bone of contention, and one my sister harbors more than I do since she's the one with children. Our mom has missed out on a lot of grandparenting time. Of course, spending more time with the kids was supposedly one of Mom's primary reasons for moving back home. We'll see how she handles two boys wrapped around her legs the moment they enter the house. Assuming they remember who she is.

"How was camping?" Lindsey finally broaches the *real* reason she's called.

I suck in my lips as my cheeks burn.

"It was good. I had fun."

She dismisses my curt answer with a hard laugh.

"Bitch, I need details. Did you?" She lets the open-ended question linger between us for a few long seconds, and I consider not answering. A non-answer is really a yes, though, so I may as well rip the Band-Aid off.

"We did."

She squeals, and I hold the phone away from my ear until her shriek has subsided.

"I want to know everything. Girl, it's been years since I've had strange dick. And a ballplayer, you lucky bitch. Is he big? Are the abs legit? Is he into wild shit or like, boring missionary style?"

"Oh my God, Lindsey. I'm not telling you any of that." I flatten my palm over my face and giggle softly at the memory of Hunter pulling my sweatshirt up my body. "Okay, okay. I'll give you one thing. Brace yourself."

"I'm braced," my sister pants jokingly.

"As skillful as Hunter Reddick is on the mound, he's ten times as good between my legs. And I mean all of him. His mouth. His hands. His . . ."

I trail off there, but Lindsey has zero boundaries and fills in the gap with a very loud, "Cock."

"Yes, that too," I admit.

I move my hand along my thigh, reaching for the memory of his hand trailing along that same path. The ache of him being inside me. The weight of his body, and the strength in his hands as he positioned me wherever he wanted. The way I let him. *Gah!*

My sister ends our call when she overhears the sudden knock at my door. I clear my throat as I toss my phone to the bed and open the door to my mother.

"I was going through my clothes, and I thought maybe you'd like a few of these things. You know, for when . . . just whenever." She hands me three garments wrapped in plastic, one of them a pale pink pantsuit that I can't imagine ever putting on my body. I blink at it a few times, then hook the hangers on my thumb.

"Thanks. Maybe."

Probably not.

I move to the closet and slide the broken door open a few inches, just enough to push the hangers through the crack. They slide in, between the door and the stack of boxes inside. I turn back around to meet my mom's gaze and pursed lips.

"If you don't want them, you could just say so," she says, folding her arms over her chest.

I chew at the tip of my tongue, imagining the version where I say exactly that and throw the garments back at her.

"I might want them," I lie instead. It feels gross. "I don't know, I just have a lot of work to do in here. I need to clear out some old stuff. I should really get to it."

I step toward her, toward the door, but she doesn't budge.

She's comfortable, standing with one foot in my room, her body leaning against the jam, her face full of judgement. As if that's the way this should go. Her judging me. *Ha!*

"Anything else?" I hold on to the edge of the door, giving her one more context clue.

Please leave now.

"Yes. One thing," she says.

I exhale, and she does the same, partly to mock me, I'm sure. Our eyes meet.

"Remember that there are two of us in this relationship," she says.

I shake with a single silent laugh.

"I don't mean me and you, though that truth works between us as well. I mean me and your dad. There are two people making decisions about this relationship, Renleigh. It's not always me deciding to stay or go."

She hits me with a hard stare that feels invasive, and I find myself wrapping my free arm around my midriff to ward off her invasion. What is that cryptic shit supposed to mean? And duh, I know there are two of them. I know he takes her back. And fine, maybe I should assign some of the blame his way and let him hear my piece, too. But what can I say/ I'm a daddy's girl. I'm always going to pick his side, even when he won't.

She backs out of my room after several seconds pass without a reaction from me, and I shut my door again the moment she's cleared the doorway.

My body is buzzing with frustration, and the pent-up anger borders on hurt. My eyes burn while I force myself not to cry. Instead, I pour every ounce of my focus into hauling boxes of worthless memorabilia, along with grade school report cards and childhood toys from my old closet, and into the garage so I have enough room to live here as a grown-up.

On my final return trip from the garage, I catch a glimpse of my father practicing his balance in the center of his makeshift room. His walker is right there, the grips within inches of his fingers so he can catch himself. His body quivers from the exertion of his muscles as he stands for several seconds at a time without help, and it makes my chest hurt.

I want to celebrate this moment. I want to congratulate him and urge him to keep going. He's working so hard. But I'm afraid he's doing it for false promises, and that's what's killing me. I know it in my gut. He thinks if he can just get back to normal, if he can walk on his own, climb the stairs to his old bedroom—*where she is*—that this time, she'll stay.

In the gambling world, they call that throwing good money after bad.

I shut my eyes and draw in a deep breath, forcing myself to leave this moment alone. I can let him have this. I can suspend my jaded heart for his sake, at least for one day. It's not hurting him. If anything, it's driving him to get stronger.

I manage to make it back to my room without opening my big mouth, but the burn in my chest is still searing.

And Hunter Reddick is calling me.

From the road.

I stare at his name in my phone, every nerve ending in my body lighting up with the memory of his touch. He's an escape. And maybe I deserve to be happy, too. At least for a little while.

"Hey," I murmur, holding the phone close to my ear, cupping the device as if it will somehow shelter this conversation and keep it a secret.

"Oh, hey. I didn't think you'd pick up. How are you?" He sounds genuinely surprised.

I can hear the rush of people filling a stadium in the background. Nashville always draws a good crowd. Hunter's not pitching tonight, but he will tomorrow. Tonight, though . . . tonight he's free. Just a flight away.

"I'm coming to Nashville." I don't wait for his invitation.

My phone is on speaker a second after the words leave my lips and I'm searching for a flight.

"Oh, wow. Really? Are you . . ."

"I get in at nine," I say, pacing my room now that I've pressed purchase and used all my points for this last-second trip.

"Okay, you're flying, then. Do you need somewhere to stay?" His shy, roundabout way of asking is sweet. But I'm not in the mood for sweet.

"I'm staying with you. And we are fucking. Text me the hotel info."

I end the call before he finishes his excited acceptance, and a few seconds later the device in my hand buzzes with his hotel address, followed by a wide-eyed emoji and a sly grinning avatar that I think is supposed to be him.

I dump a pair of jeans, a sweatshirt, three pair of panties and a clean bra into a duffle bag and zip it up, not looking back after leaving my room. I'll buy whatever else I need when I get there.

It's time to throw some good money after bad.

THIRTEEN
HUNTER

I think Renleigh might be a zombie.

That's the only explanation for what's about to happen. Or not happen. Shit, at this point I have whiplash from trying to figure this girl out. All I know is she texted me a few minutes after nine, saying she was already in a rideshare on her way here. I've been hovering just inside my hotel doorway ever since. I'm sure the guys who have seen me think I'm waiting for a hooker.

The elevator dings down the hallway, and my pulse kicks up again, the same way it has the last four times someone got off on our floor. I bite my bottom lip in anticipation, hoping it's not another dude rounding the corner. The first sign of her is her sneakers and black leggings, then my eyes trail up to her pink sweatshirt, and my dick swells. It's been trained to behave a certain way when she wears that thing. But then I get a glimpse of her expression as she barrels toward me, and all my anticipation-fueled adrenaline boils into instant, crushing concern.

She's . . . crying.

"Hey . . . hey, it's okay," I say, holding one arm out as I keep my door open with the other. Renleigh folds into me, and

I sweep her inside and let her collapse against my chest in a messy, tear-soaked ball of emotion.

"What's wrong? Are you hurt? Did someone hurt you?" The hairs on the back of my neck spike while I stroke her back as she rests her face against my chest. I inspect her clothing, at least what I can see, and am tender with my touch just in case. If someone hurt her on her way here . . . if she had an issue with the rideshare driver . . . anyone. . . I swear.

"I'm not hurt. I'm . . . I'm fine," she says, sniffling as she pulls away a bit and runs her long sleeve across her nose and eyes.

"Yeah, you seem fine." My sarcastic tone seems to amuse her, and she shakes with a single laugh before another sob takes over.

"Why don't we sit down. Come on. Let me . . . let me take this."

I pull the duffel bag straps from her shoulder and toss her light bag into a leather chair in the corner of my room, then guide her to the foot of the bed. She sits next to me, then quickly folds herself into a ball on the mattress, laying her head in my lap while she soaks my sweatpants-covered thigh with tears.

"You wanna talk about it?" I sweep her hair away from her face, combing through the wild knots with my fingers, and tucking the strands behind her ear.

She shrugs.

"I don't know what to say. It's kind of a long story." Her gaze flits to mine, her eyes red and glassy, and it breaks me to see her like this.

"Well," I say, pausing while I run my thumb along her red puffy cheek. "I'm not throwing tomorrow, so if I'm tired as hell, nobody will give a shit. Why don't you tell me about it? The whole thing?"

She stares into my eyes for a few quiet seconds without blinking, and I'm careful not to make a single sound that may cause her to hesitate about opening up. She seems fragile. Scared, perhaps. Definitely hurt. Not physically, but her heart is in pain. I can tell.

I used to find my mom like this sometimes, curled exactly this way at the foot of my parents' bed. She always told me she just got sad when my dad was out of town. She missed him. And I counted down for the day he came back home and made her seem whole again.

"My parents' relationship is just kind of . . . fucked up." She quivers with a faint laugh and bites her lip, almost as if she's embarrassed.

"I think all relationships are a little fucked up. What kind of fucked up is theirs?" I'm being sincere, and I think she can see that in my eyes as she relaxes and shifts to sit up next to me.

"I'm not even sure I understand it. They aren't married, but sometimes, when they're together, they act . . . married. And it's like my mom has this permission slip to come and go as she pleases."

She flits her hand in the air, mimicking fireworks, and I can tell her emotions are morphing from hurt to something closer to anger. I nod to encourage her to keep going, to keep sharing.

"I don't know why it makes me so mad. I'm an adult. It shouldn't, except I probably harbor a ton of resentment for all the shit she pulled during my formative years. And she did sort of fuck me over on the cusp to adulthood."

My brow furrows. "How so?"

I have pieced together some things on my own, like the fact Renleigh is living with her dad, and he's recovering from what I think was probably a stroke, or he's dealing with something neurological. But if there's one thing I learned from any argument I've ever watched my dad try to survive with my mom, it's the rule of making assumptions, and I'm not about to make an ass out of her or me.

"You know I'm twelve credit hours away from a bachelor's in psychology? From UT. A place I loved living, by the way." She blows up at the stray hairs that found their way to her forehead. I reach forward and sweep them back in place, tucked behind her ear, and the way she doesn't flinch at all feels nice. She's comfortable with me, enough so that she's sucking in a deep breath and revving up for more.

"My dad had a pretty bad stroke a couple of years ago, and I dropped out—twelve hours shy of my degree—to take care of him. And you know why?"

I shake my head and listen.

"Because my mother had an opportunity in Houston to work for some fancy oil company, lobbying for rich people and hobnobbing with billionaires. Meanwhile, my dad lives on the pathetic disability funds of a public-school teacher, and that's after months of battling way too many government officials just to get it."

I grimace.

"Okay, that's pretty shitty." I don't want to disparage her mom because that's her right, not mine. I know that people can love others and hate them a little, too.

"Right?"

Renleigh stands and pushes her hair back, tying it in a literal knot at the base of her neck while she paces. She's fully crossed over into pissed-off territory. I don't know whether that's healthy or not, but it hurts less to see her like this, so I go with it.

"That's what she does. What she's *always* done. When my mom wants to be a coach's wife, that's what she is, and when she wants to be a jet-setting, campaign-running, boardroom queen, she puts on the uniform and off she goes.

"It's exhausting, and honestly? I came to terms with how crappy it was to grow up with her a while ago. I'm just mad that she's still doing it, and that it still affects my life. Because guess what? She's back! Coach's wife again, probably because

it's convenient. Or maybe guilt finally caught up to her. Or . . .
I don't know. I don't even care about the reason anymore. I'm
just . . . tired."

She flops down in the leather chair, leaning against her
bag as her legs jut out and her hands fall on either side of the
armrests. She looks spent, like a boxer after a solid round.

"I hear you. I hear all of it, and Renleigh . . . hell, I'm
sorry. That's a lot to carry." I chew at the inside of my mouth,
eating the rest of my words despite the growing burn in my
belly. My conscience is urging me to speak some hard truth.

"What is it?" Renleigh barks.

Welp. I must have a bad poker face.

I lean forward and rest my elbows on my knees while I rub
my palms together, and steady my gaze on the gray carpet
floor between us. My gaze lifts to meet her heavy stare, and I
swallow.

"Did your dad ask you to do that?" My leg muscles flex on
instinct, like the rest of my body heard my words and took
notice of incoming missiles of attack.

"What the fuck is that supposed to mean?"

She doesn't sit up, but her head shifts forward a touch. If
she is a zombie, this is the point where she will try to eat me. I
should let her.

"Oh, fuck, I shouldn't interfere. It's just . . ."

I run my palm over my face. I have two decent skill sets—
one is throwing a baseball hard. The other? Conflict management. I've always been the peacekeeper. My sisters and I
fought like hell over everything. Same with the guys I grew up
with, my teammates. Even now, I'm constantly looking to keep
everyone happy.

Sure, it's selfish to an extent. I want Roddy to like me. I
want Brooks to like me. And Adler. And fuck, all of Texas,
when I get there. It's a complex deep and wide, and I'm aware
of it. And maybe one day if Renleigh finishes her degree and
goes into the clinical shit, she can help me dissect it. But for

right now, the need for conflict resolution is my superpower. And like it or not, I'm compelled to use it.

"You're so upset, and your emotions are valid. They are. Trust me. But is there a chance that maybe . . . I don't know." *Suck it up, Hunter. Spill it.* "That you brought some of this on yourself?"

She blinks once, then doesn't move for a solid five seconds. My insides begin to shrivel. We're not fucking tonight. Hell, I may never be seen alive again.

"I'm sorry, I shouldn't have—"

"You're right, you shouldn't. This was a dumb idea." In a single heartbeat, Renleigh is on her feet with her bag slung over her shoulder and on her way to the exit.

I fucked this up.

"Renleigh, wait—" I rush in front of her and rest my back on the door. If she asks me to move out of her way, I will. But I have to at least make her ask. I have to fight for her a little bit. I like this girl. Shit, I like her a lot. Even the ragey side. It's real. Renleigh might be the realest person I've ever met.

She doesn't push. She also doesn't speak. And those small signs encourage me. I tilt my head to one side and utter, "I'm sorry."

Her eyes fill with tears and she shakes her head, dropping her bag to the floor.

"You're right," she says.

I swallow hard, glad her eyes are on me so she can see the shock on my face. I know I'm right, but I expected her to fly all the way back to Oklahoma before admitting that.

Her shoulders lift with a deep inhale, and she lifts her gaze to me as she breathes out.

"Fuck, you're actually right. I mean . . . I *know* all of that. But also, what else am I going to do, you know? He's my dad. I love my dad. I chose him, but also . . . *I chose.*"

I nod, slowly stepping away from the door. My hands wrap around her wrists, and I bring them up over my shoulders so I can hold her against me again. She's not crying like she was before, but she seems just as spent and exhausted. A few hundred miles on a plane and a familial crisis can do that to a person.

"Who's on the mound tomorrow?" she asks as she grabs hold of my T-shirt and we begin to sway.

"Thompson. It's a rehab assignment, before he goes back to Texas. So, he'll go the full game. Why?"

Her fingertips walk up higher, tapping against my chest as her head shifts and her gaze hits mine.

"Full game, huh? So, there's no way you'll have to go in?" Her voice is quieter than before. *A whole lot* quieter. And maybe . . . suggestive.

I shake my head slowly.

"Nope. My bullpen was two days ago. They wouldn't let me throw if I gave them half my signing bonus," I joke.

She chuckles, her hands now at the collar of my shirt and working their way to the back of my neck. Our mouths are inches apart, and our eyes are locked.

We are definitely fucking.

"No curfew for you, then. Like, you can be up late." She tips her chin up, and her breath tickles against my lips. My tongue peeks out to taste it.

"As late as required."

Her eyes flutter shut, and her hands sink into my hair as I close the space between us and cover her mouth with mine. I know what this is—it's avoidance. She's using me. She wants to feel good, even if it doesn't last.

I can do that for her.

[illegible]

FOURTEEN
RENLEIGH

I'm a basket case. An actual basket case.

Yet that doesn't seem to scare Hunter off.

I suppose I should have bought into his reputation the first time we met. He proved then that he doesn't back down from a challenge, and despite every attempt I've made to cut him loose, he keeps showing up. For me.

For now.

I know how these things work. You don't grow up in Sweetwater and not learn a thing or two about dating a ballplayer. So many of the girls I went to high school with played this game, holding out hope for the pathetic pipe dreams on the other end. Land a dreamy ballplayer, become a baseball wife. Get the big house, the two-point-four kids, the fortune, travel, and easy life. And then get left alone half the year while your husband shuttles from city to city and sleeps with his side pieces.

No, thank you.

Maybe that's what makes Hunter appealing . . . *different.* I met him before he experienced any of that; before he tasted the temptations. He's still starry-eyed. Perhaps it's because he's good. Like, *truly* great. And I don't mean like nice-guy good, though he does seem to have the gentleman thing figured out. I mean good as in talent. He's the real deal.

Number one draft pick, huh? Yeah . . . I see it. And he wears that confidence like a second skin, which really fucking suits him when he's staring at me the way he is right now.

"Sit. Let me drive, okay?" He leads me to the edge of the hotel bed and gently pushes my shoulders down until I'm sitting at the foot of the bed.

Hunter grabs the remote from the TV stand and puts on a music channel before turning the volume up.

"Feel free to be as loud as you like," he says, his expression deliciously sinister.

"Okay," I murmur, my tongue wetting my bottom lip.

Hunter reaches behind his neck and pulls his white T-shirt up and over his head, dragging out the reveal of his chest and pecs as if he's a high-dollar stripper treating me in the ladies' champagne room. His hips swivel as he dances seductively in front of me, his hand drawing from the center of his chest down to his navel, then moving to the button of his jeans. He unfastens it with his right hand, then drags the zipper down while pulling his cock out with his left. He's not wearing anything underneath, and he's so hard, and way too big for his jeans to contain his length. He strokes himself as he steps toward me, kicking my legs apart so my knees widen and make room for him to stand right in front of me.

"Suck it." His husky voice scratches a hungry itch deep in my core, and my gaze flits up to his as my body inches forward and my lips part.

His hands slide on either side of my head, pushing my hair back from my face as my tongue tastes his tip. He winds my hair around one palm, getting a good grip as I bring my right hand up to stroke him and caress the ridge of his dick with my tongue.

"Do you like how I taste, Renleigh?" This alpha side of him turns me on, and I breathe out, *"Uh huh."*

Batting my lashes, I gaze up at him and close my mouth around his width. My eyes lock on his as he gently pulls me into him until I can feel him at the back of my throat. His hips rock back as he pulls my hair away from him, my mouth sucking to keep hold of his warm cock. He nearly leaves my mouth before pushing back into me and holding my head still so I can take him. My hands shift around his hips, his jeans gathered near the tops of his thighs, and I loop my fingers into the beltloops to help guide him in and out of my mouth.

A strange trust is forming between us, a wordless one that's negotiated with hooded eyes and moans that escape each of us as he slowly fucks my mouth. He holds me still when I'm full with him, dropping one of his hands down the front of my sweatshirt and pulling up the cup of my bra so my bare tit is in his palm. His hand is rough, and the pleasure from the sensation of his thumb and finger rolling my nipple makes my legs close around his. I can feel my pussy getting wetter.

"Strip," he says, backing away as his cock slips from my lips. My swollen bottom lip is wet with saliva, so I run my arm across my mouth before pulling my sweatshirt and then my bra over my head.

Hunter watches me with heated intensity, stroking himself.

"Touch your tits," he commands, and I run my palms up my ribs and over my breasts, pushing them together and pinching my own hard nipples. I never knew I would like this so much, being told what to do. And maybe it's simply the moment, or the circumstances, but I've never felt more aroused and alive.

"Touch your pussy too," Hunter says, lifting his chin.

His tongue peeks out before he bites his bottom lip as I sink my right hand into my leggings, my fingers gliding across the swollen, wet skin beneath my lace thong. Hunter pushes his jeans down completely, kicking them from his feet and pulling off his socks before nodding for me to pull my pants off too. I do as he asks, sliding the waistband of my leggings down my hips and pulling my legs free as I scoot up the mattress. I begin to pull my panties down, but Hunter shakes his head.

"Leave those. I want to see what that lace looks like on your ass." He holds a finger up and twirls it in the air, urging me to get on all fours for him. My breath hitches, a rush of heat diving between my legs as I spin for him. I should be nervous, but I'm not. I'm excited. I'm ready. And so fucking needy.

"The perfect ass," Hunter says, his voice deep, almost vibrating with his words.

"You like it?" I ask, fishing for more praise, which I get with a playful smack to one ass cheek, followed by the warmth of his palm on my skin.

"Like a fucking work of art," he says, his hand following the curve of my ass and moving to my hip as the bed dips with his weight. I drop my head to look behind me and see him on his knees between my legs.

"Can I move you . . . like this?" His hand moves up my side and toward my spine, coaxing my shoulders and head down to the bed.

I nod and whimper, "Yes."

"Fucking poetry," he says, his fingertips raking down my back until they meet the elastic band of my thong—that he pulls up to sink the thin string deeper between my cheeks. The sharp pressure cuts against my swollen pussy, and I cry out. Not from pain, but because I like it. I like what I imagine he sees. I feel like his drug, both cherished and used for pleasure. All I can think about is how I feel, how he's making me feel, and what I want next, but won't dare speak out loud or ask for. I don't want to ask for a thing. I want him to tell me, to simply give me what he thinks is right. And I want to take it all.

"Let's see how wet you are?" Hunter muses, his tone tinged with an air of authority.

His hand slides around my thigh and between my legs, his

fingers slipping under the lace triangle that conceals very little. He strokes me, gliding his fingers between my legs and drawing a deep moan out of me from the relief his touch brings.

"You are so good to me, Renleigh. Look how wet you are." He sinks two fingers into me and presses the side of his thumb into my swollen clit.

"Oh, fuck," I whimper, burying my face in the folds of the bedspread to mute my cries.

"You don't have to do that. Remember? As loud as you want."

I roll my head to the side, my cheek flat against the silky fabric as I cry with pleasure, "Yeah."

Hunter continues to work me with his hand, teasing me to the point of nearly coming more than once, always pulling his hand away and forcing me to wait with bated breath for his touch to return. Finally, he slides his hand to my backside and pulls the lacey thong to the side so he can paint my wet pussy with the tip of his cock. I try to push back into him, to trick him into letting his cock slip inside before he wants it to, and he lets out a low, rumbling laugh.

"Someone's in a hurry," he teases, finally guiding his tip inside me, but leaving me unfulfilled for long, quiet seconds while he pulls it in and out several times.

"Please," I finally whine.

He leans over my back, his mouth kissing my bare shoulder, then nipping at my ear.

"Please, what?" His breath is hot, and he smells like expensive body wash and aftershave.

I lick my lips and open my eyes to see him still close. I can barely make out his smirk, but I see it. He loves toying with me. After I rebuffed him, here I am begging for it. It serves me right, and it's a cycle I fear I may come to really enjoy.

"Please fuck me, Hunter. Please fuck me hard."

"Well," he begins, smoothing a palm along my spine as he

sits up tall. "Okay, then," he announces before driving into me, his cock filling me before he pulls out completely and steps away, leaving me cold and wanting so much more.

"You fucking tease," I laugh out.

His laugh is slightly more sinister.

I arch my back, tempting him with my ass as he paces behind me like a predator who hasn't eaten for days. After nearly a minute, he comes back to bed and tugs my thong over my ass but not down my legs. He nudges my legs apart more, then guides his cock into me again, this time holding on to my hips as he pummels me from behind. What starts as a slow rhythm quickly gains speed, and soon, his skin is slapping into mine as he makes me cum so hard that my voice gives way from all the cries that leave my lips.

His cock swells inside me, but before he comes, he pulls out and strokes himself until his hot cum spills down my ass. He paints me with it, using his dick to coat me with his slick arousal, and I'm shocked when the graze of his dick against my pussy ignites another orgasm that rushes through every nerve in my body.

My body collapses onto the bed as Hunter walks to the bathroom. The steady stream of water mixes with the hum of the bathroom fan, and a few seconds later, he returns with a warm washcloth.

"Let me care for you." His kind gaze reaches mine as I struggle to keep my eyes open, every bit of energy I had now spent from the travel, from the emotions of the day, from Hunter.

"Thank you," I whisper as he dabs my skin with the warm cloth. His eyes flit to mine, I think because he senses the many meanings I sewed into those words.

"My pleasure," he says, discarding the wet cloth to the side table before scooping me into his arms.

He carries me into the bathroom and under the warm stream of the walk-in shower. He's careful as he sets me back on my feet, placing my hands on his shoulders before filling his palms with body wash and lathering my body and hair. His gaze is adoring, painting me with affection at every curve and dip as he cleans my body, then covers each new spot with a soft kiss. When we're both showered, he cuts the water off and wraps me with a thick white robe. He leads me back to the bed and pulls out a spare T-shirt from his carry-on bag. He helps me take the robe off, then slips it over my head before pulling my body into his as we lie in the center of the king-sized bed atop the rumpled blanket and sheets we left behind.

FIFTEEN
HUNTER

"Fucking pitchers, man. I got this all wrong."

Roddy chuckles as he shakes his head at me during my massage. He's getting his wrists, left elbow, right ankle, and both shoulders taped by Becca, one of our trainers. The guy is basically a mummy at this point.

I twist my head to the side to look him in the eyes.

"You know you love the attention, throwing your mask off all dramatic before spinning around with your head back to catch the foul ball behind the plate," I say.

"*Pfft*, yeah, until I drop it, and the crowd is basically *right fucking there!*" He holds both palms out, messing up the tape job on his right shoulder.

"If you don't hold still, I'm going to boo you," Becca scolds.

"Sorry, ma'am." Roddy's shoulders sink as he locks his body back into place so Becca can finish her work. His eyes shift to me just as the masseuse digs into my scapula, and my lids flutter shut as I groan much like I did in my hotel room last night. This massage is *that good*.

Roddy flips me off. "Like I said. Fucking pitchers, man.".

My massage wraps up before Roddy's tape job is done,

and I hang around the training room in my towel for a bit before heading into the locker room to take the longest hot shower of my life. Roddy's right about some of it—I do love off days. I love on days more, though, and there's a part of me that's jealous as hell that he gets to suit up and take the field every other day. He played eighty percent of the games when he was up in the show, and while his body took a beating for it, I bet if I asked, he'd say it was worth every single bruise, cut, and tear.

"How about you actually come see me for the ice after the game today?" Becca pats down the edge of her final strip of KT, tape then lowers her head to look Roddy in the eyes.

"Yeah, I hear ya. It's just so damn cold." He slips his shirt back over his head and arms as Becca laughs and tells him, "That's the point."

She moves on to the next player, one of the rookie outfielders we picked up from San Diego last week, and Roddy hops down from the table, stretching out his arms to adjust to the compression from the tape.

"That Renleigh I see you walk in with today?" He gives me a sideways look, and my stomach rolls the way it did when I was a sixteen-year-old jumping out of my high school girl-friend's window when her father came in.

"Yeah, she's here." I don't offer details, but judging by the narrowing of his gaze, I sense I don't need to.

"It was her idea, for what it's worth." I shrug, and he shakes his head, breathing out a slightly judgmental laugh.

"I bet it was. You forget I'm from this town and know the Blackwoods. I saw Sarah Blackwood's Mercedes in town and at the house. I bet Renleigh couldn't *wait* to get out of there."

Roddy's word hit less like a joke and more like a warning, the kind that, as he said, comes from history. My chest squeezes, and I'm not sure whether it's unwarranted jealousy that he has a shared history with Renleigh, or concern that her situation is even heavier than I thought it was.

"I'm thinking about inviting her on the next road trip. You know . . . in two weeks. To Iowa? I don't know if she can get off work though."

I'm just thinking this idea through now, and my motivations are rather selfish. Other than the obvious perks of having Renleigh in my room with me, having her come on the next trip gives me a chance to really show her what I've got. Iowa promises to be a tough series for us, and I know a lot of the guys who were drafted into that organization. I'm looking forward to throwing against them. I know their weaknesses.

I realize several seconds have gone by without a response from Roddy, so I snap out of my fantasy of getting to be a big hero in front of Renleigh and instead focus on the tightness of his mouth and the wince pulling his cheeks up to his eyes. I call him out on it.

"What's that face for?"

He sighs and leans back a step, dropping his hands into the pockets of his workout shorts before popping his gaze back to mine.

"I don't know why I like you, kid."

I huff out a sharp laugh and blink away the shock from his backhanded compliment.

"Thanks?" I hike my shoulders.

"What I mean is, I feel responsible for you for some reason. I don't know why, because I'm over this shit . . . being the wise old man hanging around to mentor the up-and-comers. At least, that's how my agent pitched these last few years on my contract. The money's good, and I get to be here, which . . . let's just say, it's important to me."

He's talking about his son, I'm sure.

"I guess, thanks for looking out for me despite your best instincts to not give a shit?" I laugh out my version of what he's saying, and he chuckles as he pinches the bridge of his nose.

"Yeah, it sounds bad. I know. But I'm on my way out, and

to be real with you, kid? I'm tired. Not of the game. I'll never be tired of that. But all the other shit? Travel, and women, and all the bullshit that's about to come at you that you don't even know. I'm sick of it all. But I like you, and I like Renleigh—a whole lot more than I like you."

"Noted," I laugh out.

"And I can't just let it be without making sure you know how fucking hard all of this is going to be. How hard it is." Roddy's mouth closes into a straight line as his gaze narrows on me. I think he wants me to nod and say I understand, but I don't.

"I appreciate it, man, but you're not telling me anything I don't know."

He snickers dismissively at my response and follows up with, "You don't know shit."

I purse my lips and brace myself for him to explain.

"Let me break it down for you. You were probably, what . . . twelve the first time you won what felt like a pretty important game?"

I nod and utter, "Yeah, Little League District Championship. We went to the World Series." I can close my eyes and still hear mine and my friends' parents screaming their heads off in the bleachers. And the pizza party that night was off the charts.

"Right. Me too. Probably the same for half the guys out here. We all get it. There's something about playing this game at a high level that's this massive rush of dopamine. It gets under your skin, and it's what makes you keep stepping up on that mound or getting up to the plate. In a game of mostly failures, we come out here for the wins. Not just the day-to-day ones, but the minuscule ones. Throwing a one-hitter. Then a no-hitter. Or mastering the curve. Or getting the guy who's hitting four hundred out swinging."

My smile stretches with every new goal he states. He's basically reading my diary.

"Exactly," he says, gesturing toward me. "That smile right there. That's the one. And damn, when you get that kind of win, you want to celebrate, you know? And you might be on the other side of the country, and it's late at night, and you're hitting the hotel bar, and there she is . . . the blonde who's been staring at you from the second row for the entire game, or the sexy woman with an accent that sounds a hell of a lot better on her than it does on your shortstop. And that woman smells so good, and even though you've got one at home who was watching your game on TV, you just want to indulge this once—to treat yourself. Because you were great today. And what's one slip?"

I shake my head because I hear what he's saying, but that's simply not me. I know I'm not that guy.

"I get what you're saying, man, and I know the temptations are real. But I'm a big boy. I get what consequences mean, and I wouldn't do that to someone. I wouldn't do that to Renleigh," I say, my tone resolute.

Roddy's eyes hold on to mine for a long breath before he shakes his head slowly and pulls his mouth in tight.

"It's not just the women. In fact, the cheating bullshit that goes on in this environment is mostly a symptom, in my opinion. It's an excuse."

"Did you cheat, Roddy?" My bold question takes me by surprise, and I regret being impulsive when the two-hundred-ten-pound unshaven beast of a man steps closer to me. The only thing that keeps me still is that his hands haven't left his pockets.

His gaze drops to his feet, but I keep my focus on the fine lines etched into his face, the years of wear and tear and exhaustion and sun that have marked his jawline and eyes for good. He sniffs and bunches his lips before nodding.

"Yeah, I cheated."

I feel kind of sick for asking, and I'm not sure if I feel bad for him or disappointed in him. When his gaze lifts and hardens on mine, all those emotions morph into appre-hension.

"Not with a woman, though. Like I said . . . cheating phys-ically is a cop-out in my opinion. The real problem is that feeling—that first big win. The little wins. The chase to get the biggest win of all. The feel of that perfect leather ball and the threads against my fingertips. The dirt. Ha, even the fucking dirt. Yeah, I cheated all right. I cheated with the game, when I probably should have picked a person."

Well, damn. I can't belittle him over that. I know there's a certain level of acceptable selfishness to being the best at this sport. It's like that in most sports, I suppose, but there's some-thing about the grind of this game. The schedule. All those innings. When baseball is in your blood, you want to be in the game all the time. You never want to be taken out. It's who you are. It's who *I* am.

It's who Roddy is. A thirty-eight-year-old guy isn't catching in the minors if the game isn't both his mistress *and* his wife.

"All I'm saying, kid, is I like you. And I like Renleigh. And if this game weren't involved, I could maybe even get behind the two of you getting together. But the game is part of you. Damn, you might just be the brightest bit of raw talent I've ever caught."

I grin, but it falters quickly when I come to terms that his compliment is big, but his warning is bigger.

"You're going to live two lives in this game. One out there"—he jerks his chin in the general direction of the ball field—"and one somewhere else. With someone special . . . or with *lots* of someones. You'll never be able to give another person all of you. It's just part of the game."

Roddy's heavy hand lands on my shoulder as he leaves me with my thoughts and a mountain of guilt over the woman sitting in the baseline family section, waiting for me to smile at her from the end of the dugout.

SIXTEEN
RENLEIGH

I left without telling anyone where I went, which should be fine for a twenty-four-year-old woman to do. The fact nobody wonders where I am shouldn't be strange. Only . . . it is. Because I'm me. And my presence has been woven into routines for two years. Why has nobody noticed the disruption my being gone causes?

I'm fumbling with my phone in my lap, still dressed in a pair of Hunter's sweats and one of his training shirts that I've basically commandeered as my own for the weekend. I should probably get showered and check in for my flight. I meant to last night, but then Hunter ordered an early dinner for us in the room, and I sort of never looked at my phone again.

"You sure you don't want to head over early with me? The family room is super nice. I saw it on my way out of the training room yesterday. Nashville's got money!" Hunter rubs his thumb to his index and middle finger and flashes wide eyes.

"You mean, it's nicer than the repurposed portable class-room in Sweetwater with a few old leather sofas and a folding table with three chairs?" I lift a brow as I drop my phone next to me and pull my knees up to hug them.

"Yeah, this place has recliners and stadium-seating in front of the big screen so you can watch the warmups or a movie if you want. And there's a coffee bar with a barista and everything."

He slides a sleek copper tie into a Windsor knot as he stands before me in his fitted black pants and white dress shirt that fits every perfectly formed muscle on his body. I push myself forward and snag the end of the tie, then rock back, tugging him toward me. He crawls forward until I'm caged between his arms, and he drops his forehead to mine.

I tilt my head up, lifting my chin until our lips meet, and the warmth of his mouth over mine tempts me to untuck his shirt and work open the buttons he spent a full minute fastening.

"Careful," he says, his teeth holding my bottom lip as he presses his hard-on between my legs. "You're going to wear me out before I throw today."

I pull a knee up, increasing the pressure between us, but stop myself before I wrap my legs around him. I slide my hands up to his chest and push him away with the strength of a noodle, but enough that he moves back and abandons the bad idea I think we were both considering.

"I'll head over in an hour to watch your pre-game," I say.

Hunter straightens his tie and runs his hands down his crisp shirt. I love when the starters dress up before games. I know it's only for the walk to the ballpark, but I like the classiness of it all. The tradition and respect it brings to the game. And, my God, do I like the way Hunter looks in dress pants and a tie.

"Promise?" He quirks a brow. It's sweet how excited he is for me to watch him work again. It's a bit different this time, too, because now I know what I'm looking at. I'm possibly watching a future Hall-of-Famer. A guy who's about to change the game for the organization, at least if he keeps going the way he is now. And yeah, I kind of like that I know what he feels like against me. And that if I want to, before I leave to head back home, I can have him inside me one more time.

"I promise," I say, leaning back on my palms and crossing my legs as I stretch them out in front of me. "Just let me shower and check in for my flight."

I study Hunter as he swings his sports coat over his shoulders, looking for signs that he wants me to stay. His expression is indifferent, though, probably as it should be. We aren't anything. We're having fun. Still, I am tempted to stretch this into a longer weekend. It would only be one more night. But I've already left Daisy hanging for my shift today. I don't think she bought the text I sent her about being sick. I'm never sick. At least, not so sick that I don't suck it up for tips.

"I'll look for you. Same seat, okay?"

I lift my phone and click open the ticket app before flashing the screen at him.

"Got it."

He leans over the bed one final time and presses a kiss to the top of my head before rushing out the door. When the lock clicks into place behind him, the room becomes eerily quiet and cold. I glance around the space, the slick lines of the modern furniture and dark gray walls adding to the chill.

I sigh and drag myself out of the warm bed, padding across the floor into the bathroom. I turn the hot water up as high as it will go, filling the room with steam while I strip, then open the airline app on my phone to get my boarding pass. It's a shitty position to match the crummy seat I purchased, but when you make impulsive decisions, I guess you have to resolve yourself to middle seats near the bathroom.

I take my time in the shower, turning my skin a hot pink as my fingers prune. I finally peel myself away from the steam-filled glass retreat and twist my hair into a clip atop my head. I wrap a dry towel around my body and tiptoe into the bedroom, only to run directly into a very beautiful, very tall brunette wearing tight black pants and a Mavericks jersey tied into a crop top, accentuating her incredibly ample breasts.

"What the fuck!" I shout and clutch my chest as she does the same, both of us backing up several steps. I lean against the dresser while she moves toward the door.

"I'm so sorry. I must be in the wrong room." Her eyes are wild, searching for who knows what. This is starting to feel like a room invasion, and I form a fist with my right hand in case I need to take a swing at this lady.

"I'm certain you are," I say, steadying myself on my feet. I sure wish I wasn't naked. I'm scrappy when I need to be, but I'm pretty sure it helps to be clothed.

"I was looking for Hunter Reddick," she says, and it takes my body a few seconds to catch up with her words. I halt mid-step toward the bathroom and my phone when it sinks in.

"I'm sorry. Hunter?" I shake my head, like I'm trying to erase everything it knows.

"Yeah. I wanted to surprise him." One of her shoulders hikes up as she sucks in her bottom lip, and there's a quiet that settles in between us as we stare at one another. I'm arranging the new facts with everything I know about ballplayers, and I have a feeling this woman is doing the same.

"I'm sorry, who are you?" I tilt my head, still skeptical about her being here for legitimate reasons, though less so than I was a moment before.

"I'm Sloane. Maxwell?" She adds the last name as if that will clear things up for me. She speaks with a confident tone, as though it should.

"And you are?" She folds her arms over her chest, which makes my chest warm, and I find myself again wanting to throw a punch at her.

"I'm not telling you my name. But I was invited to be here, so . . ." I glance toward the door, but Sloane simply scoffs and moves toward the foot of the bed, where she promptly takes a seat, making herself *way* too comfortable.

"I was invited, too." She shakes her head and an incredulous laugh spills through her maroon-tinted lips.

She pulls a phone from the small cross-body purse she's wearing. I gawk at her like a fool as she slides her finger around her screen, finally opening the same ticket app I have and holding up a ticket that looks pretty much just like mine. I step forward and squint to read the date, and when I see it's today's game, I feel as though I just swallowed a boiling hot bowling ball.

"Huh." My stomach boils, caught between sickness and the tightening sensation my muscles undergo before I'm about to work out hard.

"*Yeahhh,*" Sloane says, clicking her screen off and dropping her hands and her gaze to her lap.

"I feel pretty stupid," I admit.

"That makes two of us." She shakes her head with breathy laughter, the sad kind tinged with disappointment in humankind.

She pops her gaze up to me, her lips puckered into a resolute twist, and she gets to her feet.

"I'm gonna go."

I open my mouth but snap it shut when I realize there are too many things I want to say, yet at the same time don't have it in me to utter any of them. When the door snaps shut for a second time this morning, I drop my towel and slip back into my own clothes before checking my phone app to put myself on standby for the early flight. Turns out, I'm ready to go, too.

I shove the few belongings I brought with me into my bag and give the rumpled sheets one more glance before marching to the door. My hand grips the handle, but before I can get myself to push it down and set myself free, I'm hit with a wave of emotion, and a single sob rattles my chest and weakens my knees.

I can't believe I did this. Any of it. I know better.

I'm mad at myself, but also, I feel guilty for leaving without a goodbye. How twisted is that? Hunter is the dog I thought he was from the beginning, yet here I am feeling bad about abandoning him before his game, for being a no-show, for ghosting.

I draw in a deep breath and shut my eyes for a beat, seeing my mother's face when I do. I'm nothing like her, yet here I am, somehow feeling a lot like her. If I weren't ashamed, I'd call Lindsey and get her advice. She'll give it to me after the fact when I get home, assuming she even noticed I was gone. So far, I think the only person with an inkling I'm not in town is my boss. And that's because I had to call in sick.

My eyes blink open as I let my head fall back and pivot, heading back into the room. I'm too responsible for this shit. A real woman wouldn't leave a note. She'd just go, taking her dignity and pride with her. At the very least, though, I will leave my mark.

I pull a small pad of paper from the nightstand and snag the hotel pen from the tabletop, pulling the cap off with my teeth.

Sloane stopped by.

- R

I leave the notepad right by the phone, then toss the pen into the open drawer, spitting the cap toward the bed. This time, I have zero trouble making it all the way out the door.

SEVENTEEN
HUNTER

My performance today is shit. My head's not in the game. Roddy knows it, too.

"Time out," he barks to the ump before jogging out to the mound. I pull my hat from my head and again run my forearm across my sweat-soaked brow. It's humid today. Either that, or I'm sweating bullets because I'm blowing it.

"You're all over the place. What the fuck?" Roddy slaps the ball in my mitt. I pick it out and cover my face with my glove.

"I know. Fuck! I'm just off. I keep missing low."

"And high. And outside. And inside. And in the fucking dirt. Get it together, kid!" He taps my arm with his glove, then punches the pocket with his fist before lifting his chin.

"Yeah, you're right. I got this." I sniff, then glance to my right, to the empty seat that has remained so for the first three innings.

"Hey," Roddy says, pounding his mitt again to get my attention back where it belongs. His glare says it all.

Forget the girl. Get my head in the game.

I kick at the dirt as he jogs back behind the plate, and force myself to keep my eyes locked on the dirt path from the rubber to the plate. I lock eyes with Roddy as he sends the pitch through the PitchCom, and smirk when he calls for a high fast ball. I'm either going to nail this pitch or send it into the seats. I nod and step into my windup, breathing in through my nose and holding the air hostage in my lungs until I sling the ball to my catcher.

"Steee-rike!" I haven't heard the ump say that word much today. This one is good to hear.

Roddy zings the ball back to me and calls for another fast ball, this one right down the pipe. I'm one strike away from getting out of this inning, and the last thing my ego needs is to see another ball sail over the right field wall. But I trust Roddy. It's the first lesson I learned in Sweetwater, and it might just be my last if I don't get us out of this inning.

I feel the ball in my glove, then wind up and throw the heat, holding my breath as the ball cuts through the air and just past the heavy-handed swing of Pablo Cabrera, a guy whose rookie card I have in a box back in my childhood closet in California.

"Strike three!" The ump pulls his fist into his chest with extra flair, and my shoulders drop with relief.

I keep my expression stoic as I walk back to the dugout, and Coach slaps my ass as I take the steps and head straight to the iPad to see all the places I went wrong so far today. It's a three-zero ballgame, which, in Triple-A ball is a good thing. For anyone else in our rotation, it's a great start. Three innings with two hits and a walk. It's just that those two hits happen to have been dingers, one with an RBI. But even with that, it's a solid showing. For some other guy. For me, it's a failure, and I know it's not my mechanics. They're solid. Which means . . .

"Get out of your head," Roddy says, basically reading my mind as he rips the iPad from my hands and sets it on the shelf behind the bench. He plops down next to me as he tears at the tape wrapped around his wrist with his teeth. It's unraveling.

"You're right," I respond.

"Yeah, I know I am. And quit looking for Renleigh. She probably just slept in. Or maybe she got wise and went home." He chuckles, and the corners of my mouth fall.

"You think so?" I ask.

His attention zooms back to my face as his laughter cuts off.

"Dude, I'm kidding. But maybe, I don't know. Like I said, this world? It's not good on relationships, and Renleigh knows that. Why do you think she turned you down so many times?"

"Not *that* many," I sigh, not laughing at my own joke.

"She's got a lot on her plate. Maybe her dad needed something. Her mom's a lot to handle when she's in town. Don't worry about it for now. Just focus on the game. Do your job, then sort that shit out later." Roddy slaps his palm on my thigh and uses my body for leverage as he stands.

"Maybe go get one of those runs back, huh?" I jest as he spits in his palms and slaps them together.

"I'll try. If you promise that was the last run you give up today," he says over his shoulder.

"Yeah, I do." I nod and catch Brooks's gaze as he glances my way over his shoulder. I step up next to him along the rail. He's saved my ass today, making some amazing plays at short.

"Hey, I'll try to give you a break this next inning. I'm sorry I'm giving up the middle so much." I hold out my fist, and he pounds his on top of mine before turning his attention back to the field. Something's going on with him today, too. I can tell. I'm pretty sure our expressions match.

I make it through six innings, and we end up losing by one, thanks to a home run by Roddy and some spectacular base running by Jayden Vargas.

"Good work today, Hunt," Coach says as I zip up my bag and shift it to my left side so I can keep the ice wrapped around my shoulder.

"Nah, I know I was shit. I'll do better. I promise," I drone.

I don't mean to sound like a pity party, but I can't accept compliments for what I know was a crap performance.

"Yeah, you were. But also, you battled back. Sometimes it's good to see what talent does when things don't go the way they're supposed to. You figured it out. Get some rest. You're off tomorrow."

I nod and head out of the locker room, dragging my feet as I fumble for my phone that I stuffed in the back pocket of my sweatpants. My dress clothes are rolled into a ball in my bag. I saw a few of the other guys had garment bags for their suits. I should probably invest in one of those. I should also probably get a few more suits.

The only notification on my phone is a text from my mom. It's her usual *good job, honey.* There's nothing from Renleigh, which feels . . . wrong. I hover my thumb over her name and open our last text string, which is basically her requesting a Diet Coke from the vending machine late last night when I made a snack run down the hall.

I stop at the stadium gate where kids rush around me with their own balls and mitts, most of them playing catch and pretending to snag deep fly balls like the ones I gave up today. We're out of town, so the younger fans don't recognize me, but a few teenagers stop me for an autograph while I'm mentally debating sending Renleigh a text. I finish signing a hat with a Sharpie, then hover over her name for a few more seconds before deciding to just get back to the hotel to check that she's okay.

I get razzed by a few Nashville fans on my way back to the hotel, but laugh most of the insults off. It's not until I exit the hotel elevator and some wealthy-looking guy wearing too much cologne says to his buddy, "Looks like he's going to be sleeping alone tonight," through a snarky laugh that I pause.

"What's that supposed to mean?" I fire back as the doors close, and I hear them laugh at my expense through the sealed seam.

My pulse ratchets, a little because I'm pissed, but more so, I think, because that guy was right—I am sleeping alone tonight. And I wish I wasn't. Renleigh needs to get to the airport. Or maybe she's already there. Perhaps that's why she skipped my game, so she could get a jump on things and make it back to her dad. Or what if something happened with her dad?

I flail my room key out of my wallet and slap it against the door, shoving the door open with enough gusto that it bounces off the rubber wall stopper.

"Hey, Ren?" I toss my bag on the freshly made bed. The room smells like lavender, and the television is on low, the hotel's in-room ad channel flipping through the restaurant menu to the sound of smooth jazz.

I walk all the way into the bathroom as if she could be hiding behind the shower wall, waiting to jump out and yell *boo!* Of course, she's not.

I pull my phone back out and check our text string again, hoping I missed something or that she just messaged me now, during my panic attack, but there's nothing. I sit on the side of the bed and set my phone on the night table, then catch the note waiting for me.

Sloane stopped by.

-R

"Fuck me!" I pick the small pad of paper up and stare at the three words, my eyes zeroing in on the name of the last girl I dated in college. My free hand flies to my hair, and I grip a fistful and tug just to relieve some of the pressure threatening to make me blow my lid off.

"I was being nice," I grumble, tossing the pad of paper across the room.

I grab my phone and flip through my contacts, but of course she's not in there. We never fully made it to contact status. Our last messages were all on social media, and one of those apps doesn't even exist anymore. I open the one that does and find her profile, zooming in on the part that says she's in Nashville for grad school. I sigh with a touch of relief that she's not stalking me to the point she's driving across state lines. And to be fair, I did invite her . . . sort of. I just never thought she'd actually show.

We went out a few times my senior year, and we had a healthy, physical relationship. I may have credited my successful last month of the regular season to her, but that's because I'm superstitious as fuck. I'm a ballplayer. We all are.

It was a cordial breakup, too. She was applying to medical schools, and I had just been drafted. The team sent me the link for friends and family tickets, and I wanted to keep things friendly, so I told her to come see me play anytime. And well . . . I guess she did. Or she tried to. Today. Of all fucking days.

I'll deal with Sloane later. For now, I need to figure out where Renleigh is. And what she thinks. And how the hell I'm going to fix this.

I doubt this is what Roddy was talking about during his lecture the other day, but I can't help but feel his words were a bit prescient. I dial Renleigh and pace the room while the call rings twice, then gets instantly sent to voicemail.

Maybe that was a fluke.

I dial again, but this time I'm dumped into her voicemail box without a single ring. I open our text string and shoot her a message.

> ME: Sloane is nobody.

I stare at the words for a beat, then quickly delete.

Not only is that a cliché response, but it's also demeaning to Sloane. She's not nobody. She's going to be a pediatrician, for Christ's sake. She's just not my girlfriend. Or my hook-up. Or any of the things I fear are now lodged in Renleigh's mind.

> ME: Where are you? I can explain.

I laugh out loud when I type those words, because that's probably the only *more* cliché phrase I could send. I take off the end and simply go with asking where she is, meanwhile following my gut and preparing to leave.

I pack my bags and order a rideshare while simultaneously checking the various times for outbound flights to Oklahoma City. I suppose Renleigh could fly into the small airport outside Sweetwater, too, but those routes are hit or miss. Unless she's so pissed she bribes a private pilot to take her home. Which honestly? I can see her doing. Her fire is what attracts me to her. And yeah, maybe the chase. Not *this* chase, though, because this one feels bad. She came here to get away from chaos, only to have it show up unexpectedly.

My flight app opens as I rush out of my room. There are three options before her flight, and two of them have already taken off, so I push all my chips in and bank on this last flight being the one she's trying for. I have thirty minutes to get to the airport before she boards, so when my rideshare pulls up, I toss my bags in the back seat with me and toss the guy an extra hundred bucks on the side to break a few speeding laws and get me there fast.

David in the black Toyota Camry drops me off at departures with ten minutes to spare, and I sprint to the ticket counter to plead my case. Apparently, arriving a full twenty-four hours early for a flight isn't a thing, and also, I'm not as well-known as I sometimes think I am. At least, not among the employees of Nashville International Airport.

I beg Casey, the kind, patient, but sticking-to-the-rules ticket worker, to ask her boss to make an exception, and soon a man named Thomas with hot pink wings pinned to his pocket and a mustache that twists up on the ends is also telling me the only way I can get to the gates is to purchase a ticket or apply for a special pass online. That process typically takes three to five days, so . . .

I drop my head to the counter and laugh softly. I could

move my flight up a day and bail on the team, but there's no way to do that without raising a whole lot of suspicion. The only reason guys leave early are the personal kind, reserved for family emergencies and such, or possibly an injury. I've got none of that going on, but I suppose I could lie about the family issue. I hate lying. I'm loathe to do it. But I keep hearing Roddy's voice in my head.

I cheated with the game, when I probably should have picked a person.

"Can you bump me up to the next flight, then?" I pull up my ticket info that the team travel administrator sent to my phone, and Thomas punches in my confirmation number.

"Oh, you're here with the Mavericks. How fun. Did you enjoy our stadium?" he asks.

I blink slowly, my face tight with what I'm sure is a stupefied expression.

"I did. The right field wall is a little shallow for my taste, though."

I give him a crooked smile, but my clue zooms right over his head as he replies, "Ah," and continues to punch in things on the keyboard.

"I'm a pitcher. With the Mavericks," I lean forward and whisper.

Thomas glances up but keeps typing.

"Yeah, I gathered. Good for you." His smug smile shuts me up after that, and it will be a good long while before I exploit my perceived fame to cash in favors.

"Here you go, Mr. Reddick. You'll be in a middle seat, as that's all we have available. Head to gate six once you get through security and enjoy your flight."

I slide my new boarding pass from the counter and eyeball the details. If there was room for me on this flight, then there was probably room for Renleigh, too, unless she got on an earlier one.

Or . . . I'm way off on everything, and she either took

herself to a movie or went for a long walk to blow off steam—in which case I am throwing darts at my career for no good reason at all.

Though that's also not the case. Because, despite knowing this girl for only two weeks, something in my gut tells me going the distance for her is worth it. Even if I get it wrong.

I fly through security, and sprint through the concourse until I spot the giant six lit up on the other side of the McDonald's storefront. I slip in at the end of the boarding line, and shuffle forward with my carry-on over one shoulder, a thick sheen of sweat pasting my T-shirt to my back, and sweatpants rolled to my knees because I got hot on the ride here and had no time to swap my sweats for shorts.

Once I'm on the plane, I glance at my boarding pass and note row seventeen, then pop my gaze up to manically scan the passengers ahead of me for Renleigh. I'm starting to doubt this crazy scheme I've embarked on when a familiar voice hits my ears.

"Let me move my bag for you."

Renleigh steps into the aisle a few passengers ahead of me, moving her bag so an older woman can slip into her row and take the window seat. It looks like Renleigh is stuck with a middle, too, and if my counting skills are on point, it looks as if she's assigned the opposite side of row seventeen. *My opposite*. How appropriate.

The dude in the Coors hat in front of me plops down in the aisle seat next to her, and since I've come this far, I decide there's no risk in enduring one more humiliating experience. I tap his shoulder as he hunts at his side for his seat belt, and I'm met with not only his eyes, but a pair of perfect blue ones, too.

"Excuse me, but would you possibly be willing to trade me seats?" I ask him.

Renleigh's gaze narrows, and her lips pucker with what I'm going to say might be a touch of rage.

"Uh . . . what's your seat?" the man asks.

I gesture to the middle one behind me, and he bellows laughter.

"Yeah, fat chance, buddy. Thanks, though." He clicks his safety belt in place and glances to his right to commiserate with the woman next to him, whose face has morphed from angry to rather smug.

"We need to talk," I say, sliding into my middle seat just ahead of the guy sitting next to me.

"I can't hear you," Renleigh says, pointing to her ear as if we're standing outside the plane next to the engine.

My head tilts, but my body is jostled by my neighbor, who I am guessing is a body builder of some sort with thighs twice the size of Roddy's and a tight black tank top that barely covers his bulbous pectorals that are covered with demon tats.

"Looks like we're going to be snug, pal," the man says with a grizzly laugh. My knees press into the back of the seat in front of me, and my feet are tucked under my seat as far as they can go, which isn't very far thanks to the bag slid underneath me. I gave up a first-class ticket with plenty of foot room to spend two hours sandwiched between a snoring college kid and Mr. Clean.

Renleigh has already sunk back in her seat, and the flight crew is walking the aisle, closing luggage compartments and checking to make sure everyone's seat is upright and ready for takeoff. I wedge my hand between my hip and Mr. Clean's and manage to come out with one side of my seat belt, along with my phone. I click the belt into place, then palm my phone and ruminate on the easiest lie I can concoct. My departure feels too fast for the onset of flu symptoms, and I don't own anything that could be stolen in a break-in back in Sweetwater. The only thing I own right now is my name, which, though of late feels rather worthless, is a plausible excuse to dash home a day early.

I text my coaches that someone is racking up debt in my

name and I need to get back to file reports with the police, then promptly switch my phone into airplane mode before pulling down my tray table, laying my head to the side, and staring to my right while I wait for Renleigh to crack an eyelid and glance to her left.

Newsflash: She doesn't for the entire two-hour flight.

EIGHTEEN
RENLEIGH

I could be that person who rushes from the plane, sprinting to a taxi and speeding off, hoping the boy will chase me. And I don't lie to myself—I thought about it for half the flight.

But he's on this plane. And I know he shouldn't be. So the least I can do is hang back and deplane together. And maybe —*only maybe*—listen to him.

I back into the aisle to let both passengers in front of me clear out, then wait for the hulk of a man next to Hunter to grab his bag and leave. Hunter's gaze locks onto mine as soon as muscle man's body clears a path, and he's quick to take me up on the opportunity to be within touching distance, it seems.

"Yeah?" His head tilts a smidge as he grabs his bag and walks backward.

"Go on. Don't make a big deal out of it. It's a five-minute walk from the gate to the curb. And my sister's picking me up, so you should talk fast." *Lest I signal Lindsey when she sees you and we both attack.*

"Right. Got it." He takes in a deep breath, still shuffling backward down the aisle of the plane.

"I'm a nice guy," he begins, and I laugh out so hard I snort and have to cover my face with my palms.

"Come on, Renleigh. You know I am. I'm not out here womanizing, racking up ladies in every city. That's not me. You have to know that." His head leans to one side with such sincerity, I'm forced to calm the tickle in my chest so I can hold it together and give him a fair shake.

"Hunter, I know you have a thing for IKEA furniture, and you were the number one draft pick. Those are the things you've shared with me. Sorry, but I'm not sure those qualifies as nice-guy characteristics."

I tuck my bottom lip under my teeth and shrug. That was brutal to say to him, but it's true. On top of it that, I don't trust people, especially when it comes to relationships, and it's a miracle I didn't choose to sprint off the plane, then change my number . . . and address.

He nods as his gaze drops to the breezeway floor. He pivots to walk forward, slowing enough that our steps sync up, and I open my mouth to apologize for coming off harsh, but decide against it. I want him to be a nice guy, but years of experience—of watching ballplayers come and go, of watching my own parents' toxic relationship—tells me wanting someone to be good and them actually living it are two very different realities.

"You're right," he finally says as we step into the jetway and enter the gate lounge.

I meet his gaze for a few steps and wait for the *but*. He doesn't refute me, though. He accepts my argument.

There aren't many people waiting at the gate. The early evening arrival time isn't a popular one, so there are plenty of wide-open concourses all the way to baggage claim. If I wanted to, I could hurry this conversation along and be on my way, spilling my guts to Lindsey as she drives me home. But something has me stuck when it comes to Hunter, so I slow.

"Go for a ride?" I tilt my head to the moving sidewalk, and his mouth ticks up into a faint smile.

"It's my favorite. How'd you know?" He steps onto the

moving conveyor belt first, turning to face me as I step on behind him.

"So tell me, are you normally a stand-still and ride kind of girl, or do you walk briskly and keep to the left, respecting the rules of the passing lane?" Hunter glances behind me, and I follow his gaze, confirming that right now, we're the only two on this thing.

"I'm pretty sure I can tell what version you are by the way you phrased that," I laugh out. "And I think we're of the same vein. People who impede the flow of traffic in the airport are . . . well . . . those are not nice guys, let's just say."

Hunter chuckles at my position, and nods.

"Good. One more thing we have in common." His smirk teases me, and I mimic his expression with a tight-lipped simper of my own.

"Okay, I'll give you one more check mark on the nice guy list. Now tell me something else."

I swallow as a vision of Sloane's face flashes through my mind. That's what I really want to hear about—how she fits into things and ends up in his hotel room. But I'm willing to give him the trip out of the airport to lay out his case with more personal facts.

"*Hmm,* well. My parents have a strange relationship, too. Not quite like yours. You take the gold in that," he says, and I sashay a hand across my midriff before taking a bow and accepting the worst top prize ever.

"Why are your parents strange?" I push him to keep sharing.

"Well, they aren't in the same place a lot. My dad travels for work six months out of the year, and my mom gets lonely. I'm pretty sure she struggles with depression, though she's never come out and talked to me about it. I should probably ask, but I don't really know how. And part of me doesn't want to know for sure because I feel guilty for leaving her alone, too." He draws in a sharp breath and widens his eyes before blowing out. "Wow, that was a bit of a breakthrough for me."

My gaze narrows with a touch of skepticism, but I quickly see he's being genuine.

"I get how your mom feels. I felt that way too, when my mom would take off for months or years at a time. It's why my dad and I are so close."

Hunter nods, shifting the weight of his travel bag on his shoulder as he drops his gaze to his feet.

"It's probably why I'm so close with my mom. When Dad was gone when I was in high school, it was just us. My sisters were out of the house, in college." He brings his attention back to my face, his smile urged on by something distant. And maybe precious. "She was there for every practice, every game, every tryout and college visit. And when I went to college, she sometimes dropped by unexpectedly. Oftentimes. Basically, every other weekend," he laughs out.

I snicker, picturing a woman who looks a lot like him barging into a single college guy's dorm room. That thought quickly morphs to Sloane.

"You have a habit of women just dropping by unexpectedly, it seems."

I press my molars together and stretch my lips into a tight smile, not exactly proud of my passive-aggressive segue, but not exactly backing off from it, either.

Thankfully, Hunter breathes out a soft laugh through his nose and quickly nods in agreement.

"It seems I do. But I swear, there's an explanation for Sloane showing up to the hotel today."

"To your room, you mean," I correct.

Hunter's spine straightens, and his head jerks back a few inches, as if I hit him with a blast of air. He didn't know that part. Or he's a great actor.

"Oh, yes. She was in your room, Hunter. I walked out of the shower in nothing but a towel, and there she was."

I leave out my commentary on her being drop-dead gorgeous. Besides, he seems in shock, and I don't think he's blinked since I broke the news to him. Either that or he's dwelling on the part about me being naked. We're approaching the end of the moving sidewalk, so I gesture behind him to pay attention. I don't catch him quite in time, however, and he backpedals several feet with his arms swinging to keep from falling and cracking his head on the terrazzo floor.

"Renleigh, I swear to God. I swear on my arm, on my future, on everything that's important to me, Sloane showing up today was just the culmination of a lot of poor communication on my part. I did tell her she was welcome to come see me play . . . anytime. We dated my senior year, briefly, and I may have chickened out when it came to a hard and fast closure to the relationship."

"You mean you wanted to keep the booty-call line open," I challenge him.

Hunter winces at first, but his expression morphs into one of resolve, his mouth heavy at the corners and his eyes not able to fully reach mine.

"I probably did, yeah. No . . . I know I did. But that was just stupid plans hatched in the brain of a single guy hyped up about his future, fantasizing about a glitzy lifestyle, parties, fast cars, and—"

"And women," I cut in.

His lips twist, and he lifts a shoulder.

"Yeah. I guess so."

He blinks slowly, bringing his gaze fully to mine, and it's heavy with guilt. He's being honest; it's written all over his face. But also, I don't think he'd have said everything he just did if he were trying to pull one over on me.

"So, what changed?" I ask.

His eyes dim, and his brow lowers, his expression puzzled.

"Huh?"

"Eight months ago, you wanted all those things—the fast cars, the glitz. *The booty call.* What changed? And when you say you aren't that man, that you're a good guy, why should I believe you?"

My body is buzzing suddenly at uttering those words. I'm scared he's going to tell me nothing's changed, that he made a mistake—that *we* were a mistake.

Hunter takes measured steps closer to me, though, and at first, I back up, keeping pace with him. Eventually, I hold my ground, and his hand moves to the side of my face, his thumb stroking my cheek.

"I met you, Renleigh," he says. "That's what changed. And you believe me if you want to. What kind of guy would I be if I treated this thing between us like a negotiation?"

Well . . . damn.

I suck in my bottom lip as my eyes flit to his mouth, then back to his gaze. I lift on my toes and move my hand to his jaw, closing my eyes as my lips press to his. His body quivers in reaction, the tremor tiny but present, and his breath hitches from my touch. I'm not sure if it's surprise at being kissed or relief at being forgiven. And I'm not completely sure I have just yet.

But I do know I believe he's trying to be a good guy. It's not his fault that I don't believe it's possible for people in his line of work. At least, not all the time. But I can let this thing with us play out a little longer. Until the next time something hurts.

NINETEEN

HUNTER

My little white lie about identity theft turned into an entire organizational—*and mandatory*—training on best practices for keeping your personal information safe. I think Roddy's on to my lie, because he keeps using me as an example every time he asks or answers a question from our facilitator.

This is *not* how the guys wanted to spend their day off.

"Now, remember to keep your passwords protected—"

"You got that, Hunter?" Roddy hollers from the other side of the room. I don't make eye contact.

"Yup, already secured. Thank you, buddy," I respond.

He's pissed.

"Sure thing, *buddy*," he replies.

Very pissed.

The facilitator walks the aisles of the lecture-style meeting room Coach rented at the university for today's workshop, passing out packets with more information along with her company's services to help clear names in the event of identity theft. She pauses at my desktop and taps on the phone number at the top of the brochure.

"They can really do a number on your credit. Call if we can help, or if you find things are worse than you thought."

I force a pleasant smile and nod.

"I will. Thank you."

I fold the brochure in half and stuff it in the back pocket of my jeans as I get up from my table. A few of the guys sitting near me pound fists and offer their condolences for my financial loss. *Fucking hell.*

Roddy maneuvers his way from the other side of the room, his eyes focused on me like angry little laser beams. I try to look away, but his giant frame cuts off my exit, and soon his hand is on my chest.

"Hang back a second. I have some questions for you." He nods goodbye to the stragglers leaving the room, then tugs me by the sleeve of my Mavericks hoodie to the back corner of the room, away from the facilitator packing up her projector and business cards.

"What's up?" I drop my hands into my front pockets and force my eyes wide and interested, but Roddy calls bullshit right away with a quick smack to my chest.

"Knock that shit off. Nobody believes you left early for identity theft. What's really going on? Are you working a trade? You knock someone up from your past? Spill it, kid."

I shake my head wildly, trying to wrap my mind around some of his theories.

"What? No! I did not *knock someone up.*"

I mean . . . I don't think I did. Renleigh and I have been pretty active, but she said she has an IUD, and—

"Man, stop putting that stuff in the universe. No, nothing like that at all. I had someone hack my bank card," I lie. One more run up the flagpole with this plan.

Roddy's hand thumbs my chest again, and this time it hurts because he literally flicks my breastbone with his fucking enormous fingers.

"*Owwww,*" I whine, rubbing the spot.

"Are you two all right?" the facilitator asks, eyeing us.

We both hold up our hands.

"We're fine. Just debating the next game. Sorry," Roddy says, tugging my sleeve again and pulling me out of the room and onto the sidewalk outside. College kids are scurrying in all directions, and it feels odd to be in a place like this now that I'm a pro. It also feels strange to be lectured by a forty-year-old man who is six inches shorter than me.

"For the love of God, Hunter. Why did we all spend our day off taking your punishment? You know Coach put this together to call you on the lie. This isn't a thing they do. Ever."

My eyes freeze open, and my stomach tightens.

"It's not?"

Roddy's chest rumbles with frustrating laughter, and he takes a few steps back as he shakes his head.

"You're like this naïve little kid, I swear. No, Hunter. This was put together to make you feel uncomfortable. And yeah, the other young guys probably think it's normal and that it was the team looking out for them. But the rest of us? We know better. This is what they do when they want to make a point. And that point is, you don't bail on the team unless you have a damn good, unselfish reason. So, one last time, Hunter. What was yours?"

I hold his hot stare for a few quiet seconds, until my mouth waters the way it does before I throw up. I think I'm afraid he's going to punch me. I lift a shoulder and bunch my guilty lips, and give it to him straight.

"Renleigh."

"Well, no shit," he fires back. "But what about Renleigh? What did you do?"

I pinch the bridge of my nose and squeeze my eyes shut.

"Man, I don't even know how it all happened, but basically, there was this girl I hooked up with in college, and she showed up, and somehow got in my room, and Ren was there, and then—"

Roddy's heavy laughter cuts me off.

"It's not funny," I protest.

He holds up a palm and bends in half, laughing even harder. His cheeks are actually turning red.

"Come on, Roddy. It's not funny." I rock back on my heels and tilt my head, giving him the hard stare this time.

"Oh, it's funny. But also, it was bound to happen. Hunter, you're going to need to learn a thing or two about being *the guy*." He straightens his spine, then slings an arm over my shoulder, urging me to walk along with him back to the parking lot. "Come on. You're buying my beers."

"I can't," I utter, my shoulders low and ego deflated. "I told Renleigh I'd be over to watch the Texas game with her and her dad."

"Good. We'll sneak Dale a beer too. You could probably use the tutelage of a couple of wise, older men."

I give in and let Roddy lead me to our trucks, then hop in with him to go to the grocery store about a mile away from the Blackwood house. By the time we leave with a fruit platter to make Renleigh happy that we're following her dad's diet, along with the twelve-pack of Sam Adams meant to counteract the health effects, I feel as if mastering my pitching technique was nothing compared to the minefield that lies ahead.

Sloane was a friend, or at least a genuine person from my past. The next woman to show up in my room, especially when I get called up, might be a complete stranger. And while sixteen-year-old Hunter would have rubbed his hands together excitedly at the prospect, twenty-three-year-old me is bloody terrified.

"You really had a woman fake a pregnancy to get you to marry her?" I respond to Roddy's latest story as he pulls up in front of the Blackwood home.

"Sure did. And when I tell you that's just the tip of the iceberg when it comes to my crazy-ass journey . . ." He settles into a sad sort of laugh, flopping his hands over the top of his steering wheel as his focus drifts to something far away, beyond the Blackwood home, I think.

"Maybe one day you'll fill me in on the rest."

It takes him a few seconds to answer.

"Probably not, kid. Probably not. Let's go eat." He ends the view into his life there, effectively cutting my questions off with a swift exit from his truck and a slammed door.

I snag the beer and fruit, then follow along behind him to the screen door propped open with a faded wooden porch chair.

"Well, look what the cat dragged in!" Roddy puts on his thick Oklahoma accent as he stretches an arm out and hugs a woman who is almost the spitting image of Renleigh, only twenty years older. It's clear this is Renleigh's mother.

"Roddy, I heard you were back in Sweetwater. Good to see you." Her mother's gaze stops on me as she hugs him.

"I hope you're planning on hiding that beer from the man parked in front of the big screen," she says.

"Did I hear beer?" Dale chimes in.

I hike my shoulders up and smile through gritted teeth, feeling instantly guilty, which I think was Roddy's goal in making me both buy the beer and carry it in.

"Sorry, Dale. The mean old women in this house said *no*," Roddy says.

"We'll see about that," Renleigh's dad adds over his shoulder.

"No, we won't," Renleigh cuts in, putting a definitive end to the entire conversation as she takes the twelve pack from my right arm and carries it out to the garage.

"Oh, now, *that* stuff? That he can have," her mom says, taking the fruit tray from me. She rubs her free hand along her tight-fitting jeans, drying her palm, I presume, before holding it out to me. "I'm Sarah. It's nice to meet you . . . *Hunter?*"

"Yes, ma'am," I confirm, taking her hand. Her grip is

solid, and it makes sense that she puts some muscle behind it. Her daughter is the same.

"Make yourself comfortable," she says, motioning to the living room. Roddy takes the easy chair next to Dale's and quickly pops the recliner back to talk with his old coach.

"I'm just gonna see if Renleigh needs a hand," I say, gesturing toward the garage door. Nobody seems to care, so I slip out quickly and find Renleigh pulling the last two beers from the carton to tuck them behind some meat in the outdoor fridge.

"Hey, mind if I have one of those?"

I startle her, and she jumps as she turns, clutching the beers to her chest.

"Sorry," I wince.

"It's fine. I've been on edge a lot today. Not used to having so many bodies in this house. Lindsey's upstairs putting the twins to sleep. Her husband is coming later to barbecue, so I hope you're hungry. And then, of course, my mom was here when I woke up. And when I got off work. And is still here . . . for now."

I take both beers from her hand, pull the cap off one, and hand it back to her. "I'm pretty sure you need a beer, too."

A faint smile plays at her lips as she pulls the beer to her mouth.

"Thanks." Her raspy voice scratches an itch deep inside my chest.

"Let's get some space, yeah?"

She tilts her head back, toward the open garage, and I nod. We move out of the garage to a stone path on the side of her house, and I trail behind her to a round patio with grass poking up between several of the bricks. She takes a seat in one of the wooden Adirondack chairs, and I do the same. A well-used metal fire pit holds burnt log ends in the center. It's a little warm out today, but I could get used to sitting by this thing at night.

"This is a nice spot," I comment, taking a swig of my beer.

Renleigh lets out a heavy sigh and rests her beer on the armrest while sinking back in the chair and closing her eyes.

"My dad built it when I was in high school. I used to come out here to read. The trees block it from most of the yard, and there isn't a single window in the house that views this place.

"So, what you're saying is, this is where you did all your devious behavior?" I wink at her as she pops an eye open at me.

"Some of it," she says, her lips tight with a guilty smile.

I chuckle, my lips resting on the rim of my beer bottle.

"I meant smoking pot and drinking underage, Renleigh. You're the one making it dirty."

My eyes remain on her as I tilt the beer back and swallow.

"I never said I was dirty back here."

Fuck if my cheeks aren't hot.

"You sort of insinuated it," I say, setting my beer on the ground beside the chair, then folding my hands across my chest.

"Did I?" Renleigh's gaze narrows on me as her tongue pushes into her cheek, and I suddenly feel the need to sit up taller and adjust the fit in the crotch of my jeans.

Renleigh takes one more sip of her beer, then rests it on the arm of her chair before standing and stretching her arms over her head. She pivots slowly, scanning the pathway we took to get here before bending down to eyeball the yard beyond the heavy cover of trees.

"What are you doing?" I grab my cock under my jeans this time, adjusting it as it gets hard.

Renleigh steps in front of me and bends over, dropping her palms to my thighs and squeezing. She lifts her chin to meet my gaze, which is temporarily hypnotized by the white lace trim of her bra spotted through the deep V neck of her

T-shirt. Her palms travel up my legs slowly, until one covers my hard cock over my jeans, and I groan.

"Devious behavior. Isn't that what you called it?" She presses against me, and I grind my hips up toward her palm as my eyes flutter shut.

"See, I knew you were dirty back here." I sit up on the edge of the chair, my hands grabbing the back of her thighs as I press my mouth between her legs.

"You wet for me, Renleigh?" My teeth snag the black fabric of her leggings, pull it away from her pussy, then let it snap back.

"Maybe," she hums, her hands moving into my hair. Roddy is going to give me shit when I walk back inside after this, but I don't really care.

"Let's see," I say, my fingers curling into her waistband before slowly dragging her leggings and panties down her hips. As soon as the thin trail of hair comes into view, I lean forward and slide my tongue between her legs and taste her.

"Shit," she mutters, her hands pulling my hair as she holds my face to her swollen pussy.

"You are wet, you dirty little girl you," I tease, pulling her pants and underwear down enough that she can spread her legs for me and give me more access.

My tongue sinks into her, probing her sensitive skin before I suck her clit into my mouth.

"Oh shit, Hunter. Shit, shit, shit."

Her muffled cries make me harder, as does the sharp feel of her nails against my scalp. I want to give her bliss out here, to give her a new memory beyond the books and escape from her family. I want to make this place carry thoughts of me. My hand trails to the inside of her thigh, inching higher as my tongue continues to pleasure her. When my thumb reaches her swollen clit, I rub in slow circles until her legs quiver from overstimulation.

"You want to come in my mouth, Renleigh?" I look up at

her, and her hooded eyes open just enough for her to whimper, "Yes."

"Come for me," I say, flicking her pussy with my tongue as my hands move to grip her ass. I hold her hostage against my face, my fingers digging into her from behind, and she grows wetter against my mouth until she writhes and depends on my body to hold hers up.

"That's it, Renleigh. Let go," I say, sliding my hands deeper into her ass until my fingertips feel her wet center from behind. I sink one inside her pussy, and another teases her asshole as she hums through every wave of her orgasm.

When her arms go limp, she falls back on her heels and steps a few inches away. I run my sleeve over my face, which I'm sure glistens with her arousal. She's fucking delicious.

"Was that good for stress relief?" I ask.

She nods slowly, still drunk from pleasure. Her hand comes up to my face, sliding along my jawline and back into my hair as she urges my head back so our eyes meet.

"I'm not done," she says before dropping her gaze to my hard cock, which is threatening to poke out of the top of my jeans.

"You want me to—" I tilt my head to the right, still holding her eyes as my hands move to my zipper.

"Pull it out," she commands.

A nervous laugh hits my lips, and I glance back down the path, the coast still seemingly clear. Though anyone could venture out here while we're not looking and get a pretty full show.

"You sure?" I check.

She nods and whirls a finger in a circle toward my dick.

"Pull. It. Out." Her sharp tone is sexy as hell, so I yank my zipper down and lift my hips enough to tug my jeans and boxers down my hips. My cock springs free. I wrap my hand around my length and stroke myself while reaching for her lowered pants and tugging her close enough that I can slide my hand between her legs, rubbing her soaking wet pussy while she licks her lips and stares at my cock as if it's her favorite dessert.

Without me asking, she turns so her ass is facing me, then slowly backs into me and sits on my lap as I guide my dick into her. She sinks down slowly at first, a rather loud *ahh* escaping her mouth.

"Fuck, you feel good like this," I say, lifting my hips into her and sinking in deeper.

"*Ooooh*," she moans, palms flattened on either armrest and lifting herself.

Her rhythm picks up, and she's soon slapping her ass against my abdomen and thighs while I continue to thrust up to meet her every move.

"I'm going to come so fucking hard inside of you, Renleigh. So fucking hard," I grunt, my cock swelling as she continues to slide down my wet shaft.

As her cries pick up, I lose my edge, and need overwhelms me as I fill her with my hot cum. She sinks down on me one final time, grinding against me as she whimpers, then falls back against my chest.

"Fuck, I needed that," she says as I wrap my arms around her. She covers my hands with hers and guides my palms to her breasts, urging me to squeeze her tits for her own release as she lets out a languid moan.

"We didn't even get to these," I say.

She giggles softly and utters, "Next time," then slowly lifts herself from my cock.

My cum paints the inside of her thigh, so I pull my sleeve over my palm and clean her before helping her balance and pulling her panties and leggings back into place.

"You want me to run that through the wash?" she says, tugging on the strings of my sweatshirt.

"Probably should," I say, pulling my sweatshirt over my head and letting her take it with her back to the garage. I linger behind for a few seconds, reveling in a new level of best sex ever before tucking my cock in my boxers and pulling my zipper back up.

I run my hands through my hair before I pick up my beer and finish it off as I make my way back to the garage. Renleigh is already inside, it seems, so I scan the garage for a recycle bin, toss my bottle inside, then take one more deep breath before reentering the lion's den.

This time, when Roddy spots me from across the room, he shakes his head and laughs before silently clapping in my honor. He's right to do so. Because that moment outside? It deserves plenty of applause.

TWENTY
RENLEIGH

I see the way Daisy, my boss, looks at me. Like I'm opening an enormous can of future heartbreak and trouble. I get where she's coming from. She fell in love with a ballplayer, then spent the next twenty-plus years trying to get over him, only to have him come back.

I'd like to say my story is nothing like hers, but I bet she thought the same thing when she was my age, and someone warned her about getting involved with a pro athlete. I do believe this thing I'm in with Hunter is different, though. I know the rules. I'm the one setting them. This is a good time. And I know it will end.

"Someone left something for you this morning," she says, pulling an envelope from under the register and sliding it across the bar toward me. I slap my hand on top and say, "Thanks," before tucking it in my apron.

It's a pair of tickets for me and Lindsey. If I'm being replaced at home by my mom, then I may as well enjoy the free time with my sister while I have the chance. Lindsey's taking her up on her babysitting offer, too. There's a chance an afternoon helping Dad with home rehab while running after those boys might be enough to send her packing again, so we may as well get the free time in while we can.

"I heard them talking about him this morning. You know, on the news?" Daisy says.

She leans over the bar and rests her head in her palm while she taps her long red nails of her other hand on the tabletop. *She's judging me.*

"Yeah? *Sports Center* on because Roddy was there?" I purse my lips and glower at her, because two can play at this game. Her gaze narrows on me, but she doesn't answer. I know he's been spending the night at her house. And there's a lot of messy history for them to unpack. None of my business. Just like Hunter is none of hers.

I pick up a bar towel and move toward the table just abandoned by a group of fans. I bus the glasses, then wipe the surface down, only to turn around and find Daisy's glare still waiting for me.

"I guess this is a big start for him today. They're talking about calling him up early. Guess one of the starters went on the injured list, so this would be his shot. Just . . . something to consider."

By *consider* she means weigh against getting involved with him further.

"Yeah, I hear you," I say. And I do. I don't need the warning, though. I'm going into this with wide-open eyes and a guarded heart.

"*Mmm hmm,*" she says, leaving me with one final rap of her fingernails on the counter before going back to tending bar.

It's a steady stream of fans and college kids for the next hour. There's a band coming in to play tonight, so the place is getting packed by the time my sister shows up and I clock out. I'm glad I got the night off, though my coworker, Brandon, is going to kill it in tips tonight. Whenever Earl's has live music, the take goes way up.

I change in the back room, slipping on the new Maverick's

jersey Hunter gave me yesterday. I feel a little self-conscious wearing his last name on my back, mostly because I know the look I'm going to get from Daisy when I walk by, but I keep it on. It was a thoughtful gift, and truthfully? It feels nice to have a man's attention. I'd forgotten what it was like.

"Look at you," Lindsey teases as she greets me by the exit. I glance over my shoulder and am relieved Daisy's busy with customers.

"Yeah, Hunter got it for me. Do I look like a bimbo?"

My sister snorts.

"That's such a *Mom* word."

I roll my eyes, but she's right. My mom used to call the girls who hung around Earl's trying to get ballplayers to hook up with them bimbos all the time. We used to laugh when she did. And now here I am. *Bimbo.*

My sister leans into me as we walk along the small businesses that are slowly flicking their neon signs on as the sun goes down.

"You're not a bimbo," she whispers. I suck my bottom lip in as I smile in return.

"Thanks."

Night games in Sweetwater are special. We didn't always have lights in the stadium. It was a big deal when the first night game was played about ten years ago. It revived the downtown strip in many ways, spurred on a late-night vibe that kept Earl's alive in many ways. Without the college in session, things at Earl's would get pretty slow. Now, though, the Mavericks games fill the bar all summer long.

We get to skip the line outside, thanks to the special tickets Hunter gave me. We're closer to the dugout tonight. I think he didn't want my father to have to take many steps when I came last time. It was thoughtful, and of everything that's attractive about him, I think it's the little things Hunter does that catch me off-guard and hook me deeper than I want to be. Still, he is thoughtful. And it is striking.

"Girl, I could get used to this," my sister says as she settles into the seat beside me. We both prop our feet on the dugout.

"They're really nice seats."

Lindsey snickers under her breath, then echoes my words in a mocking tone.

"Okay, okay. Don't act like we've never been here," I say, brushing her thigh with the back of my hand. She laughs louder at that remark, and I give in and join her.

The front rows at Mavericks games are strictly VIP. The seats are extra wide, with leather cushions that get covered after every game and polished before the starts. We also get our own servers who will take concession orders and deliver the food directly to our seats, just like they do in the majors. And as if the leg room and food weren't enough, there's also a special tunnel to a private bathroom and access to chat with the players anytime we want. And one of those players is crooking a finger at me right now.

"You're being summoned," Lindsey teases.

"Shush. That's worse than bimbo," I chastise her.

I skip down the aisle to Hunter, and he leans over the short wall to press a chaste kiss on my mouth that earns a few whistles from the fans nearby. My cheeks burn, but I smile right through it. Turns out I kind of like this attention.

"You ready tonight?" I tug down the brim of his hat, and he chuckles before adjusting it.

"Yeah, I'm ready." Of course he is.

"Daisy said it's a big game tonight. She heard something on the sports show, I guess?" I squint from the glare of the lights as I look up at him. He shifts so he's blocking the bright beam from my eyes. *Thoughtful.*

"It's just like every other game."

He sniffs as he shrugs, but underneath the bravado, I catch a glimpse of his nerves. It's in the way his upper lip twitches, fighting against a nervous smile, and the rapid blinking as he glances around.

"Hey," I say, centering his gaze back on me. I grab hold of the collar on his jersey, the top two buttons open, exposing the thin silver chain he always wears. It was a gift from his mom in high school, and he said he never pitches without it. I tap my finger on the chain link and he tucks his chin, glancing down.

"You're gonna be great," I assure him.

He gives me a crooked smile and utters, "I know."

I shake my head and laugh, the cocky young hotshot still beating strong inside him.

"Hi, Hunter!" My sister waves behind me, and Hunter leans over the wall further to wave back.

"Thanks for coming, Lindsey. I'm gonna need you to keep your sister in check tonight. Things are gonna get a bit intense."

My sister gives him a thumbs up. He leans back and shifts his gaze back to me before darting it over my shoulder again. He's a lot more nervous than I thought he would be.

"Why is it going to be intense?" I chuckle.

"Oh, no real reason. Just . . . well . . ." His eyes lock on something behind me, and I follow the path of his gaze until I see a man and a woman waving at us as they take the steps toward us two at a time. They're both incredibly tall. And they look strikingly similar to Hunter.

Oh, fuck.

I swing my gaze back to him and lean in close.

"Did you invite your parents to this game? Is this a parent meeting ambush? Hunter Reddick, I swear to—"

"There he is," the woman says, stepping into the space next to me. I shift to the side as Hunter envelopes the woman —clearly his mom—in his arms and kisses the top of her head.

"You look good in blue," his dad says, taking Hunter's hand for a shake before the two of them pull each other in for one of those back-slapping man-hugs.

"If they wanted me to wear hot pink and neon green to pitch in the big leagues, I would," Hunter says.

His dad laughs, and the sound it makes is eerily similar to his son. My shoulders hike up. I think I may be a bit freaked out.

"Mom. Dad. This is Renleigh. Ren, these are my parents, Allison and Chandler."

I blink my gaze from Hunter to his parents and laugh through my freaked-out grin.

"Hi! It's so nice to meet you both," I lie. I mean, it's lovely to meet them. And I wouldn't have minded. But a warning would have been nice. Plus, meeting parents is an extra level of intimacy. I mean, sure, he met mine, but still.

"Renleigh, it is so nice to meet you. Hunter tells me you grew up here in Sweetwater?" This sweet woman is softspoken and warm, and her son's blue eyes are clearly the carbon copy of hers. All I can do is stare at her with wide eyes and my dumbfounded expression.

"I did. Yes." My gaze flits to Hunter, but all he does is offer a tight-lipped grin.

He told his parents about me. Facts about me.

"Hey, I gotta warm up, but Renleigh can show you your seats." Hunter's gaze shifts to me. "They're next to you and Lindsey."

Hunter backs up a few steps, and once he's out of view from his parents, he mouths, "I'm sorry."

I'm gleaning that their attendance was a bit of a surprise for him, too. I guide his parents to our seats, then introduce them to my sister, whose expression is a lot like what I imagine mine was. The four of us settle in, his mom next to me, and his father next to her. I'd love to trade places with Lindsey right now. She's better at small talk. Also, she's not the bimbo fucking this woman's son.

"You know, he told us he was going to be a starting pitcher when he was five years old. He refused to play by the rules in tee ball," his mom says, the proud smile of a mother denting her cheeks.

"He insisted on pitching to the other kids. They kicked him out of the league," his father adds with a chuckle.

My gaze drifts to the field where Hunter is starting his long toss with Roddy, and I smile.

"I could see that," I say.

The four of us watch him stretch his throw across the outfield, and his dad says his wife was better at catch than he was. She makes a remark about being around more, and I sense a heaviness in the air when she does, but it dissipates quickly when his dad leans over, kisses her cheek, and whispers, "I love you." It's sad and sweet at the same time.

"Hunter says he met you because of a bet," his mom finally says.

"Oh, well, sort of. He lost that bet, but it did break the ice," I say.

"She took him for a hundred bucks," my sister adds.

"Linds!" I nudge her, not-so-gently, with my leg.

"What? You did," she says.

Hunter's parents laugh, and his dad holds out a fist for me to pound. I do, and he winks, adding, "You should have held out for two hundred."

By the time the game starts, his parents have filled in most of the gaps from his childhood, all the pleasant things parents like to brag about their child, and I mesh the fondness he seems to have for them with the stories they tell. It's a beautiful adolescence, and they seem like a beautiful family, despite the challenges Hunter confided in me. They are nothing like the messy relationship my parents have, and as warming as it is, it also sits heavy in the pit of my chest.

I'm jealous.

"You've seen him throw this spring. What do you think? Does he really have it?" Chandler's hands are clasped across his belly, and he's wringing his hands. I think maybe he's nervous, even after all these years.

I nod and shift my attention to the tall, stoic man on the mound. Hunter pulls his hat off to run his arm over his forehead, then pushes it in place, the curled ends of his hair poking out the back and sides. He feels the ball in his glove and nods to Roddy before zipping his last warm-up pitch into the glove.

"Yeah. He's got it," I say.

He's got me, too. And that's definitely not part of the plan.

TWENTY-ONE
HUNTER

I talk a big game, and I know it. I've been my own biggest hype man for years. It started when I was in junior high, and I watched this video by a guy named Derrick Lujan. He was an all-star shortstop for Seattle, and he went on this crazy hit streak where he got a hit for fifty games in a row. Not quite Joe DiMaggio's stat of fifty-six but still flirting with greatness. His videos focus on mindset, and he said the biggest muscle a player can work is his ego.

I took that advice to heart that night, and the very next day, before I took the mound, I told myself I was the best in the county. I threw my first complete game. A year later, I had two no-hitters. Then in high school, I set a record for strike-outs and even threw a perfect game.

All because Derrick Lujan taught me to exercise my ego.

Well . . . that ego just landed me in Coach Shuster's office after throwing a one-hitter against the toughest team in our division—with an open slot in the starting rotation in Texas. And my parents both here because someone told them to fly in.

I pretty much put it together about an hour before I took

the mound, but I didn't dare utter it out loud. I feel it in my bones, though. I'm getting called up.

"Hunter, great game tonight, son," Coach says as he slips into his office, along with Coach Burdick. They close the door, and Coach Shuster motions for me to take a seat on the bright orange couch. Everything in this stadium is either blue or orange, I swear.

"Yes, sir," I say, doing as he says. I ball my hands together and rest my elbows on my knees, my gaze bouncing between my two coaches. My palms are so sweaty, and my mouth is watering again. If I vomit through this news, I'll never live it down.

"You know why I called you in here, Hunter?" Coach Shuster says.

I start to nod on instinct, and my eyes prick with tears.

"I think so, yeah." My voice is suddenly hoarse. Fuck, this is hitting me harder than I imagined. I worked so hard for this. I can't believe it's really happening.

"You're going to need to pack your bags this weekend. Come Monday, you're on a flight to Dallas, and you're starting in Arlington."

His words come at me through a narrow tunnel, everything in the room muffled by the sudden thumping of my heart. I nod more aggressively now, and tears fall down my cheeks as an elated sob shakes my chest and I stand.

"Shit, this is embarrassing," I laugh out.

"Meh, we all do it. It's a big moment. Marriage. Baby. Getting called up. And not necessarily in that order," Coach Burdick says.

I hug him first, running my fist over my nose while he can't see me.

"Go make me proud, Hunter," he says.

"Yes, sir. I will. I promise."

I turn to face Coach Shuster next, first gripping his hand, then embracing him.

"Thank you, Coach. Thank you for everything," I blubber. He chuckles at my breakdown and slaps my back a few times with a heavy hand.

"I didn't have to do much. You came ready to go. You were ready for this in college, Hunter. You're going to do great. Just try not to come back here to rehab an injury, huh?"

I breathe out a laugh as we part.

"No, sir. I mean, yes, sir. I mean . . . fuck. I'll try not to get hurt."

Both coaches chuckle at my sudden inability to speak in coherent sentences, and then Coach Burdick cracks open the office door, and my parents step inside to share the news.

"You two knew, didn't you?" I hug my mom tightly, the tears flowing good now. My dad's hand rests on my shoulder, and the shuddering in his palm clues me in that he's probably crying like a baby, too. My mom's the only one with dry eyes, which is hilarious, because if this were a situation to place bets on, her crying would have been a sure thing.

"I'm so proud of you, Hunter. So incredibly proud," my mom says, holding me at the elbows and stepping back so she can study me the way she did before sending me off for picture day at school.

"Thanks, Mom. Dad. Just, oh my God, I'm making the show! Woo!"

I pump a fist, and my coaches start clapping. Roddy peeks his head in, and the moment our eyes meet, his mouth stretches into a wide grin. He rushes at me, wrapping me in a bear hug that knocks the wind out of me.

"Fuck, yeah! I knew it! I fucking knew it!" His hands slap my back after he drops my feet back to the floor, and he moves on to shake my parents' hands next.

"You two have a great son. He's one hell of a talent. I loved catching for him."

My dad's eyes widen as he shakes Roddy's hand, probably because my dad has one of his jerseys at home.

"Thank you for dealing with him," my mom says, hugging the sweaty, dirt-soaked catcher.

Roddy chuckles as he points to my mom over her shoulder and meets my gaze.

"I like her," he says.

"Yeah, I figured you would. You can commiserate over dealing with my know-it-all attitude, I'm sure."

"Meh, you were easy to break. I just had to let an All-Star hit a homer off you, and you got right in line," Roddy says, recalling our first outing at the start of the season.

My body is tingling with excited energy, and I practically skip my way out of the locker room to where Renleigh and her sister are waiting in the administration lobby. The smile plastered on Renleigh's face seems caught between something real and a forced expression. My parents probably clued her in on what was coming. I wish I could have given her a better warning. I didn't want to jinx it, though. Plus, sometimes my head tells me a story that isn't really rooted in facts. I felt as though the winds were shifting. My agent told me to be ready the moment Riggs went down for a shoulder injury in Texas. But still . . . there were a lot of options besides pulling me up early. It's rare for a rookie to get the call before the All-Star break. *Very* rare.

"Holy shit, Hunter!" Lindsey says as I pull Renleigh into a hug, smashing her face against my chest.

"Yeah, I'm having a hard time wrapping my mind around it all," I say.

"Bullshit. This is the dream. Boy's gonna be a legend!" Roddy shouts as he passes by, his gear bag slung over his shoulder as he heads out to his beat-up truck. I know the man's a multi-millionaire. And as prickly as he is, I hope I can be a lot like him with this ride.

"Congratulations," Renleigh says, her voice muffled against my shirt.

I drop my hands to cradle her face and meet her wide

eyes. She's freaked out, and the rush of her reaction crashes into the excitement bubbling in my chest so hard my heart stops for a second.

"I don't leave until the weekend. We can talk about this, how it works. It's going to work out. I promise," I say, dropping a soft kiss on her lips.

She nods, her mouth moving against mine as she utters, "Yeah."

I don't believe her, but there really is time for us to talk. We just need to get out of here.

The rest of the team spills out of the locker room, and I take turns shaking hands and hugging a lot of the guys, but I make sure my free hand is always tethered to Renleigh's. She doesn't pull away, which means she's open to fighting for this little thing we just started. And I do intend to fight.

"Let's celebrate, brother! Come on, Roddy said he's buying," Jayden says as he slings an arm around my neck. I duck just as he nearly pulls me away from Renleigh, and his gaze shifts to her. "You're coming too, right? I mean, you deserve to enjoy Earl's from our side every now and then. You in?"

"Hell, yeah, we're in," Lindsey says, despite the frantic darting of Renleigh's eyes.

"I don't know. I should get home," she says, pulling my hand closer to her.

I step in and drop my head lower to give us a small private space amid the rowdiness around us. She shakes her head, her smile more of a straight line as her eyes flit from focusing on mine to the rest of the world around us.

"My dad had in-home rehab today, and I'm sure he's tired. I don't know, I just—"

"Mom is there," Lindsey says, stepping into our space. Renleigh winces, and I want to push her sister away, but also, I'm on Lindsey's side. The relationship between their family is complicated, but Renleigh owes it to herself to have her own life. And maybe this timing is the universe's way of giving us a shot.

"Just one drink. I won't drink at all, and then I can take you home. I'm too excited to drink anyway. I want to keep feeling this natural buzz. What do you say?" I sway in my stance, drawing her eyes to mine, and finally she nods and lets her mouth break into a faint smile.

"Yeah. You're right." She glances to her sister. "I'll come. For a little while. I want to."

"Good! Now, let's go order some expensive shit and make Roddy pay for it," Lindsey says, looping her arm through her sister's and leading her out of the building.

"I'll be right there," I say, noticing Brooks finally trailing out of the locker room. He's been so quiet lately, and while he was never the crazy, wild guy in high school, he wasn't a hermit, either. I feel bad that I haven't spent a lot of time with him since we both landed here in Sweetwater.

"Hey, you hear the news?" I say, pulling his gaze up from the ground. He has a massive duffel bag slung over his back, which is weird for a guy who isn't a catcher.

"I did. Wow, that's . . . I knew you'd be the first to get called up. Good for you." He lifts his chin, and the corners of his mouth turn up slightly, and I swear he might be jealous. He's going to get his shot. He'll be in Texas with me next season for sure. Maybe even for a few games this year if he keeps raking at the plate.

"We're going out to celebrate. I'd love to catch up with you before I go. Let me buy you a beer," I say, nudging his bicep with my arm.

He winces and glances off to the side, into the dark parking lot that's generally littered with beer cans from tail-gaters who broke the rules and came out here to pre-game. He waggles his head side to side, seeming unsure.

"I don't know. I got a lot going on." His gaze snaps back to me, and there's a flash of something behind his eyes. More jealousy, perhaps.

"Yeah. Okay. Raincheck, then," I say, holding out my fist.

He drops his gaze to my hand and bites the inside of his cheek as he nods, huffing out a short, breathy laugh.

"Sure. Raincheck." He drops his fist on mine, and his eyes never quite make it back to my face as he utters, "Congratulations, though. For real. I mean it."

He heads out to the parking lot, toward the black SUV he bragged about buying for himself when we first got here.

I think about shouting after him, assuring him his time is coming soon, but something about his posture urges me to let him go. He's got some shit he's working through, I think, and doesn't need my chaos busting through it.

Lindsey and Renleigh are waiting at my truck when I get to it, and I open the passenger side for them to slide into the front seat. I love that Renleigh sits in the middle, close to me, but I don't like how still and quiet she is. I appreciate Roddy and the team wanting to celebrate me, but right now, all I want to do is drop Lindsey off at home and take Renleigh somewhere far away, where we can be alone, and I can get her to believe me that she and I are more than a fling. That my opportunity doesn't have to mean the end for us. I know that's where her head is. I can *feel* it.

It's clear I'm not going to get the opportunity to talk it out with Renleigh anytime soon. The moment we pull into the lot at Earl's, the three of us are swept into the roaring bar crowd for a toast. The band playing on the corner stage fills the space with a freight train of sound, chugging out classic Johnny Cash songs with a healthy dose of rock behind them. It's a great vibe, and normally, I'd be all over this kind of music. But right now, I wish they would go on break.

"To Hunter!" Adler says, holding up his mug as he shoves one in my hand. I shake it off, but he keeps forcing it at me. I take a small sip with him to keep him happy before discarding my pint on the nearby table.

"Aww, don't be a pussy, Hunt. I know you can drink! I saw you the night we all got here. You were keeping up with me."

Adler slings an arm around me and shares stories about our first night in town, when it was just me, him, and Brooks at the local inn before we got our rentals squared away. We partied hard, sure, but it's not the kind of thing I do every day, and I know Brooks doesn't. Adler, however? Adler might have a problem.

"Maybe I should just . . ." Renleigh says as she hugs my free arm and nods toward the exit.

My brow furrows and I shift away from Adler, hunching to bring my eyeline to hers.

"We won't stay long. I promise. Please stay," I say, lifting her chin with the tip of my finger. My eyes drop to her mouth, and her lips twitch into a timid smile.

"Yeah, okay. For a little bit. But then . . ."

I kiss her softly and cup her face.

"Then we go home, and we talk. All night if we have to."

She nods, and I can still sense the reservations wreaking havoc in her mind, but she's still open to listening.

My parents finally make it to Earl's in time for the team's second toast, and I'm careful to keep myself far away from Adler so I can be ready to take Renleigh and her sister home the second a good opportunity arises. My parents, however, are more than happy to toast their son. They're staying at the inn down the street, so no driving necessary for them. And if anyone in this room deserves to drink up Roddy's kind gesture, it's them. My mom, especially.

"Hey, one round. What do you say?" Jayden hands me a pool cue, then nods toward the back of the bar, where the billiards and darts are. Adler is holding a stick alongside a few of the other guys, along with a crisp hundred bucks. I don't need his money, but I want it. Mostly because I'd like to knock him down a peg. He can be . . . *a lot.*

"Sure. But just one," I say, taking the stick from Jayden and turning to encourage Renleigh to join me.

"We can go after this. Yeah?" I offer.

She nods and glances behind her, searching for her sister.

"I'll be right there. Lindsey got a call and stepped outside."

I follow her gaze and spot Lindsey holding one hand over her ear and pressing the phone to the other as she pushes through the exit.

I nod.

"Okay. But you're my good luck charm, so don't take long," I tease.

She gives me a lopsided smirk.

"I don't want to be your lucky pair of socks," she replies, I think referencing my superstitious habits—*aka Sloane.*

"You are not a pair of socks, Renleigh Blackwood. You are my non-negotiable." I back away slowly, leaving her with a sure grin that, for the first time tonight, seems to etch one on her own face.

"You rack," Adler says, thrusting the triangle at me when I step up to the pool table.

I hold his gaze, and I can tell he's already beyond buzzed. I have a feeling he played that way, and I'm starting to think he does that quite often.

"Yeah, okay," I say, keeping my eyes on him as I round the table. I plunk the rack down and sort the balls inside, setting up the game.

Adler chalks the end of his cue, dropping his attention to the table, biting the tip of his tongue as he bends down and lines up his shot to break. He sends the balls spinning around the table with a clatter, and I scan every pocket, pleased when he doesn't sink a single ball.

I round the table, eyeing the best strategy to get this table cleared and be on my way. As I bend over one of the corner pockets, though, a slender hand lands on my shoulder.

"Hunter," Lindsey says.

I spin to face her, relieved it's not a stranger, but a little disappointed it isn't Renleigh stepping up behind me. My eyes dart over her head at that thought, in time to see Renleigh rushing out the exit, and my gaze drops back to Lindsey's worried-looking face.

"Mom called. Dad fell. He probably broke his leg. We gotta . . ." She's breathless with panic as she points over her shoulder with her thumb.

"Yeah. Absolutely. I'll be right there," I say, dropping the pool stick on the table behind me, flicking a few of the balls when I do.

"Hey, what the hell?" Adler slurs. I hold up a palm, cutting him off and giving my attention to Lindsey as she pushes up on her toes and cups her mouth to talk to me over the band.

"Ren's got the Jeep parked here from earlier, so we're going to take off. But come to the house after you're done here. I'll tell Ren to text you updates." She backs away as I nod.

"I'll be right behind you," I say. I have zero intention of leaving them to handle this alone. I might not be able to do much, but if there's something I can do to lift their dad or run errands so they can stay where they're needed, then that's what I'm going to do.

"Okay," Lindsey says with a nod before turning and sprinting out the door in her sister's wake.

I pull three twenties from my wallet and toss them on the table, keeping most of my promise for the bet.

"Sorry, dude. We'll have to have a rematch sometime. I gotta go," I say.

Adler grabs the cash off the table, bunching it in his fist as he laughs.

"Dude, what the fuck? Are you seriously running off on

the biggest night of your life because of some chick? Didn't I let another woman into your room in Nashville for you? I mean hell, dude. This one's just our fucking bartender."

Less than a second passes before I lunge at Adler and send a fist into his face. He spins and braces his fall on the table, his nose bleeding into his hand as he stumbles back a few steps and calls me a *motherfucker*.

"Hey, no. We aren't doing this," Roddy says seconds later, his hand on my chest. He points a finger at Adler as he pushes me back toward the bar.

"You need to sober up. Then, you need to apologize. Clean yourself up, you worthless piece of shit." Roddy's vitriol feels personal, but my heart is racing so fast with my own fury right now that I don't have time to dig into it.

"Come on. You need ice," Roddy says, dragging me to the bar where Daisy is already waiting with a bag full.

"I was never this bad," Roddy says to her. She chuckles, and there's a fondness to her expression as she gives him a crooked smile.

"You were so much worse," she says, reaching for my left hand. At least I was smart enough to swing with my glove hand.

I flinch as Daisy presses the ice to my knuckles. She pulls it back, then dabs my skin with the cold compress a few times until my skin adjusts to it. My knuckles are bruised for sure, but I don't think anything's broken. I wouldn't tell a soul if it were.

"Now, why are you starting fights in my bar, hon?" She bats long lashes at me as her smirk settles in. I'm sure she's seen lots of swings thrown at Earl's, and I sense Roddy's thrown his fair share of them.

"Adler opened his big mouth and said some shit about Renleigh," Roddy says for me.

I purse my lips and nod.

"Pretty much," I confirm.

"Ah. Well, then . . ." She pulls the ice back again and blows on my tender knuckles before flitting her gaze over my shoulder. "That was a good reason. I think the real doctor is here now, so I'm gonna let her take over."

I twist to make room for my mom to step in beside me. She holds the ice bag to the back of my hand as she shakes her head with silent laughter.

"Haven't done this since you were nine, when you pegged that kid with a fastball on purpose, and he stormed the mound. Pretty sure you knew enough to punch with your left hand then, too." My mom's gaze lifts to mine as she gives me a wry grin.

I shrug.

"I might be a rock head sometimes, but I'm not stupid."

"To be determined," my dad adds as he steps in behind me.

I endure the ice—and the well-deserved ridicule—for a few more minutes, but my pulse won't slow until I know everything is all right for Renleigh and her dad. I hand the ice pack back to Daisy when she stops in to check on me, then kiss my parents and let them know Renleigh had a small family emergency.

I catch their shared look, which I'm sure is some silent parent language about their son falling for a girl, and they'd be right. Thankfully, though, they let me go without grilling me for details on the emergency or the girl, which is good, because right now, I'm not sure I have answers on either. And the unknowns scare me more than I thought they would.

TWENTY-TWO
RENLEIGH

I need everyone to get out of my way. I just need this house empty for one minute so I can think.

My fingers sink into my temples, rubbing tight circles to fend off the migraine itching to take me out. Hunter is lifting my father's favorite chair the way a child hugs an enormous stuffed animal and carries it around. All I can think is, he's going to hurt himself and not be able to play for Texas this weekend. Plus, he still hasn't explained the bandage wrapped around his left hand. Lindsey says it's on the knuckles and he probably punched someone, but I don't think he'd be stupid enough to do that after getting called up.

"I don't think it will be a problem to fit the ottoman in here, Renleigh." Hunter wipes his brow and moves to the next piece of furniture so my father can relax, though his leg is going to be in a cast for six to eight months.

"I just don't know," I say, staring at the space to imagine how it's all going to work.

It's not the chair. Or the bed. Or that we're regressing back to the wheelchair because he can't drag a cast on a walker, and he was making so much progress. It's none of that, but it's all of that. And it's the fact if I were here, maybe it wouldn't have happened.

"Hey, let's take a break," Hunter says after setting the ottoman in place. He's right. There's plenty of room.

"I don't have time for breaks," I bite out.

I spin in the room, my eyes darting to my sister, who is leaning against the staircase banister while snapping off a piece of carrot between her teeth. It's the most annoying sound ever. I'm pretty sure she knows it, too.

"Are you going to help?" I hold out my open palms, and she shakes with a silent, single laugh.

"Absolutely not. You're a tornado." She snaps off another bite and smiles as she chews with tight lips.

I glower at her, and Hunter palms my shoulders and redirects me to the sofa, forcing me to sit. He's probably right. I'm on edge. But also, he's leaving, so what does any of this matter?

"Do you want me to get your dad in here, and we can see how this works out? I can help him. You just sit, maybe manage the situation from here, huh?" He covers my balled hands with his massive palm, stopping me from fidgeting. My gaze flies to his.

"My mom didn't know what to do. She still doesn't. She's just sitting in there at the kitchen table, making *important* phone calls while he sits in his wheelchair and waits for her to get done with her oh-so-vital work," I scoff.

Hunter chuckles, which sets me off even more.

"Stop it. You know I'm right," I snap, getting to my feet. He grabs my hand before I make it a full step away, and despite my best effort to finagle my grip away from his, I'm forced to pause and meet his gaze.

"This was not your fault," he says.

I blink without breathing as I stare into his eyes. I don't believe him, but also, I don't think it was *only* my fault.

"I wasn't here, Hunter. And she had no idea what to do.

He just lay there, by the tub, waiting for the medics to come and help. Because she sent the home health nurse home. She wanted to help him bathe on his own, and then—"

"She wanted to try. And your dad is a grown-ass man, Renleigh. I don't think he tried hopping into that tub just because she told him to. Falls happen."

Hunter takes a deep breath, and I match it with my own on reflex. It helps calm my nerves, but tears threaten to break through again, so I glance to the floor between us. I'd rather be angry.

"Falls can be prevented," I murmur as he pulls me into his embrace.

Fuck. Now I'm crying.

"Probably. But we're here now, and the doctors said he'll heal. And it won't set his recovery back more than a few months. He just needs to do other things to keep his strength and coordination improving. He will. Your dad is anything but lazy."

I shake with a small laugh.

"He's a little lazy," I tease.

Hunter's soft laughter vibrates in his chest as he sways with me in his arms.

Lindsey passes through the living room and pops the end of her carrot into her mouth "I'm gonna get Dad. You two work out whatever—" She swirls her finger in our direction.

I lean out of Hunter's embrace when her back is to me, then arch a brow at him.

"I hope she chokes on that thing," I say under my breath, which makes him laugh even harder.

"Okay, settle down. The *last* thing you need is another medical emergency. Also, I threw the rest of the carrots away outside, so she won't be getting any more." He smiles down at me, and I rise on my tiptoes to kiss him with my own grin.

"Bless you, Hunter Reddick."

My sister wheels our father into the room, and my mom

lingers behind, holding her laptop in one hand while bouncing her gaze between the present world needing her full attention and whatever *important work* is on the screen.

"Let me try . . . to do it . . . on my own," my father says, swatting my sister's hand away. Lindsey grimaces at him but backs off after rolling her eyes at me.

"I'm just going to stand close as a precaution, if that's cool with you, Dale?" Hunter doesn't wait for my father to say no, stepping within a quick grasp of my father as his forearms flex with his own weight. He manages to move himself from the wheelchair to the edge of the upright chair he's going to have to deal with for the next several months. He scoots himself back, then pulls the strap fixed to his cast to lift his full right leg up to the ottoman. He looks utterly ridiculous, sunk into the chair and not scooted back completely, but he folds his hands over his belly and looks up at me with such pride, I can't help but clap.

"You did it on your own, all right. How's the fit?" I glance from him to the TV, which, thankfully, he can see from this spot in the room.

"I'm miserable, but it . . . will do," he jokes.

"I think we'll manage just fine," my mom says, setting her laptop down on the ottoman next to my father's feet and leaning over him to kiss the top of his head.

I stare at the scene for a bit, fully aware of the disgust weighing down the corners of my eyes and mouth.

"I'm going to the store to get a few things. I'll be back," I say. "Lindsey, you staying for dinner?" My fuse is already short from the fact my sister isn't paying attention to me, but rather is staring at the stupid social media apps on her phone.

I snap my fingers and she glances up.

"Huh?" She clearly didn't hear me. Her face is devoid of absolutely every emotion. She's basically here to take up space.

I shake my head. "Never mind. Just go home," I say, heading out the door.

"No, wait. I'm sorry." She rushes to catch up to me, pushing her phone into her back pocket before snagging her purse from the hook on the coat rack.

"You stay here. I'll go get some easy stuff for dinner. I just wanted to know if you'd be staying, is all." She gives me a blank look but then shakes her head, almost as if she's a robot needing a reboot.

I lean in close.

"Is something going on?" I ask, breathing in to see if she's drunk or something. She smells fine, though, and I know she drove Dad and me home from the hospital an hour ago.

"I got some upsetting news," she says, quickly snapping her mouth shut, as if she regrets speaking the words in the first place.

"What's going on?" I pry.

My sister's expression deflates, but her wry smile comes back into play.

"I'm not laying one more burden on you, Ren," she says with a short laugh.

"Oh, come on. I mean, what's one more thing, right?" An exhausted half smile hits my lips as I loop my arm with hers. "Let's go. We'll hit the store together."

I nod to Hunter and he winks softly, signaling he'll handle things here while we're gone. Of everyone in this house, I trust him the most. In less than a month, he's become dependable.

And he's leaving.

I stuff the sick feeling eating up my stomach back down and turn my attention to my sister as I drag her out the door with me to the Jeep. We both hop in, and after she buckles her safety belt, she tosses her phone in my lap. It's a text string with a number I don't recognize, and it ends with a set of digital photos.

"What is this?" I glance at her with a squirrely expression.

"Just open them," she says, her voice suddenly monotone.

I look back at her phone screen cradled in my palm and open the first photo, zooming in to be sure that my eyes aren't lying to me. Unfortunately, they aren't. Her husband, Brandon, is in a full-on lip lock with a woman who is very clearly *not* my sister.

"Oh, Linds," I sigh out.

"Yeah, I've had a feeling for a while," she says, stretching her hand toward me and flipping through the photos on her screen. They're all with the same woman, but the clothes change, which means the days change. The one thing that doesn't is my sister's husband is having an affair.

"Hey, on the bright side, if you leave his ass and move back home, the two of us can bunk in our old room again, just like when we were kids." I slap her phone back into her open palm, and she puffs out a hard laugh.

"What's sad is that really is the bright side. For both of us." She squeezes my hand in silent acknowledgement of my own aching heart.

Lindsey knows it was hard to open myself up to feeling for someone. She also knows when Hunter takes off for Texas, I'll lock down my heart so it never feels again.

TWENTY-THREE
HUNTER

This is supposed to be the moment of my life—the culmination of years of grinding on the ball field and pushing my arm to the max on the mound—and all I need to do is get on this plane. Yet here I am at gate six in the OKC airport, my lucky glove in the bag on my shoulder and a start in Texas waiting for me in the morning, and I can't seem to get myself to board the damn plane.

"Why don't you come with me?" I've asked Renleigh no less than a dozen times to make this trip with me. I have the means to make it happen. I can buy her a first-class ticket. I have a seat for her in at the stadium in Texas. My parents are going to be there, too; she won't be alone. Hell, I'll get Lindsey here, too. And her boys. It sounds like she needs an escape from Sweetwater as much as Renleigh does.

"I need to be here for my dad," she says, the same answer as the last ten times.

I nod, my fingers tangling with hers until she slips her hand away. My group boards next. I have only *minutes* with her until I either come back or get her to come visit me.

"Your mom seemed willing to—"

"She can't take care of him," she cuts me off. "Or I can't rest easy for thinking she won't. Too much history."

Her lips quiver. She's quitting on us. She warned me about this. Not directly, but she was clear about her feelings when it comes to long distance relationships. But it doesn't *have* to be long distance. Not if she comes with me. She can have her own life. Go back to school. I don't need her in my apartment as badly as I want her there. I just need her fewer than five hundred miles away.

"What if your mom proves you wrong? I don't mean that to sound so challenging, but what if? She might?" I lift a shoulder, but her sour expression makes me drop it again.

"You have to board soon. I promise I'll watch the game. And I'll wait up so you can call me as soon as you get back in. I'll be rooting for you." She throws her body into mine, wrapping her arms around me but burying her face. And as she pulls back, she turns to walk away.

"Wait a second, Renleigh. You aren't leaving like that," I say, reaching for her arm, my fingers brushing along the back of her elbow. She stops after a few steps and buries her face in her hands, so I step in behind her and wrap her in my arms again, slowly turning her until she's looking up at me.

"This doesn't have to be a sad thing," I say, cradling her face. My thumbs sweep her tears away.

"I don't see how it can be happy, Hunter. It's fine, though. We knew what this was. It was fun. I enjoyed being the Oklahoma side piece."

I laugh at her dramatic words, but that only makes her eyes drop with more pain.

"No, Renleigh. Please don't cry. You're not a side piece. You're the only piece. I mean, my only piece. I mean . . . you aren't a piece. *Fuck*, this isn't coming out right." I pinch the bridge of my nose, and she shakes with a single, sad sob.

"It's okay, is all. If you can't come back, or we don't talk every night. You're going to be busy, and I've got to figure out my life and what I'm going to do with my dad. I should be open to trusting my mom, but I simply can't. Not yet. She's let me down too many times."

"I won't let you down, though," I say, breaking through her words and sweeping the tears from her cheeks again.

She blinks her eyes dry as they call my boarding group, her gaze shifting to the small line at the gate behind me. I shift my body to block the view, keeping her focus on me.

"I'll call you the minute I land. And then again before bed. And in the morning. Say you'll answer." I stare into her eyes, my stomach twisting with so much doubt.

"Why are you working so hard to hold on to this?" she asks.

"To us. I'm holding on to us. Because I feel it in here," I say, pressing my fist against my breastbone. "I'm young, Renleigh, but I'm not naïve. I know what special feels like. And what we have is special. It deserves more time."

She glances around again, and the attendant clearing her throat, waiting for me—the last passenger—to get my ass on the plane. I'm tempted to sit right here on the floor in protest, just to prove to Renleigh what lengths I'm willing to go to.

I wouldn't give up my shot. That wouldn't be healthy for either of us. But I don't believe I have to. That *either* of us have to give up anything. We just need to be honest. And care about each other. That feels like the easiest thing in the world to do.

"I'll answer the phone. I can do that, Hunter. And I'll be watching you throw. Me and my dad. And my fucking mom, probably," she says, a half-hearted laugh vibrating her voice.

"That's enough," I say, pulling her mouth to mine for one last kiss.

I hold up my phone as a visual reminder as I walk backward to the gate, not turning till the last second so I don't miss any seconds of seeing her. Once the attendant scans my boarding pass, I glance over my shoulder. She's walking away. I type out a text for her to read, hoping it will be before I take off, so I'll get anything she decides to text back.

> ME: Would it help if I said I am falling in love
> with you?

I smile at my own words the moment they're sent, and stare at my screen, waiting for any digital clue that she's read them. But the only thing I get before takeoff is the little tag that reads *delivered*.

For now, that will have to be enough.

The delivery notice changes to *read* by the time I land in Dallas, but there's still no response from Renleigh. It was probably a pretty heavy confession to throw at her, but time was running out for us. if I don't say it now, I'll regret not taking the chance when I could.

I don't prod her about my words while I wait for my checked bag. I simply send her a short note letting her know I landed. That message shifts to *read*, too, which feels somewhat lacking in closure, but maybe she's busy.

It's evening in Sweetwater, and it will be sundown here in minutes. I picture her arguing with her sister over how her dad should or shouldn't get into his wheelchair, and the imagined bickering amuses me. I don't think Lindsey knows that Renleigh filled me in on her husband's affair, and I wouldn't break Renleigh's trust by mentioning it without either of them inviting me to. I think it sticks in Renleigh's mind, though, and probably heightens her anxieties about relationships.

The team sent a pretty sick car to pick me up. I've never actually sat in a Bentley before, but now I can say I have. I'm not sure I'm dressed nice enough for it, though. I never went shopping for more suits, so I hope I can stretch the one I've got through two games until I have time to shop.

I pull my phone out, and there's still no response from Renleigh. I decide to keep filling her in on my progress and my thoughts.

> ME: I need more suits. Maybe we can do some online shopping together tonight?

I send it and wait for the notice to shift to *read* just like the other times. It takes a minute or two, but eventually it does. And like before, she doesn't send a response.

I tuck my phone into the side pocket of my leather travel bag and stare out the window at the passing subdivisions and full freeways as we weave our way toward Arlington. The team has an apartment set up for me, fully furnished. They have a few of them at a weekly-stay building near the stadium. It's for situations like mine, the last-minute call-ups. Sometimes there's more than one player bouncing between Sweetwater and here. I hope I get to stay and find a more permanent address; maybe a condo for now. And one day, a dog.

I pull my phone back out and shoot another text to Renleigh.

> ME: What are your thoughts on dogs? I'm not much of a cat person, but I could be persuaded if necessary.

I don't bother to wait for her to read it before tucking my phone back inside my bag and continuing my trek to my new job, in a city I don't know, all alone. I should be terrified. I should be thrilled. Yet right now, I feel neither.

The driver pulls up to my building, and my agent, Shawn, is waiting for me in a car parked out front. He approaches as I lift my bag out of the back and hand two twenties to my driver. He pushes my hand away, though, explaining he's on staff with the team. I still feel as though he should get a tip. I don't want to be known as the cheap asshole, so I glance at Shawn for approval before reaching forward and tucking the money into the breast pocket on the driver's jacket.

"Thank you, Mr. Reddick. That's very kind," he relents, covering the pocket with his palm and nodding once before rushing to the driver's seat to head out for his next task.

"Okay, so here's your key. And that car over there . . ." Shawn presses the lock button on a key fob and flashes the lights on a dark blue Honda Accord. "That's yours for now. The team will get your truck up here for you—"

"Can I drive it myself?" I quirk a brow.

"Uh, I think they want you here. It's a pretty strict schedule, a lot more rigorous than Triple-A ball, but . . ."

I continue to stare at my agent, my eyes wide with hope.

He sighs and makes a note on his phone.

"I'll ask," he says.

I pat his shoulder.

"Thanks, Shawn. I appreciate it."

I really want a reason to go back to Sweetwater. I need this second chance to plead my case and talk Renleigh into coming with me. I checked the schedule, and if I head back to Oklahoma after my arm care on Tuesday, I'll have all day Wednesday to wear her down, then drive my ass back here for my bullpen session on Thursday morning.

"You need help with any of that?" Shawn glances at my checked bag and the small leather travel one dangling from my fist. I lift it like a kettle weight and smile.

"I can handle it," I say.

"Okay, man. Wow! This is huge. I hope you know that." He laughs nervously, probably because he knows if I'm up here for fifty innings of work, then his power of negotiation on my behalf gets a full season head start.

"Get ready to earn your keep," I say, tremors of excitement tickling my belly. We grasp hands, then he pulls me in for a hug, slapping my back.

"I'll work my ass off, Hunt. You do your job, and I'll do mine."

We slap hands and he heads back to his car as I make my way to the elevator to get to my new home for, well, probably a week. My phone buzzes in my bag, so I fumble the key to unlock the apartment while also grabbing for my phone. In all my scurrying, I answer, expecting it to be Renleigh.

"You're a cat person, aren't you?" I smile, proud of my easy banter in the face of telling her I'm falling for her.

"I am not. I'm a kid person. And the thought of adding a pet into my mix right now sounds terrifying."

I deflate when my brain catches up. It's Lindsey's voice on the other line. I pull the phone away from my ear to verify the unknown number, then put her on speaker.

"Sorry, I thought—"

"I know," she says. "And don't worry. When you call later, she'll answer. And if you tell her I called you, I will end you forever. Hear me?"

I swallow hard, then laugh.

"I hear you," I confirm.

"Good. Now, I only have a second before she meets me on the porch for wine. I need to say a few things, and I simply need you to listen."

"Shoot," I say, picking up my phone and carrying it with me to the basic gray loveseat sitting in a very empty, very basic room.

"Our mom fucked my sister up good, and she doesn't trust relationships because of it. But she trusts you, Hunter. And that scares her. If you're really invested in this thing with her, I'm asking you to be patient. And to not give up. Because I haven't seen her open to the possibility of finding her person, well, ever."

I sit with her words for a beat, then utter, "I get it. And I am. I'm invested."

"Good. Now, call her in an hour. Right now, my sister and I need a drink." With that, she ends our call.

TWENTY-FOUR

RENLEIGH

There's an empty wine bottle on the porch table, and I am only responsible for a single glass of it. That was enough for me. And while my sister can be a sloppy drunk, she has earned the right be sloppy a few times before she has to get her shit together and take her soon-to-be ex-husband to the cleaners.

"Come on, Linds. Let me do the heavy lifting."

I duck under my sister's arm and help her stand, sort of. She's wobbly, so by the time we get inside, she has to lean against the entry table for balance. She spots her keys in the tin bowl and clutches them, so I promptly take them from her hand and tuck them in my pocket.

"Nope. You're staying here tonight, remember? The boys are on the pull-out sofa." My sister giggles and wanders toward her twins, so I steer her back toward the stairs. "No, babe. Let them sleep."

This was so much easier when I was a freshman in high school, and she was a senior. Seven years of life has made her more gangly, a bit heavier, and stubborn.

"Let me help. Here," my mom says, swooping in and taking my sister's other side. My face goes stoic, but I accept her offer as my sister rolls her head to my side and holds her finger to her lips.

"*Shhh*, be nice," Lindsey says.

"I am, Linds. I am," I reply.

The three of us take the steps one at a time, and after a few minutes, my mom and I manage to get my sister into my bed and pull her shoes off. I throw the quilt over her, and she's snoring by the time I slip back out the door with my mom.

"You're a good sister. I hope you know that," she says.

I pull my lips into the familiar forced smile and nod.

"Thanks."

My chest is tight for lots of reasons. I feel unsettled, for sure, but nothing makes my chest tighter than being alone with my mom. To end this moment on the positive, I decide it's best I leave her with that small token and kindness and slip downstairs so I can make myself comfortable on the blow-up mattress next to the boys. *This house is too small for this many people.*

"Renleigh, hold on a second," she says, her fingernails grazing the sleeve of my sweatshirt.

I should keep going.

I sigh softly and turn around to face her, my tight, forced smile now clearly a pretense.

"Can we?" She nods over her shoulder, toward her bedroom, which was mine a week ago.

"Sure," I relent.

I'm too tired to fight.

I follow my mom into her room, and she glances over her shoulder as she sits on the foot of the bed.

"Close the door a little," she says.

I do, leaving it cracked enough for an escape, I suppose, then join her on the bed. She pulls a cardboard box from the center of her mattress to her lap and flips open the lid. I recognize the photo of me and Lindsey in the baby pool instantly. We're maybe two and five, respectively. Our hair is covered in mud, and Lindsey pushed my short hair into a mohawk with it after attempting to do the same with her own. I was too young to fully remember the moment, but I have heard the story many times. And this picture has always been one of my favorites.

"I love this photo," I say, taking it in my hands.

My mom leans closer but doesn't touch me.

"Yeah," she says. I glance at her in my periphery, and she's smiling softly. She smiles a lot. More than I give her credit for.

She pulls out another photo, this one of the four of us at an amusement park. I'm in a blue wagon. I vaguely remember this one, too. Again, I was little. Not much older than the mud photo.

"Where was this?" I ask.

She runs her fingers over the yellowing photo, still smiling.

"Upstate. It was high school baseball playoffs, and there was a carnival. The team got knocked out early, so we stretched the weekend into a family trip. We didn't get many of those."

She's right. We didn't. Because she wasn't here for them.

"Why are we looking at these?"

I level her with a frank gaze, and she draws in a deep breath before letting her shoulders sag and putting the photos back in the box, seemingly filled with so many more.

"I wanted you to see that we were happy. Your dad and I. We *are* happy. We've never been enemies. I love your father very much. And he loves me."

I shake with a silent laugh.

"Sure," I utter.

"No, Renleigh. We do. We did, even then. It doesn't mean that I don't have regrets. Because I do. I regret leaving after his last stroke. That wasn't right of me. But—"

"But you had *work.*" I emphasize that word, punching it out.

She's quiet, her lips mashing as her eyes flit to her lap, her mind seeming to sort through how to respond. Her lips part with a breath, and it takes her a few more seconds to look at me again.

"Your dad told me to go. Every time. Your dad asked for the divorce, and not because he was bitter or angry, or because we didn't get along. He wanted to force me to pick me. Because he knew I wouldn't."

My mouth hangs open, and I laugh once without sound.

"That makes zero sense." I shake my head and rack my brain for the any evidence I have that supports her version.

"I know it doesn't. And I probably shouldn't have gone along with it. It took some convincing, for sure. In fact . . ." She pulls the mud photo out again and flattens it on her thigh.

"This was about the same time I was offered the Chief of Staff job in Tulsa. The new mayor was a friend of mine from college. She knew I was trying to break into the politics and PR world, so she reached out with an incredible offer."

I don't remember my mom ever working in Tulsa.

"You didn't take it?"

She shakes her head, confirming so.

"Your dad was the new coach, and he was so excited about it. And you guys were young. I would have had to spend weeks away and weekends in Tulsa, or we would have had to move. I couldn't do that to your dad, and I didn't want to leave you. So I turned it down."

My gaze drops to the floor as I consider how that decision squares with everything *I* know about my mom. She's always been selfish. I can't imagine her turning down something so huge. It doesn't jive with who she is.

"Your father didn't know I had the offer," she adds. My gaze flashes to her face, and her expression is resolute, mouth a solid line, eyes unflinching. "And when he found out about it, and that I turned it down, he felt . . ."

"Guilty," I say.

My mom nods.

"Among all the other emotions in that family of feelings." She sighs and shifts so she faces me more head-on. I do the same.

"I told him it wasn't a big deal, that I would take the next one. And the woman who did work for Lianna—that was my friend, the mayor—she ended up running for Congress a few years later. She won."

"Allysa Saunders," I hum. I remember my mom helping with her campaign. We had posters all over the house, and I liked coloring the letters in. I probably wasted a dozen of those things with my markers. My mom never got angry at me for it, though.

"Yep. Alyssa wanted to take me with her, but your dad had just won state. So, I didn't tell him. *Again.*"

"But you ended up in Washington around then. I know you worked for Alyssa," I contradict.

Her gaze falls again, and a sad laugh leaves her lips with a tiny breath.

"I did. Your dad pays more attention than any of us gives him credit for. He figured it out, and when I insisted I didn't want to take the job, he saw through my bullshit and asked me for a divorce.

"That was probably the first real fight we ever had. But your dad knew I would never leave this—him, my girls, Sweetwater—unless he forced me to. And he knew I would have probably resented him for it one day. My work gives me so much joy, Renleigh. I know it's hollow sounding, but you never knew your grandmother.

"My mom? She was a housewife, and my father was so stifling. She had this incredible mind, and she tried to volunteer for community groups just to use her voice. He never let her. He made her small. And I was so afraid of feeling the way she did. Your dad was the opposite of my father, though. And he'd rather make life hard for him than limit my potential."

She pauses with a soft laugh, shaking her head before looking up at the ceiling.

"I know how self-centered it all sounds, but the way my self-esteem blossomed when your dad pushed me to pick myself. It was . . . addictive. I became the person I sketched out in my mind when I was a teenager, the strong personality my mom buried. And even though we weren't still legally married, I had this man—my best friend—who rooted for me the whole way. Who was the best girl dad around. Who loved his life in Sweetwater, and coaching those boys, so much he knew he couldn't give that up to move to Boston, or Washington, or Houston.

And you and Linds . . . you had friends here. You were happy. It worked. And maybe it only worked for me, and I've made all of that up to justify the life I've led. But you girls turned into incredible people. I've done enough for me now. It's your time, you and Lindsey. Though your sister is going to need some help."

I gurgle an irritable laugh over my sister's situation as my mom leans into me.

"She'll get through it. She's better off," I say, shifting my gaze to my mom's.

"She is," she agrees. "And now, it's my turn. I should have taken it sooner. I didn't realize how much like me you are."

I bristle at the comparison, and I think she notices as she rests a palm on my knee. I don't recoil from her touch, which maybe surprises both of us a little.

"You would pick anyone else rather than choose yourself."

Her words hit my chest like Thor's hammer just as my pocket vibrates with a call from the one person I want to pick for myself, more than anything. And even with my mother's truth bomb giving me permission, I still don't know if I can. Because he's always going to be somewhere else more often than he's not.

I pull my phone out and stare at the single H that comes

up. I couldn't even bring myself to type his full name into my contacts. That felt too permanent. I haven't answered his texts today either. I'm sure he's confused by it because I said I would. But I don't know what to say.

"You deserve to let yourself answer that," my mom says, placing a hand on my leg again and squeezing before getting up and leaving me alone in her room—*my room.*

Five rings have buzzed, and I know the call is going to disappear into my voicemail soon. My thumb is vibrating with fear as it hovers over the answer button on the screen. I close my eyes and wet my dry lips with my tongue before my thumb presses the screen and accepts the call.

"Hi."

"Hi." His reply is swift. He sounds excited. Maybe relieved.

"I'm sorry I haven't texted back yet, I—"

"It's okay."

It's not, but I take his out. He's giving it to be kind.

"How was your trip?" I pull my feet up and scoot back, making myself smaller in the center of the bed.

"It was fast. Weird. I feel a bit like a commodity," he laughs out. "My agent met me in the parking lot downstairs. I'm in an apartment that looks like it was ripped straight out of a catalogue."

"Was it an IKEA catalogue, by chance?" I tease.

"I wish!" His laughter is soothing to my ears. I hold the phone close, wanting to capture it to remember later.

The quiet filters in between us, and I wonder if his lips are parted like mine are, his mind riffling through what to say.

"I was just—" I stop.

"How would you feel about—" He starts.

We laugh as we talk over each other, and my cheeks rush with heat, the nervous, flirtatious feeling trickling down my spine. Hunter does this to me. Nearly every time I see him there's a physical reaction. A giddiness, perhaps. Attraction, definitely. But there's also this want for more time. With him.

"You go first," I say, unsure of what I was going to say anyhow.

"Okay, well. I was wondering if you'd like to ride to Dallas with me next week? I have to come and get my truck, and it's a pretty easy drive, but I sure could use company. I'd let you pick the playlist and everything.

"Ooooh, playlist perks. That's . . . that's tempting, Hunter." It *is* tempting, but not because of a playlist.

"Yeah? What do you think?"

I breathe in deeply and look out the open bedroom doorway toward the room I'm sharing with my sister for, well, who knows how long.

"I don't know. What would I do when we get there?" I mean, *I know what we would do.* But then what?

"I thought maybe you could check out the area with me. There's a psych program at UT Dallas I was just looking at, and since you were already in a Texas school, I thought—"

"Hunter, that's . . . I can't move to Dallas. I'm not starting school now. I can't leave here," I explain.

"Okay. Yeah. I get that," he says.

The quiet creeps in again, and it's heavier now. I glance at the box still resting on top of the bed. My mom picked those moments. And then she picked others. I still don't know how much I believe my dad pushed her to leave, but at the same time, his affection for her has never wavered. She made so much money in her line of work. Meanwhile, life here stayed simple. Dad barely got by.

"Why?" Hunter breaks into the conversation happening in my head.

"Why, what?" I ask.

"Sorry, I was wondering . . . why can't you leave now?"

I laugh softly, mentally lining up all my reasons before saying them.

"Well, let's see. My dad has a broken leg and is going to need to start back at square one when it heals. And my sister has twins she'll be raising on her own. She has zero time to work to support them, and she doesn't have a college degree, so she'll probably have to take shifts at Earl's, which means someone has to watch the boys when she works. And my mom—"

"Renleigh, I know your thoughts on your mom. But your parents are adults, and your dad is a lot stronger than you give him credit for. Besides, what if your mom stays this time? What if you stick around and it turns out all you're doing is observation?"

"But what if she leaves, and he falls again, and—"

"He won't. I mean, sure, there are infinite possibilities for several things happening, but those are all outliers. And no offense, but you aren't carrying everyone on your back. Your mom and dad are figuring it out without you. And your sister? She's not going to want you stepping in and taking over. I don't know her well, but I know enough about her to know she's as independent as her sister. Just maybe less—"

His words stop there, and my hair stands up on the back of my neck.

"She's less what, Hunter?" I get to my feet so I can pace.

"Less scared, Renleigh. Your sister seems to be taking this shit head on, and she's a little fearless about it, despite how scary it is. Maybe you should take a page out of her book? Take a chance."

"On you? You want me to take a chance on you. Is that it?"

I hear myself, and I don't like it, but my feet are dug in. What's the difference between being here for my family or being in Dallas for Hunter?

"For you, Renleigh!" Hunter says. I don't know if I've heard his tone so bold before.

I sit back on the edge of the bed.

"For the love of God, Renleigh. Don't be scared of what *you* want. I mean, damn—I would love for you to be here with me, for us to decorate my next apartment together. For it to be *our* apartment. We can get a cat, or a dog, or a fish. Or *fuck!* I'll get you a damn lizard, or an imaginary friend.

"All I want in the world is for you to pick something *you* want. For you to do life *your* way . . . for you. Not for *anyone* else. For you. And if that means you don't live here with me, and instead you go back to Austin and finish school there, well then, I'd be pretty fucking sad here alone with our pet lizard, but I'd be happy."

There's a stark silence on the line, so I utter, "Why?"

Hunter chuckles, the tone noting his frustration.

"Because I meant what I said when I wrote that text earlier. I'm falling in love with you. Hell, fuck that. I'm *in* love with you. And when you love someone, nothing makes you happier than seeing them live their best life. Even if that means you can't be in it all the time."

Well, goddamn.

This time, we both let the silence take center stage for nearly a full minute. It doesn't feel strange, and the need to feel it isn't suffocating. We give each other time. No deadline. No rush.

"I'll think about it," I finally utter.

Hunter sucks in a sharp breath, then blows out heavily.

"That's good enough. Yeah, that's . . . that's amazing, Renleigh. Thank you."

I can picture him pacing in a beige apartment with generic Southwestern-style tiles and tan walls as he grabs at the back of his neck. It's one of his cutest habits. The way his fingers fiddle with the curls that tickle the back of his neck. I miss that, and I just saw him do it this morning. I miss it already.

I miss him.

TWENTY-FIVE
HUNTER

It's the same ball.

Same dirt.

Nothing has changed in the measurements. Still sixty feet, six inches from here to the glove. It's not Roddy's glove, but Kyle Durbin is a lot like Roddy. He's thirty-three and pissy. I can pretend.

"Batting for the San Diego Padres, number sixteen, Miguel Arenas."

It's a home game, so it's our announcer, and he's pretty straightforward as he announces our opponents. It's almost comical because Miguel won a Silver Slugger award last year, and he has fans everywhere. The applause and screams as he steps up to the plate sure feel like I'm in San Diego instead of Texas.

But I'm not.

And it's still sixty feet, six inches to strike one.

I dig at the dirt in front of the rubber to get the perfect feel, the right balance of traction and release. My cleat settles in, and I lean forward to study my first situation. My first pitch in the majors. My mom is holding her breath somewhere. My dad is holding my mom.

"Let's do this," I whisper.

The call comes through the PitchCom. Fastball. High and outside. I nod and bring my glove into my chest, feeling the ball in the leather. My first pitch in the majors, and fucking Kyle Durbin wants me to throw a ball.

I wind up, my mind races as my motion takes over, and I release the ball straight into Kyle's glove. Only it never snaps into the pocket. It cracks off Miguel's bat, and I flip around and try not to throw up all over the mound as a hundred-and-four mile per hour liner zips down the third baseline and lands . . . five inches foul.

"*Fuuuuuck*," I mutter as my eyes shut.

I pull my hat from my head and run my forearm over my forehead. I'm sweating more than usual. That was a close one.

I pivot in time to catch the ball Kyle fires back at me, his mask up on his forehead, his frown set into his cheeks. Yeah, he may as well be Roddy.

I lift my glove in apology. I'll tell him I missed my spot. I'll blame it on nerves. But the truth is, I did it again. Just like Roddy said. I didn't fucking listen.

The PitchCom comes in with another fastball, high and outside, and I chuckle to myself. My first pitch was a strike of sorts, but not the kind I want. High and outside it is. Right you are. *Listen to your catcher, Hunter.*

I wind up and fire the ball to Kyle, and Miguel swings through it for strike two. The crowd roars. Most of the fans behind the plate on their feet. It's my first start. I'm the guy. The best there ever was or will be. And they are all behind me.

My upper lip flickers with the need to smile, so I give in to the asshole smirk I know it must look like to Miguel. I'm sure the commentary about this first batter, my first faceoff, is full of color. I'm sure my reputation is being set right now. I'm all right with being the guy who smirks his way through trouble, as long as I'm the guy who comes back stronger. Who throws harder. Who pitches smarter.

The PitchCom calls for the slider, and I feel the threads of the ball in my glove. I keep the smirk in place as I imagine the words they're saying in the booth.

You have to wonder when it's a kid like this on the mound. So much hype. Can he handle it? Twenty-three is young to be facing guys who have World Series rings in their vaults. And Silver Slugger awards, to boot. Then there's this guy—Hunter Reddick—number one draft pick. And despite all the experience standing at the plate in front of him, he seems cool and unfazed. He seems ready. And I gotta tell you, Texas fans, I believe he is. This is our guy. And he's going to make this a summer to remember.

I wind up, my body following the years of training that led me here, my arm stretching back, my step forward strong, leg straight, quads engaged, elbow like a rubber band, ready to work. The ball flies through the air, the threads spinning so fast there's no way Miguel can get a read on this. He's going to swing. He's going to miss. And then . . . he does.

"Hell, yeah!" I pump my fist as Miguel shakes his head and glances at me on his way back to the dugout. He touches the brim of his hat, a tiny tip for respect, and I nod back at him.

"I want that ball!" I shout, and Kyle tosses it to the coaching staff to put somewhere safe for me to give to my mom. She deserves this token. It's hers as much as it's mine. Dad can have the next one.

"Pretty solid way to introduce yourself to the fans here in Arlington, Hunter Reddick," Amy Tidings, the local affiliate reporter says before pushing her microphone toward me.

I chuckle and glance over my shoulder where Kyle is still changing out at his cubby.

"I'm only as good as my catcher, really. I feel lucky to have a guy like Kyle Durbin catching for me. I was in good hands. Though, I missed my spot that first pitch. That one . . . That scared me," I say through a nervous laugh.

"It scared all of us, I think," Amy says. "It's nice to hear such respect for your teammate already. I know you're the new guy here, but that has to go a long way in the clubhouse, I'm sure. What has the welcome been like so far?"

I glance around the locker room, and most of the guys are busy in their own worlds while I'm chatting with a reporter about my seven-inning outing.

I shrug.

"Good, I think. It will take a while to not feel like the new guy. As long as I do my job and help the guys get the win, that's all that matters."

"Well, you certainly did that today," Amy says, her eyes shifting to my left just in time for me to catch sight of the cooler about to be tipped over my head.

"Oh, damn!" I shout and try to duck out of the way. It's no use, though, as the ice-cold water soaks me from head to toe. It's colder than the wrap around my arm.

"Yeah, he's ours. Atta boy, Reddick!" The praise comes from all directions as my teammates pile on, slapping my soaking wet jersey against my skin and ruffling my hair. They push me around like I'm their little brother, which, in the hierarchy of this locker room, I suppose I am. I love it. Every second of it. Even the ice.

"I'd say you're part of the family. How about you?" Amy says.

I laugh hard as I pull a chunk of ice from the inside my jersey and throw it toward Kyle.

"I guess so," I say.

"Well, you heard it here, Rob. Texas has a new starting

pitcher in town, and this city—this team? They like him. I like him. And I know you boys in the booth like him. You talked him up all night."

Amy nods in response to whatever the rest of the media team is saying. I pull the mic clipped on the collar of my jersey free and hand it to the cameraman about three feet away from us.

"Thanks for that," I chuckle, meeting Kyle's grinning face.

"Hey, you earned that bath. Now, let's make it a habit, huh?" He holds a fist out for me, and I tap my knuckles to his.

"Go on. Hit the showers. You're going to freeze your dick off."

He snaps a towel at me, and it stings my back.

I wait for the guys to clear out a little more before I check my phone. My heart does a double beat when there's a text waiting for me, but then I realize it's from my agent, not Renleigh.

> SHAWN: Thanks for making my job easy. Tremendous, bud. What a start!

I smile to myself, and his words solidify my opinion on my start. That first inning was tough, but once I settled in, things started to feel natural. The stadium felt smaller, more intimate. Kyle felt more like Roddy. And in my mind, I was back in Sweetwater, or on the mound back in San Diego. It's the same game. The players may be mightier, but the rules still stack up. The ball is round. The bats are heavy. The yard is deep.

And listen to the catcher.

I snicker to myself, wondering if Roddy watched the game. The Mavericks are traveling this week, but it's a scheduled off day for him, and part of me really hopes he found a way to watch.

By the time I shower and change, then check in with Coach, most of the friends and family waiting for other players have gone. It's just my parents and Kyle's wife left in the family room that leads to the secure exit to our garage. The three of them are in deep conversation when I enter the room.

"The star of the show," my dad says as my mom leaps from her seat and dashes into my embrace.

"I'm so proud of you, Hunter. You did it. You really did it," she says through sniffles.

I pull the ball out of my hoodie pocket and hand it to her, and she studies it, scrutinizing every stitch.

"That's the first strikeout. I signed it and dated it, which I guess somehow makes it worth more, but I don't know. The guy put a sticker on it. You can sell it one day." I shrug, but my mom clutches it to her chest and stares into my eyes.

"No way! I am never selling this."

"*She* might not, but how much are we talking about?" My dad's joke earns him a swift jab in the ribs from my mom's elbow. "I mean, we'll keep it forever. Of course. Just like how we will never change anything in your old bedroom, despite what a great man cave it would make."

My dad steps back this time, avoiding the jab, but he can't escape my mom's glare. He chuckles and says, "Kidding. Of course I'm kidding." He flashes me a look over her shoulder, though, that reads, "Phew!"

"You had a great start, Hunter. You should be very proud. Kyle was excited to catch you tonight," Kyle's wife says. I met her, briefly, before the game. I think her name is Stephanie, but I'm not sure, so I don't want to guess and get it wrong. Besides, it looks like she and my parents have already made their own introductions.

"Thank you," I say, taking her hand for a shake.

I swing my arm around my mom's shoulder just as Kyle pushes through the door to the family room. He gets a lot of post-game work done on his knees, so he's always the last guy to leave.

"Your son had quite a game," he says, weaving his hand

into his wife's. I notice the way they instantly connect and don't let go. There's genuine affection between them. And Kyle's wearing his ring. It's one of those silicone ones. I paid attention because he wore it during the game, too. A lot of guys take them off, but not him.

"He's been waiting for this moment for, well, twenty-three years," my mom brags.

I lean toward Kyle.

"Maybe sixteen. For the first seven years of my life, I wanted to be Spiderman," I confess.

Kyle and his wife laugh.

"Well, who didn't?" Kyle adds.

"We've got an ice cream party to get to, and then homework," Kyle's wife says. Her husband follows along with her itinerary, his expression morphing from elation to dread in a way I'm sure his kids will the moment they get home.

"How long have you all been married?" my dad asks. I'm glad it was him and not me. I don't like being invasive. Chandler Reddick, top software salesman for QLM Solutions for six years running, has zero boundaries. It's part of the job, or at least what makes him so good at it.

"We're about to celebrate eight years in August," his wife says. "It was easier when it was just the two of us, but when we started having kids, I couldn't really travel with him anymore. I'm so busy with the rugrats, though, it makes the road trips fly for me."

"Not so much for me, though," Kyle says, pulling his wife in close and kissing the top of her head. "I miss them when I'm gone. But that's the game, isn't it? Not quite ready to give it up yet."

I think of Roddy as he speaks, and I wonder where their paths diverged. How Kyle and his wife ended up making it while Roddy and Daisy didn't. One day, I'll need to get the scoop on his story. Maybe Renleigh can fill me in during our trip to Dallas, which she's still thinking about.

A wave of adrenaline sweeps over me at the thought, and I shiver from it. My mom twists her neck and scans my face.

"You all right?" she asks.

I smile and nod.

"Still cold from the ice, I guess," I lie.

She clearly doesn't buy it, but she lets me off with a "*Mmm hmm.*"

The five of us walk out to the garage together, and my parents manage to work their way into a dinner invite before they head back to California late tomorrow night. I'll be on the road by then, heading to Oklahoma for the fastest overnight and turnaround of my life. All worth it, though, if there's even a chance I won't be driving back alone. And if that isn't what happens, I'll just have to leave something else behind so I can keep coming back.

I snuggle into the gray sheets and comforter on my queen-sized bed. I spent the end of my last conversation with Renleigh giving her the rundown of everything gray and beige in this apartment. It's quite a list, with the only outliers being some tumblers in the cabinet—they're bright green—and the overabundance of throw pillows. None of them match.

I ordered in tonight, a massive grilled vegetable platter with chicken that one man shouldn't be able to eat alone, yet I did. With my belly full and my heart hopeful, I dial Renleigh and hold my breath as I pray she'll pick up. She answers almost immediately.

"Seven innings," she states.

She watched.

I grin.

"What did you think?" I care about her review more than anyone's, even the ownership.

"I don't know, that was more of a second-round draft pick kind of outing," she teases.

I push a laugh through my tight lips.

"You jerk," I say.

"Kidding. You were really great, Hunter. Really, *really* great." The pause and silence after her compliments feel hopeful, and I bite my bottom lip in anticipation.

"Roddy called," she says, and I let my lip slip from my hold. Not where I saw this conversation going, but okay. "He wanted to talk to Dad after they pulled you, and he said he could tell you listened to Durbin. He knows him. Dad says he and Roddy are a lot alike."

I laugh and utter, "They are."

The silence slips in again, and that same trembling in my chest crawls up my throat. *Please say you're coming back with me. Please.*

"Oh, I have more gossip for you. Or, I guess it's gossip. I don't really know the Mavericks guys that well, but I know you and Brooks are close."

My pulse picks up at the mention of my friend, so I sit up.

"Is he okay?" He's been so quiet, and he seemed off the other day.

"Well . . ." She exhales, and my head gets light in that small pause. "Turns out Brooks is a dad."

"What the—"

That's not what I was expecting at all. My palm flies to my forehead as my mind spins with this news.

"Yeah, I thought that might shock you. I'm pretty sure it shocked the hell out of Brooks, too. I only know about it because Linds ran into him at the grocery store. He was trying to buy diapers, and the boy didn't have a clue. She helped him out."

I wouldn't have a clue either.

"I should probably give him a call. We didn't really get to talk before I left. He was . . . distant. Guess I know why now."

"Yeah," she hums.

"And your dad? He's doing all right?" I hope she's given everything a lot of thought and has realized her parents have this under control.

"It's been thirty-six hours, Hunter. He's the same as he was when you left." Naturally, she gives me a snarky response, and absolutely nothing that gives me a clue as to what she's thinking about, well, about us. I suppose I should suck it up and ask.

"And yes, I'm still thinking about it," she says, somehow reading my mind.

I sink into the bed, a little deflated but not despairing.

"Okay, I'm glad. Anything I can do to . . ." I stop myself from saying the words *persuade you.*

"I promise I'm really giving it serious thought, Hunter." Her response feels final, and I mean to let it drop. But then I squeeze in one more little thing—in my favor, I hope.

"I'll see you tomorrow," I say. "And I love you."

TWENTY-SIX

RENLEIGH

I flop back into the double bed I'm sharing with my sister, and she purses her lips as she stares at me. I'm not sure if it's because she heard that last bit from Hunter through the phone or because she's mad I won't let her have more than one glass of wine tonight.

"You told him you were taking this seriously," she says, holding up the blue crayon and the pad of construction paper she and I are using to make my *very serious* pros and cons list. I lift my head from the mattress to meet her gaze.

"The list is serious. It's not my fault we don't have the best tools to work with." I lift my palms, then let them flop down on the bed on either side of me.

"Renleigh Jamison Blackwood, your serious list includes the following phrases: He has abs. I like his eyes. The sex is mind-blowing. Texas is far from home. Dad needs me. Lindsey needs me. This is not a serious list, Ren."

"How is it not serious?" I challenge as I push myself to sit up.

"Well, first of all, I do not need you," she says.

I let my head fall to one side as my mouth makes a straight line, and my eyes haze.

"Don't you look at me like that. I'm not fragile. I'm going to figure this out." She draws a line through that item on my list. "Dad also does not need you. He never has."

Her chin drops as she hits me with a hard stare this time, the same kind she uses on the boys when she wants them to knock it off and listen. It's effective, even though she's wrong again.

She draws a line through my Dad item, and I hiss.

"We'll come back to that. You'll lose. Next."

She taps the crayon on Texas being far from home and pops her gaze right back to mine, drawing a line through it without looking.

"It is far, Linds," I whine.

"Hey, Salt-N-Pepa?" That's what Lindsey calls the voice system on her phone. It's a hack her husband—correction, *soon-to-be-ex-husband*—did for her. "How long does it take to drive from Sweetwater Springs, Oklahoma to Dallas?"

"By automobile, the trip to Dallas from Sweetwater Springs, Oklahoma, takes approximately three hours and fourteen minutes."

Lindsey's lips twist as she looks up at me from her phone.

"Girl, that's not even half a season of binge TV. You're being crazy." She draws a line through my last con, then circles all my pros before adding a string of bullets I can't read upside down.

"What are you doing? Lindsey, we're going to have to start over. This is my list, not yours." I reach for the tablet, but she pulls it to her body, out of my reach, as she finishes scribbling her edits.

"There." She tosses the crayon toward the box on the bed, then flops the paper pad in front of me.

If you go to Texas, you can finish your degree, and then maybe you can figure out what is wrong with your own damn brain. Kidding. But seriously? You should go because Hunter makes you happy, and you deserve to be happy. And also, because you love him.

My gaze flashes to my sister, and she hits me with a smug grin.

"You know you do," she says.

I leave the bed and huff, my hands scratching at my scalp.

"I don't love him, Lindsey. I . . . enjoy his company."

It's such bullshit. I can't even keep a straight face after uttering it.

"Fine, I like him a lot. And I could see maybe, if we were in different places, or if I was not locked down here—"

"You aren't," she fires back.

My shoulders drop, and I pull my Earl's shirt from a hanger and glare at her on my way to the shower.

I haven't showered in two days. Maybe three. I like to say it's because I'm busy, but it's because I'm a little depressed and anxious. I don't need to finish my psych degree to tell me that.

My fingers massage a healthy dose of shampoo into my hair, and I push the sudsy pile into a pyramid on top of my head, pressing my palms together to recreate the little girl with the mohawk. The wall of hair flops over my right eye in seconds, but for a moment, I think I had it. I was her. A sweet, innocent toddler who didn't know any better, and who was happy to have two parents who loved her, and a roof over her head, and a sister who shared her room.

I still have all those things, just not the way I imagined I would. My mom's words have haunted me ever since she shared them with me. My dad has never been hostile to my mom, and I've always wondered why. He wanted my mom to feel whole, and sometimes that's hard for a woman. I get that. Maybe more than most.

"Hey, ass face, I'm taking the boys out for burgers. We'll revisit this thing tomorrow," my sister says after rapping on the bathroom door.

"Okay, I love you even though you make me nuts," I holler.

"And I love you, too. Just like Hunter Reddick!"

"Lindsey!" I shout after her, popping my head around the shower curtain. I can hear her laughter in the hallway as she rushes down the stairs.

I'm going to miss having her as a bunkmate, though it would be more comfortable in that room if we had actual bunk beds. Two grown women in a double is tight. And my sister likes to kick. But I cherish those bruises for now. She's already hunting for a place to stay longer term. Work is going to be a little harder to come by, but she should walk away from Brandon with a good chunk in her checking account.

The steam fogs the blue tiles on the shower wall enough that I'm able to draw lines in the condensation. I make a box first, then write the word abs next to it and check the box for my own amusement. I wipe the evidence away, though, then force myself to think about what my *real* list is—the reasons why I want to take a leap of faith, and what's holding me back. When I'm honest with myself, it's a pretty simple scale. I think I might be in love with him. Also, I'm really scared he's going to leave.

I finish my shower and dry my hair, but I still have a solid hour before my shift tonight. I love Sweetwater, but it's also not the kind of place with a lot to do on Tuesday night unless you're into bars. I already work at one, and I'd rather not clock in early, extra tips or not.

I'm tempted to text my sister and horn in on her burger date with the boys. If she took them for burgers, it's probably at that place off the highway with the arcade and prize booth. It's about ten miles out of town, though, and I don't have *that* much time to spare. I tiptoe my way down the stairs, the flickering light from the television bouncing off the walls. I hear my mom laugh and stop. It's more of a giggle. Something about it makes me curious, so I sit down about five steps from the main floor and peer at them through the railing.

My dad is in his second-favorite chair, his leg propped up on the ottoman, with my mom sitting next to him on it, her hand on his cast. She has a marker in her hand, and she's drawing something, or maybe writing. She has her reading glasses on the tip of her nose.

"O in the upper . . . right corner," my dad says, and my mom draws something on the cast. I think they're playing tic-tac-toe.

"You keep using the same strategy, and you keep losing, Dale." She laughs her raspy sound, and I find myself smiling at the two of them.

"I like to think I'm . . . wearing you down," my dad says. My mom pops her head up and peers at him over the rim of her glasses, and within seconds, the two are laughing so hard I think there are tears involved.

"Fine, put it . . . in the middle," my dad finally says.

My mom shakes her head.

"No, I already drew it in the corner. It's not your turn."

My dad lets out a well-acted *humph* as my mom draws a small X on his cast.

"Well, hell, you . . . stole my strategy," my dad says, drawing even more giggles from the woman he's loved, in his own strange way, for my entire life.

"All part of my insidious plan," she says.

I get to my feet and take the final few steps with a little extra thump to my steps to give my parents a warning. I'm not sure I can handle seeing them kiss right now, though I've caught them a few times. It's strange. I don't remember seeing it before.

"Hey, Ren. You off to work?" My mom puts the cap on the Sharpie and drops it in a cup on the fireplace mantle.

"I start in an hour. I was just killing some time. Is that—?" I gesture to my father's leg, about a dozen tiny games of tic-tac-toe drawn around the knee area on the cast

"Oh, yeah. It was your dad's idea," my mom says.

"I kinda thought I'd have . . . more wins to show off." My dad cranes his neck to look me in the eyes.

"How many of them are yours?" I ask.

He holds up a tight fist to signal zero, and I snort-laugh in reaction.

My father's breathing has gotten stronger, and even though his cast limits what he can do with his legs, he's aggressive with everything else. My mom doesn't take it lightly on him, I've noticed. Not that I did when I was running the show, but I was probably a little quicker to let him call it a day when he could maybe do more. His arms have gotten stronger in the last ten days. And I caught him messing around with a baseball the other night, practicing his grips. He misses it.

"Do you want something to eat before you go?"

My mom moves around the chair with a hopeful posture, her hands clasped in front of her and her lips sucked in tight. She's trying.

"Uh, maybe a sandwich?" I know there's some of that in the fridge.

"Coming right up. Have a seat." She gestures to the ottoman, so I snag the marker, sit down, and eye my father in challenge.

"Don't take it . . . easy on me," he says.

I smirk. He knows me better than that.

I draw the grid, then lift my gaze and my brow, offering him the chance to go first.

"Upper right corner," he says, and I shake my head with soft laughter. He is stubborn and relentless. They are not the same thing.

I give my father the X in the corner, then draw an O in the middle for my turn. He studies my work, as if there are a lot of options when it comes to this game, then tilts his head to the side.

"Opposite corner?" I ask.

"Uh huh." His eyes dim, like he's up to something. I draw an O between his marks, and his smirk immediately falters.

We carry on for another minute or two, until every square is filled and the game ends in a tie. He has a few of those on the cast, but a lot more losses. He falls for the traps. So appropriate. At least, that's what I always thought. Lately, though, I'm not as sure. Maybe he knows exactly what he's doing all the time.

"Hey, Dad?" I cap the marker and scan the kitchen area for my mom, keeping my voice low.

"What do you need . . . to know?" He's so intuitive. People have always underestimated him because he was a PE teacher and a baseball coach, but I know how much calculation must live in the mind of a baseball manager. It's a constant state of odds, and a fucked-up game of geometry and physics. Throw in the wild card of coaching teenagers, and my dad's ten-year winning record for a high school team looks mighty impressive. That same instinct has always been a part of his parental toolkit, too. He's using it now.

"Mom made a lot of money over the years. But when you had to quit coaching, things got tight here. I'm just wondering . . ." I twist my head to check on my mom, but I still see her floating around the kitchen, zipping from the counter to the fridge and back again.

"You want to know . . . why I didn't force her to pay . . . for me?" He quirks a brow, a bit of a superior tilt to his smirk.

"It sounds bad when you put it that way, but also . . . she told me the real reason she left the first time. And why you guys lived the way you did."

I shrug, still a bit baffled, but less so than before. Especially after Hunter hit me with his words earlier.

When you love someone, nothing makes you happier than seeing them live their best life. Even if that means you can't be in it all the time.

My dad nods and reaches an upturned palm to me. I lay my hand in his and smile as his fingers wrap around mine. His hands have always been twice the size of mine. Like Hunter's. Pitching hands.

"She told me you talked. I'm . . . glad. And as for your mom's . . . salary? How do you think . . . we paid for your college? Or . . . Lindsey's wedding. And now . . . Lindsey's lawyer."

I stare into my father's eyes and unravel my entire life. My sister's life.

"I thought I qualified for financial aid. That I had scholarships?"

My father's lip inches up on one side, and he shakes with a silent laugh.

"I know you did. And it was . . . a scholarship of sorts. We call it . . . the Sarah Rasmussen-Blackwood . . . fund for girls."

My eyes sting from the air because I can't seem to close them. I can't blink. I can't speak. I had no idea.

"And the wedding? It wasn't money that Aunt Beth left for us?"

"Renleigh . . . did you ever meet an Aunt . . . Beth?" He chuckles, almost proud of this massive fraud he and my mother pulled over on us. It was for our own benefit, but still!

"You made her up?" I lower my head and cover my mouth, realizing my volume.

My dad nods, and I'm about to grill him more when my mom appears behind him with a paper plate in her hand, and a triple-decker sandwich complete with toothpicks holding the pieces together.

"One turkey, bacon and tomato, coming right up," she says.

It's my favorite sandwich. I *know* my mom used to make it for us when we were kids. It's the reason I love club-style sandwiches.

"You toasted the bread," I say, my eyes stinging with a massive desire to water. I push the sensation down. I'm not ready for any of this.

"Hope you like it," she says, eyeing my tic-tac-toe game on my father's cast.

"She totally took it easy on you," she snickers, winking at me.

She's right.

I did.

TWENTY-SEVEN
HUNTER

When I told Kyle I was making this drive, he laughed and told me to stay awake. Coach's reaction was similar. I heard a lot of warnings about the crowded highways on my way out of Dallas and the sudden dearth of topography. But I have to say, coming from the congested freeway tangles of Southern California, the wide-open spaces and lush green feel kind of nice. So do the small towns along the way.

It's been a four-hour trip, but I feel like I've seen a thousand places, all of them different. Maybe this will get old eventually, but it's going to take several passes for me to find any of this boring.

I roll into Sweetwater just as the sun is setting. The sky is swaths of purples and oranges. I get similar paint strokes in Dallas, but it hits different out here. Less urban. In Oklahoma, you can almost *smell* the sunsets.

I arranged to swap out my rental car here in Sweetwater at a small car lot that mostly serves the university. Brooks brought my truck up for me, but I'd be lying if I didn't have ulterior motives with the ask. It's an excuse to check in on him. I didn't have to pry much when we talked, either. There was a baby crying in the background, and that's kind of hard to explain away when you're a single dude playing for a farm team.

I park the Honda near the rental office and turn in the keys while some dude walks around the car with a clipboard to make sure I brought it back in one piece. Other than bugs smashed on the windshield, it's pretty much the same as it was when it was delivered to me.

"Hey, man. I got someone for you to meet," Brooks says, swinging a carrier around his body as he steps around the front of my truck.

"My goodness," I coo. It's funny how a tiny human can literally bring two massive dudes to their knees.

"Brooks, buddy. She's precious," I say, careful to keep my voice down so I don't wake his daughter.

His expression still seems gobsmacked. He's as white as a ghost, and the dark circles under his eyes are prominent. But there's a smile under all that exhaustion. He's doing this. He's actually doing this.

"So, this is Holly?" I glance up at him briefly, immediately dropping my gaze back to the angel snuggled in a pink blanket.

"This is Holly," he says, taking a deep breath.

I don't know all the details, and I won't push him. He's still overwhelmed. But from what he shared, Holly was the product of a one-night stand, and her appearance at his doorstep with a note was a massive surprise.

"Here's the keys to *your* baby," he says, handing over my extra key fob.

"I think mine is a little easier to handle for me," I say, hoping the joke isn't too much.

"Oh, me too. But I don't think you want to trade," he says, immediately adding, "Kidding. I'm kidding. I would never . . ."

"I know," I say. "Come on. I'll give you a lift back to your place."

We pile into my truck, and Brooks fastens the baby carrier into the middle seat with some clip that connects to my seatbelt. I stare at his hands as they work, much the way I do when my mom operates her sewing machine. It's like sorcery to me.

"You'd be amazed what you can learn on the internet," he says. He gives the seat a little tug, then nods, satisfied Holly is secure.

His place is only a few blocks away, so he's undoing his work within minutes. I reach an arm around him for a half hug in front of my truck, and I pat his back, hoping he figures out a plan soon. He needs a nanny, stat. And then it hits me.

"You know what? I have someone you should reach out to. She's good with kids. And she's looking for a job that might let her stay at home. Interested?"

Brooks hands over his phone at lightning speed, and I pop open my contacts to send him Lindsey's number. It's a fluke I have it, and it's only because she called me the night I got into Dallas. But my half-hatched idea isn't so bad. They could help each other out. And I'd like that, for both of them.

"I'll call her today. Thanks, man. You're a lifesaver."

I hug him one more time and reassure him that he'll be playing up with me soon enough—even if it takes him a season of raking down here to get there. And maybe he'll have things sorted out about Holly by then, whether she stays with him permanently or not. I saw the way he looked at her, though. He's letting her go.

"Say hi to the guys for me. Especially Roddy. Let him know I listened to the high and outside. He'll know what it means."

"Sure thing," Brooks says.

I pull away as he heads into his apartment with his daughter, and on my way to Renleigh's place, I take the route that runs by the stadium. The lights are on, though there's not a game tonight, so it must be the field crew. I'm tempted to pull over and ask if I can drive the mower, just once. It's like the Zamboni in hockey, and I'm sure I'd fuck up the pretty lines in the grass. But it would grow back. And I'd have a check on my bucket list.

While that urge is strong, the one calling me to keep heading west is stronger, and soon, I'm pulling up outside the Blackwood home, and Renleigh is on her way out to me.

I roll my window down and kill the engine.

"Well, shoot. You're all dressed up and pretty." She's wearing a white cotton sundress with a blue sweater over it. She reminds me of summer.

"I was hoping we could go on a date," she says, her lips puckered as she lifts herself up by the running board to kiss me through the window.

"Date, huh?" My brow lowers with skepticism. If we're heading out together tomorrow, it feels strange to go on a date tonight, which fills my belly with worried butterflies. But this is Renleigh, and nothing about our relationship has been by anyone's book, not even those romance ones on her shelves. Well, *my* shelves.

"Hop in," I say, leaning my head to the right as I smile. I'm doing my best to ignore the fast pitter-pattering in my chest, but my stream of worried thoughts is making it impossible. I can't handle the anticipation, so the minute she slips into the passenger seat, and I get us a mile away from her house, I blurt my inner thoughts out.

"You're not coming to Dallas, are you?"

Renleigh

Nothing like this ever goes the way you imagine. I rehearsed this talk with Hunter a hundred times, and always got to gently let him down. That method, however, was imaginary. And this one, the *real* one, is going to hurt.

I suck in my bottom lip, and his eyes fall along with the corners of his mouth. He hangs his hands over the steering wheel and sighs before rolling his neck and meeting my gaze.

"Why?"

I match the tilt of his head.

"You know why," I croak.

"Your dad isn't alone, Renleigh. And if your mom leaves, you can come back. Or I'll hire a home health aide to come, someone who can stay with him, maybe help him rehab faster."

His offer warms my heart, and I have to brush away the tears that rapidly form in my eyes as I shake my head.

"It's not my dad, Hunter. You're right. Someone else can care for him. My mom can care for him."

He deflates, physically, his body sinking into the driver's seat and his neck hunching.

"Then, what is it? What's in our way? Because I want this, Renleigh. I want you. *Us.*"

He bites his bottom lip, and I'm so tempted to crawl over this center console and bite it back, but I don't. I have to say my own hard truth out loud.

"I can't come with you because I'm not sure I'm strong enough in here"—I pat my hand on the center of my chest—"to handle you leaving week after week, and month after month. I can't . . ."

I'm having trouble breathing, and Hunter pulls his seat belt off and pushes up the center console, sliding closer to cradle my face with his warm hands.

"I know, I get it. I understand," he says, bringing his forehead to mine.

I wrap my hands around his wrists and breathe with him, my heart pounding so hard that it nearly drowns out my thoughts. If only it pounded harder, and maybe then I would think about how terrified I am to be alone.

"Maybe eventually. Maybe . . . I don't know." I start to cry at that reality. What if I'm broken beyond repair? What if I've pushed myself into this coping box that I'll never get out of?

"So I'll wait. And I'll drive to Sweetwater. I'll drive down here every goddamn week if that's what it takes. And I'll call you from the road. And I'll—"

"But you have your life, too. I don't want you taking care of me and my fucked-up head and heart," I choke out.

"Ren," he says, his lips brushing mine. I hold on to the soft kiss, memorizing the brush of his lips. "I do have my life, and this is what I want for it. I want you. And us. I want our shot. And if that means I drive through small-town America a million times a year . . ."

I blubber out a pathetic laugh.

"I'll do it," he says.

I swallow the sharp, invisible rocks terrorizing my throat and nod before kissing him harder, and soon, he sweeps me into his lap, my back against the steering wheel. He maneuvers his seat back more, and my hands fight to unbutton his jeans and work the zipper down. He helps, pulling his cock out and gripping it while I tug the skirt of my dress up my thighs and drag the cotton strip of my panties to the side with my finger so he can guide himself into me. I sink onto him, his cock flexing inside me as I roll my hips and hum into his mouth. He deepens our kiss, his hands sliding under my dress and grabbing my ass, pulling me into him as his hips thrust upward.

"I want to have this. I need this," I say at his ear, his mouth hot on my neck. His teeth graze my ear as he pulls me onto him harder.

"You can have me. All of me. And this is enough for now, if it's all you can give. I won't stop trying. I won't stop waiting. I will never not fight for you," he mutters against my skin.

The build between us is swift, our bodies hot with sweat as the first wave sends shocks down from the pit of my stomach to the wet center between my legs. I moan as I search for his mouth, and the moment we kiss, my orgasm rocks through me, taking my breath with it. A deep groan vibrates from the depths of Hunter's chest as he fills me with his warmth, thrusting into me one final time until he's emptied every bit of himself inside of me.

Instead of climbing back to my seat, instead of feeling the cool burn of embarrassment on my cheeks for not being able to control myself when it comes to him, I revel in where I am. I stay here in his arms, with him inside me, for as long as it takes to not feel the hole in my heart that formed the minute he got called up to Texas.

There's nowhere for us to sleep together, not in that house, anyway. Too many Blackwoods in too many of the rooms. So I stay in Hunter's truck, holding on to him, and letting him stroke my hair and tickle my spine until the sun peeks over the horizon.

Now, I can barely keep my eyes open, and I have to rally and clock in for my shift.

Hunter left me just after six in the morning with the promise that he'd be back in Sweetwater in a week. The slight bit of furniture he accumulated here in town is at Roddy's place, in the garage, so that's where Hunter headed when he left. He said he couldn't live without the bookcase we picked out together, but I think he simply didn't want to build another one.

I knot my hair at the base of my neck and push through the door to Earl's, glad to have the breakfast crowd here to greet me instead of a hopping Friday night.

"Mornin', Ren," Daisy says as she flies by with a plate filled with hashbrowns and eggs. She carries the order to a man at the end of the bar, then makes her way back to me, punching in the keys on the register over my shoulder since I'm struggling to get my number right.

"I love you, doll, but you look exhausted. Are you feeling all right?"

I nod, but the moment I pivot and meet her gaze, the weight of everything combusts inside of me, and suddenly I'm sobbing.

"Oh, honey. Come on," she says, taking my hand and guiding me to the kitchen, where she holds me to her chest while I let everything out.

I cry for a solid ten minutes, and every time I try to stop and explain why I'm such a mess, I get to Hunter's name and fall apart again. Daisy gives me a glass of water, and I clutch it between two hands, terrified I'll drop it and send shards of glass flying in all directions. I take tiny sips until my breathing regulates, then hand the heavy glass back to her so I can press my palms to my puffy eyes.

"My God, that was a lot. I'm sorry," I say through an embarrassed laugh.

"Looks like you needed that," she says, her hand wrapping around my bicep, then sliding down my arm until our hands meet.

"You said Hunter. I'm guessing he's . . ." She narrows her gaze on mine, studying me for clues, and I'm sure she's drawing the typical conclusions. I don't want her to think Hunter's someone he's not, so I shake my head.

"He's wonderful, actually. He asked me . . ." I quake with a heavy breath, then bite my lip to steady myself and focus. "He asked me to go to Dallas with him, to move in together. Or to go back to school if that's what I want. Or to let him come back here every week or two, as long as he could see me."

Daisy's mouth morphs into a laughing smile, and my head falls to the side.

"Don't laugh at me," I beg.

"Oh, no. Ren, hon. I'm not laughing like that. It's just, my God, are you me or what?" She laughs a bit harder this time, but I can read the empathy in her eyes, so it doesn't sting as much.

"Come sit," she says, moving me to the business office at the back of Earl's. She hands me her makeup bag, then rolls two chairs together and grabs a small mirror from her desk drawer.

"Here, I got you. Do your thing," she says, holding the mirror up so I can fix the mess I made of the little makeup I *do* wear.

"How am I you?" I ask as I run a cotton swab under one eye, cleaning up the smeared eyeliner from my meltdown a few moments ago.

"You know, Roddy asked me to come with him when he got called up, and I didn't go. Sure, we were different. And he wasn't ready the way Hunter is, but still. I can't help but wonder sometimes—a lot of times—*what if?*" She shifts the mirror so our eyes meet.

"What if?" I echo.

She shrugs and holds my gaze, mashing her lips with her thoughts.

"What if I got it wrong?"

She draws in a deep breath through her nose, and I hold

my lungs full at the same time. That's a huge confession for Daisy to utter, and I feel honored, and a wee bit terrified, that it was my ears she gave it to.

"Are you saying maybe *I'm* getting it wrong?" Because I'm sure I am. No matter what I choose, it's going to be wrong. I've become a self-defeatist. And that's part of my problem.

Daisy takes the makeup bag from me and moves the mirror to her desk before pulling out a small eye pencil.

"Shut your eyes," she says, and I do as she asks. My skin pricks with the sharp edge of her eyeliner, but I hold still as she does my face for me, dusting my cheeks with a bronzer next, then touching the corners of my eyelids with a faint gray shadow that gives my face just enough color to look like it's attached to someone who slept.

"Here," she says, holding up the mirror for me to inspect. I look nice. A bit extra than I'm used to, but nice. And alive.

"All I'm saying, Ren, is that this is Sweetwater. It ain't far from Dallas. So if you get it wrong, you can always come back."

Her eyes level on mine with a hard stare, one forged in kindness for sure, but it's not wrapped in kid gloves. It's honest. And she's right. And that's exactly what I needed to hear.

"Daisy, I think I . . . I think . . ." I get up from the chair and look around the office, at the calendar where my name is scribbled so many times. My pulse is racing again, but I don't feel like I'm going to faint this time. This feels like I need to run. And fast.

"I think I quit," I blurt, and a manic laugh follows that I cover with my palm.

"I kinda thought you might," Daisy says, getting to her feet and opening the office door.

She leans her head to the exit, and I wrap my arms around her, uttering, "Thank you," into the crook of her neck.

I sprint across the empty bar, pushing through the front

door and letting bright sunlight spill inside as I race into it. I pull my phone from my pocket and dial Hunter immediately, fumbling for my keys to the Jeep, then fumbling them again to get the damn key in the ignition. I redial when the call goes to voicemail, and at the same time, press the gas and reverse my way out of the Earl's parking lot. My tires squeal on the roadway as I shift into drive and race to Roddy's house, where I hope I find Hunter's truck parked outside.

As I round the corner, the street is empty, but I hold out hope that maybe Hunter pulled into the driveway or the garage. But the closer I get, the more reality hits me. I missed him. He's already gone. My heart breaks by the time I pull to a complete stop, and I drop my face into my hands as I ruin my makeup for a second time this morning.

"You all right, Renleigh?" Roddy's voice hits my ears through the ragtop of my Jeep, and I shake with exhausted laughter. I peel my fingers away to find him standing in the middle of his garage with a broom. His truck is covered in dried mud, and he's sweeping up the chunks.

I get out of the Jeep and let my feet plop onto his drive-way, then let my arms hang at my sides, threatening to pull me to the ground.

"I missed him, huh?"

I know he's not gone forever. I know I could barrel down the highway after him, honking my horn. Or wait for him to answer his phone and call me back. But I'm afraid I'll miss this sliver of bravery, this caution thrown to the wind. What if I can only say yes to this right now? What if—

Roddy's bellowing laughter rips me from my personal spiral, and my spine straightens as I snap, "What?"

"Ren, he just ran to get gas. He's got more shit here to move, and he'll be back in, well, there he is." Roddy points over my shoulder, and I spin slowly until I see the front of Hunter's truck. His engine roars as he presses the gas, zooming down the street to get to me faster, and when he reaches the end of Roddy's driveway, he flies out, leaving his truck door wide open as he races to me.

"Please say you're here because—"

I don't give him another moment of air. I launch myself into his arms and steal his breath for my own, our lips crashing into one another as if this were our last chance to kiss. Instead, it's the first. The first kiss when I pull away to breathe and utter, "I love you." It's the first kiss on our way to Texas, together. It's the first chance I'm taking for me, a risk of the heart.

And it's the only time I've ever felt safe enough to try. And that . . . that doesn't just mean *something*. That means everything.

EPILOGUE

HUNTER

18 MONTHS LATER

Renleigh couldn't get that gold graduation cap off her head fast enough. For a girl who's not much into hair and makeup, she's pretty picky about the hats that go on her head. If it's not Texas, it's not touching her follicles. Unless they trade me, of course. Then, I think she might burn her Texas hat and curse the owners for life.

So far, though, the Texas management is safe.

"You didn't have to come to my graduation. You're going to be late," she says, fidgeting in the passenger seat as I race from her university graduation ceremony to the ballpark, where she thinks I'm starting today. When she realizes I'm not, I fear this entire plan will fall to pieces, but I have to try.

Surprising this girl is impossible. I guess a year and a half of grad school makes for one astute mind, and Renleigh has become about as observant as a renowned detective. She's going to make a great child therapist. I've seen the heart she brings to every case. Her clinical studies are where she shined.

Probably because she relates so deeply to the young girls she's trying to help. The nonprofit she's joining is lucky to have her. And I love that she is stepping in to serve families who can't afford the kind of mental health care their kids desperately need. It's one of the reasons I'm asking her to marry me, among about a billion other.

Of course, if I blow this surprise and she sees it coming, she might run. It's still a bit of a thing, and it's part of what makes her . . . *her.* She's cautious with her heart. She gave hers to me, and I'll never misuse that trust. Now, though, I'm asking for a big, public promise. That's going to scare her deep down, so if it's a no today, I'm good with it. I'm good with what we have. It doesn't mean I won't ask again, when or if she tells me the time is right. It's about comfort for her, and sometimes comfort takes time.

"Your parents are going to love their seats," I say, glancing at her as she wriggles her hips and pulls her jeans up her bare legs. She insisted on changing in the truck. I think she just likes to torture me by making me watch her strip when my hands are tied up.

"You really got my dad front row behind the plate?"

She snaps the button on her jeans, then sinks back into her seat, adjusting the seat belt I never let her take off. She thinks she's invincible sometimes. I won't take that chance.

"I sure did. You think he'll forgive me for stealing his daughter from Sweetwater because of it?" Her dad doesn't really think that, but the man can tease pretty good.

Renleigh's lips bunch.

"Uh, maybe. It might take more than one game."

I roll my eyes and return my attention to the road.

Renleigh just wants to sit there with him. I know how her mind works. She hates that the family section is on the third baseline, far from a good view of the ump's bad calls. She wants to give our umps shit when they screw me over, but if I get her within earshot, she'll say something that will get *me* ejected. This is also another reason why I want to marry her, of course.

"Your parents should beat us there by a bit. They got out of the university lot fast."

It was by design, of course, but Renleigh doesn't seem to realize that. I purposely parked in the worst spot to buy her parents time to get to the stadium. They'll be in their seats with phone cameras at the ready when I pop the question.

"You know, the last game my dad came to was the first time he took the stadium steps without his cane. He's doing so well." She beams.

I reach over and squeeze her hand.

"They both are."

She nods, and for once, doesn't temper the acknowledgement with a *for now*. Renleigh's mom kept her word. And it seems the story she shared about why she left in the first place was rooted in truth. I'm sure there were ugly parts of their marriage. But fate found time for them now, it seems. And they appear happy.

Dale is even traveling with Sarah to places that don't revolve around baseball. They have a trip planned to Washington next month, to see the buildings Sarah worked in. Part of me thinks she might not quite be done with that place. But I also think Dale is willing to leave Sweetwater this time and head east with her.

Lindsey couldn't make the trip. Too many logistics with the twins and taking care of Holly, plus there's the scrutiny she'd face by possibly showing up with Brooks. As observant as Renleigh is, I'm surprised she hasn't questioned her sister's relationship with her employer. I could be wrong. Maybe it's nothing. It sure feels like *something*, though.

My parents have our sisters covered, though. My mom loves a good livestream, which is what she thinks FaceTime is. If she ever veers into actual livestreaming, we're all in trouble. She does not self-edit her words. Ever.

My parents are sitting right next to Renleigh's. I called in all my favors for this game. It helps that we're no longer in contention this season. That's why one of our prospects is getting a start, and I'm getting an extra day of rest. The next three weeks are experimental for us as a team, which makes it the perfect time for me to take a big swing with Renleigh.

I reach my left hand along my hip, feeling for the ring. I know it's there, but I keep checking as a creature comfort. It's become my worry stone today, though a lot more jagged on the edges. I hope Renleigh likes it. She mentioned it once when we were walking downtown. It was in the Harry Winston window, and it's the only ring on display that isn't big and square. It's subtle, quietly elegant, and bold in its simplicity—kind of like the woman it's meant for.

We pull into the players' garage, and I rush around my truck to open the door before Renleigh can. It's a game we play, and I only win half the time. And only because she lets me.

I take her hand, helping guide the heels of her boots to the concrete floor. She's wearing the black leather ones that hug her calves, and I have every intention of begging her to keep them on—and nothing else—when we get home later. All of this, of course, is contingent on her not punching me in the nose when I propose. I'm prepared for all possibilities.

We walk through security and head right into the waiting elevator. I'm not smooth enough to have that timing planned, so it's a gift from the universe that gets us to the club level without interruption. The restaurant area is buzzing with executives. Our crowd is thinner now that we're not in the hunt, but the high-dollar fans and sponsors still love the atmosphere. The game is more of a party to them, and since their dollars pay my salary, I say *drink up, my friends.*

We reach the tunnel where I would normally send Renleigh up to her seats by herself while I peel off and duck into the clubhouse, only that's not how today is going to go.

"Don't you need to get in there?" She points to the club-house door; I can tell her suspicions are already raised.

"I'm just going to say a quick hi to your parents, make sure the seats are good." I'm fumbling, but I smile through it.

Renleigh's forehead dents. That's doubt right there.

"Of course the seats are good, Hunter. They're behind home plate." Her tone is a bit indignant, but I let it roll off me as I march ahead of her, up the stairs, and to the front row where her parents are sitting next to mine. I feel the side of my pocket again, checking to make sure a hole didn't suddenly appear, but the ring is still there.

"Hunter, why are your parents . . ." She turns to her right, toward the family section, where a ball cap is being passed among the players' wives. They're stuffing it full of twenties, and it takes Renleigh less than five seconds to piece together what's going on.

"What's the bet?"

She turns to find me on one knee, and her hands fly to cover her mouth, even though she likely saw this coming.

"Ren, the wives and I have a bet. They don't think I can get this ring on your finger. So, what do you say? Will you do this life thing with me forever? Will you marry me?"

My throat is so dry, but I don't dare breathe or utter another word. I simply wait while the woman who owns me calculates her next move. When her hands peel away from her mouth one at a time to reveal a hint of her familiar smirk, I exhale the small bit of oxygen left in my lungs. But I don't yet celebrate. Or relax. Not yet.

"How much is in that thing?" She tilts her head toward the hat, now held at the end of the row. Kyle's wife walks it over, riffling through the bills and counting on her way.

"Looks like two hundred and eighty," she says, holding the hat by the bill as she presents it to Renleigh.

"Well, then," my girl says, scooping the dollars into her fist and shoving them in the front pocket of her jeans. She next takes the ring from my hand and slides it on her left-hand finger, admiring it as she stretches her arm out between us. Her eyes flit to mine, and her lips tick into a tight, perfect smile.

"I guess I win," she says.

I'm on my feet in half a second and spinning her in my arms the next.

"I love you, Renleigh Blackwood," I say against her lips as I break our kiss.

I set her feet on the ground and press my forehead to hers. She gathers the front of my shirt in her fists, holding me close.

"And I love you, Hunter Reddick, number one draft pick."

<h2 style="text-align:center">THE END</h2>

Ready for more Sweetwater Springs? Fall hard for shortstop Brooks Callahan as he navigates life as a single dad. And thank goodness Lindsey Blackwood is looking for a job and is the perfect nanny! ;-) Preorder Hey There Slugger now! Releasing March 19, 2026! That's soon!

ORDER ON AMAZON: Hey There Slugger

If you enjoyed Easy Tiger, I have several other sports romance series you might enjoy. Check out the following:

VARSITY HEARTBREAKER - BOOK 1 in the VARSITY SERIES
READ NOW IN KU: Varsity Heartbreaker

Lucas Fuller is a lot of things.
He's the boy next door.
He's the first crush I ever had.
He was my first kiss.
He's also the only person who has ever broken my heart.
For two years, I've wondered what happened to the us I used to know.
We were best friends, and then suddenly…we weren't.
I tried to run away from it. I even changed schools just to make the hurt disappear.
But no matter how hard I tried to not think about Lucas, I

just couldn't stay away from the high school quarterback with perfect blue eyes and so many secrets.

I'm back. We're seniors now. We've grown—all of us. And Lucas Fuller might be different, but I'm different too.

This is my time to take risks, to experience life and to fall in love for real.

I want Lucas Fuller to be a part of my story, but I know for that to happen, I need to know the truth about our past.

THE TOMBOY AND THE CAPTAIN Book 1 in the FINAL SCORE SERIES
READ NOW IN KU: The Tomboy and The Captain

It was supposed to be my year, but then he made a bet that I couldn't refuse...

A star senior on the Tiff U volleyball team, it's been my goal to come back strong after an injury that nearly took me out of the game. But I'm Laney freaking Price, and I'm taking my shot to make it on the new pro women's team, despite the lack of support from my father.

The problem? Cutter McCreary. He is the Captain of the Tiff U hockey team, all-around loveable guy, and a total player. And did I mention a complete thorn in my side since freshman year? Yeah…that guy. His charms don't tempt me.

Until…a mix up with our housing situation forces us into a bit of a predicament. We were both promised a room. The same room.

His proposal? A bet. We split the room in half—for now. Whoever falls in love with the other first has to move out. The winner gets to stay. But when strategic glances turn into late night talks, and fake kisses start to feel real, I'm finding myself without a game plan. And winning suddenly doesn't feel like the only thing that matters.

ACKNOWLEDGMENTS

If you've been a reader of mine for long, you know how I feel about baseball. I don't think there's a sport that's more romantic. My love for this game runs deep. And that's why this series? I plan on making it epic. And I'm talking 6 books kinda epic!

Hold on tight, because the boys of Sweetwater are going to take you for a ride. I hope you enjoyed this first installment. I loved every second of it. But man did I go all 9 innings to make it come to life. And I couldn't have done it without my team.

Everyone needs an Autumn in their life. I'm not sure I'd make it over the finish line sometimes without you. I love you more. Brenda, my editor, I must bless you for your patience and brilliance. You always make my stories better, and I learn so much from you. I try my damnedest to make those lessons stick, too.

I had a writing buddy that was my constant in bringing Easy Tiger to life. Kacey Shea, you know I couldn't have done this without you. I'm ready when you are to do it again. And then again. LOL. I love that we push each other. Likewise—Mom, Tim and Carter—thanks for making sure the other things in my life kept going.

Lastly, to my incredible readers, I will never be able to repay you for the gifts you give me. Every time you dive into one of my stories, you send my heart soaring. You are my extra innings. My perfect game. My MVPs. Thank you, forever. Always.

If you enjoyed Easy Tiger, please consider leaving your review anywhere you would like. It is the best way you can boost an author, and the difference it makes is enormous. Now, who wants to find out what Brooks is up to?

ABOUT THE AUTHOR

Ginger Scott is a *USA Today, Wall Street Journal* and Amazon-bestselling author from Peoria, Arizona. She has also been nominated for the Goodreads Choice and RWA Rita Awards. She is the author of several young and new adult romances, including bestsellers Waiting on the Sidelines, The Hard Count, A Boy Like You, This Is Falling and Wild Reckless.

A sucker for a good romance, Ginger's other passion is sports, and she often blends the two in her stories. When she's not writing, the odds are high that she's somewhere near a baseball diamond, either watching her son swing for the fences or cheering on her favorite baseball team, the Arizona Diamondbacks. Ginger lives in Arizona and is married to her college sweetheart whom she met at ASU (fork 'em, Devils).

FIND GINGER ONLINE: www.gingerscottbooks.com

facebook.com/GingerScottAuthor

instagram.com/authorgingerscott

tiktok.com/@authorgingerscott

ALSO BY GINGER SCOTT

The Boys of Sweetwater Springs

Easy Tiger

(The full 6-book series coming soon)

Final Score Series

The Tomboy & The Captain

The Wallflower & The Running Back

The Best Friend & The Short Stop

The Boys of Welles

Loner

Rebel

Habit

The Fuel Series

Shift

Wreck

Burn

The Varsity Series

Varsity Heartbreaker

Varsity Tiebreaker

Varsity Rule breaker

Varsity Captain

The Waiting Series

Waiting on the Sidelines

Going Long

The Hail Mary

The Waiting Series - Next Generation

Home Game

Game Face

Final Down

Like Us Duet

A Boy Like You

A Girl Like Me

The Falling Series

This Is Falling

You And Everything After

The Girl I Was Before

In Your Dreams

The Harper Boys

Wild Reckless

Wicked Restless

Standalone Reads

The Older Brother

The Moon and Back

Southpaw

Candy Colored Sky

Cowboy Villain Damsel Duel

Drummer Girl

BRED

9 781952 778476